MOON
PATH

A Novel by
STEVEN GREENBERG

FIRST EDITION SOFTCOVER
ISBN: 1622532252
ISBN-13: 978-1-62253-225-4

Editor: Lane Diamond
Cover Artist: Kabur Shah
Interior Designer: Lane Diamond

EVOLVED PUBLISHING™

www.EvolvedPub.com
Evolved Publishing LLC
Butler, Wisconsin, USA

Printed in Book Antiqua font.

BOOKS BY STEVEN GREENBERG

Enfold Me
Galerie
Moon Path

DEDICATION

*In loving memory of Michal Greenberg, my first inspiration.
You are always with me.*

For my brother.

PROLOGUE
Samuel

Pechora River Gulag Transport Ship - Soviet Union, January 1941

My hands... I saw these most vividly. I looked down at them in wonder as it happened.

Because they weren't really *my* hands. They were not the hands I'd brought from Vilnius, and certainly not those I'd had in Warsaw. The dirt on *these* hands had colonized the depths of the ragged fingernails, had swarmed into the vein-ringed chasms of the chapped skin. *These* hands were calloused, sickly, rough.

My hands were familiar with the cool obsidian of a fountain pen, with the warmth of coffee shop porcelain. They knew the silkiness of Danuta's inner thigh much better than splinter-infested shovel handles, dented tin cups, and sweat-slick cervical tissue.

For *these* hands, I discovered with horror, were locked tight around a human neck.

I never knew the man's name. I never cared. I'd woken with a start from a deep slumber, a sleep fueled by *gulag* exhaustion and starvation, and by the gut-wrenching seasickness from which I'd suffered since we came aboard the prison ship. But I hadn't slept so deeply as to shut out the man who tugged at the rag-wrapped bundle on which my greasy head rested. That bundle contained my solitary remaining collared shirt, my spare socks, and the crusted oilskin that embraced my letters.

My letters!

I was on him in a moment, with an energy that rose from somewhere unnamed, somewhere I—even then—hoped never to revisit. I, who scarcely ever hit a man, found myself pinning this one to the floor with suddenly elephantine weight, born not of the NKVD-supplied ration of moldy bread, river water, and thin soup, but rather of sheer fury.

My thumbs pressed deep into his windpipe, and at some point, he stopped struggling. The arms that flailed futilely at my grimy hands stilled. The contorted back straightened, the knees bucking my coccyx reposed, and his eyes, betraying unmistakable clarity and unimpeachable relief, begged me to continue.

Kill me, they said. *Show me this one decency, will you not?*

The man had allowed himself to be murdered, and *those* hands — not *my* hands — obliged.

The foulness of the man's final breath still stung my nostrils, and the cramped muscles of my hands — *those* hands — started to ache. I turned my adrenalin-engorged eyes to the hundreds of dirty faces peering down from three levels of roughly welded bunks. I clutched my bundle to my chest, and turned to the rust-sweating wall.

"My letters... *my letters!*" I hissed viciously in the momentarily silent hold. Then, as the men turned back to their gambling, masturbation, petty arguments, and lice gathering, my softening voice intoned as if in whispered prayer to the implacable iron wall, "*My Danuta.*"

CHAPTER 1
Samuel: I Am My Words

Warsaw, Poland, November 1937

"Would not Brzozowski's anti-determinism preclude your assigning us homework this week, professor?" I stood from my chair on the left side of the steeply-tiered lecture hall as sparse winter sunlight angled in from the hall's narrow windows, illuminating galaxies of dust motes in its beams. My folding seat retracted suddenly as I stood, making a crash that was a finale in the silence following Professor Lutoslawski's solemn closing remarks.

I turned to face the other students of Introduction to Modern Polish Thought, as they started to gather their things in anticipation of the lecture's end. I put on my most inquisitive face, widened my eyes innocently, opened my hands in a childlike 'why not?' gesture, and turned back to the Professor. "After all, if the *experience* of work follows from the physical act of working, would it not be overtly deterministic to actually *do* homework in order to, shall we say, 'experience the experience'?"

A titter of laughter flitted from seat to seat, echoing up and down the tiers of the lecture hall. This was not going as I had hoped.

The Professor looked up from his crumpled lecture notes and stroked his goatee pensively. The hint of a smile crossed his stern lips.

Perhaps there's hope?

No, for then his eyes narrowed, and his booming voice shook the smirk off my face. "The utterly flawed logic of your statement, which I assume was on some pubescent level intended to amuse, is actually an excellent argument for *extra* reading, young man. You may add Chapters 51 through 54 to your reading list and summarize these for the class next week. Good day."

The titter swelled to a hearty collective guffaw, quickly swallowed by the snapping of a hundred retracting seats, heels against hardwood floors, and the rustling of books being stuffed into canvas rucksacks.

Jacek looked over at me from his seat across the hall, shaking his dark curls with a smile. *Again?* His look said, *Must you?*

I smiled back from my place on the "ghetto bench." *Yes, I must. I must, because you don't become the youngest staff writer at Nasza Opinia, which is my plan, by holding back.*

Even from the side of the lecture hall newly designated for Jews only, I expressed my thoughts and hoped like hell that someone wanted to listen. Because if I didn't express them, I would *know* that no one was listening, and *not* being listened to....

Is there really anything worse? If I'm not listened to, who am I?

Because I *was* then—had always been and would always be—my words. I was Samuel Katz, but I couldn't actually say I was born of great words. I'd have loved to claim I was the son of a writer whose words illuminated thousands of nescient eyes, but no. In fact, my father's words, tripping eloquently across the carbon-copied quarterly employee newsletter in the Praga branch of Bank Zachodni, which he'd managed for these past ten years, may have moved some office drones to giggle around the water cooler, but they were never of greater impact. This happened not because he lacked thoughts of inherent value or the eloquent words with which to express them, but because he chose—from timidity or humility—*not* to share them. He *chose* to remain unheard.

How can one with the ability to move mountains choose not *to do so?*

My father once did move mountains, in his quiet way. He moved himself from the raucous *shtetl* of his childhood to Warsaw. He chose to raise his family in the secular vibrancy of Warsaw's up-and-coming Praga neighborhood. He insisted we children speak only Polish at home, despite the fact that he and Mother regularly slipped back into their childhood Yiddish, especially when they argued. He made the break with what he called the Dark Ages of Jewish life in Poland, into what he called the "enlightenment of equality and mutual respect." We were to accord ourselves always, he reminded us nightly over family dinner, as "Poles of Jewish extraction, not Polish Jews."

As the students filed out past me, I still smiled sheepishly while making a tidy stack of my textbooks and sliding the pile smoothly into my faded canvas rucksack.

The majority of students had already left the hall, and Jacek waited for me just outside the door, smoking, his eyes lowered to the floor. The heel of one foot casually supported his weight as he leaned against the wall in a ne'er-do-well pose. He'd adopted this "bad boy" persona as subtle compensation for his short stature, perhaps, or his entirely urbane upbringing, or some combination thereof. He pinched his cigarette so tightly between thumb and forefinger that its tip flattened into a narrow oval, on which he sucked with the intensity of a hungry infant at a nipple.

He looked up as I approached him. He peered around quickly and—he thought—surreptitiously. Jacek never realized that I knew of his embarrassment at being friends with a Jew, even though we *had* been friends since kindergarten.

"That was a stupid joke, *malpeczko*, he said. "Aren't you ever going to learn to keep your mouth shut?" He'd called me *malpeczko*—monkey—ever since I'd revealed, over too many glasses of vodka one evening, that it was the diminutive of my favorite stuffed animal as a child.

"I'll keep my mouth shut if you keep your finger out of your nose in lecture, you pig. God, it was so far up there, I swear I could hear you scratching your brain."

Now it was his turn to smile, but only for a moment. He lowered his voice further. "Seriously, you need to watch your mouth. You don't hear the whispers on *my* side of the lecture hall. The only reason they're not louder is because the professor is a Jew, too." Jacek got that look that always reminded me of the squirrels we loved to feed in Lazienki Park—wide-eyed, wary, concerned.

That look was the inspiration for my own hastily conceived pet name for him. "Relax, *wiewiorka*," I said, far more loudly than necessary. "After all, I'm a citizen of the Great Second Republic of Poland. I have full legal rights and civic obligations, and am entitled to do or say anything that a fellow Pole unfortunate enough to have a foreskin can do or say. As long as I do it *from my fucking side of the lecture hall*, that is." I looked around brazenly, hoping for an audience. There was none, but I still felt vindicated.

I'd been stunned to be relegated to the "ghetto benches" in Warsaw University lecture halls. I could think of no allegory to use, no children's fable to quote with a moral that illustrated my point. Only these words came to me: stunned and infuriated. The order had come directly from the Polish Ministry of Education, and the university Rectors had seemed eager to comply. The decision had been, after all, widely popular among non-Jewish students. So, I'd filed into the Student Administration office one grey day last month, together with a long line of Jewish students, so a bored secretary could stamp my student ID card with the innocuous-looking and euphemistic purple stamp: "Seated on Odd Benches."

"This is the undertow, Samuel," my father had told me over dinner that evening, his calm voice doing little to assuage my boiling anger. "Yes, it is unpleasant, even dangerous, but it is a natural part of the tide of enlightenment on which we now float. Of course, there are those that have trouble accepting our integration into Polish society, but we have the legal and social tools to fight back, do we not? We have rights, and we must never fear to exercise them."

By "we," my father had apparently meant "you." He had yet to join me in demonstrating against this affront to the enlightened Polish society in which he purported to believe. He had yet to sign his name to any of the petitions against the ghetto-bench, or to lend his words to my occasional articles in *Glos Gminy Zydowskiej*, the Voice of the Jewish Community. He had to consider his position in the community, he claimed. He had to consider his increasingly tenuous position at the bank.

Once again, he'd chosen to withhold his words, instead of putting them to good use.

Jacek lit another cigarette, flipping the lock of hair from his eyes to avoid singeing it as he did so. He adamantly refused to trim his bangs, thinking it lent an air of mystery to his otherwise plain visage.

I thought he looked like a poodle on a bad hair day, but had learned to hold my tongue.

"On a different note, *malpeczko*, why don't you come out with us this evening? There's a poetry reading, drinks afterwards. Would it add an extra crack to your Semitic ass if you spent one evening away from your notebooks? Maybe you'll meet a girl, and be able to spend a few less hours in the bathroom with the lingerie catalogs."

I stuck my tongue out at him. "I'll leave my notebooks if you agree to finally get rid of your dolls, little girl. And don't tell me again how they're miniature cast-whatever soldiers. They'll always be dolls to me." Grinning, I turned to leave for my next class.

I did indeed have plans that evening with my notebooks. I'd reached a key juncture in my play, and had spent the day running the next scene's dialog repeatedly through my head, but it hadn't fully formed yet, not quite ready to come out. So, on a whim, I turned back.

"Fine. You know what, *wiewiorka*? I will come out this evening. Let's see if your gentile poetry holds more my attraction for my mammoth foreskin-free *putz* than the pictures of your sister I've got under my mattress. Should I come by at 8:00, or will you still be having your diapers changed then?"

I walked away, trailing the glow of our friendly banter behind me like a cloud of sweet pipe tobacco smoke.

I never even considered that the evening would, defying all physical and temporal logic, never come for me. My clock stopped that afternoon, and in many ways never restarted. It stopped just after they grabbed me, pushed me against the wall, and pulled out that knife.

More accurately, it stopped when *she* first spoke.

CHAPTER 2
Samuel: The National Interest

Pechora River Gulag Transport Ship, Soviet Union, January 1941

The giggles grew louder as Danuta gave me butterfly kisses, her feathery eyelashes fluttering against my forehead and cheeks. Now she showered my face with rose petals, laughing as she did so. The petals bounced lightly across my eyelids, then slid, burning, into my nostrils. I snorted reflexively, and they hit the back of my throat like pepper, causing me to sit up so rapidly that I banged my head on the bunk above. Still the petals crawled over my face.

I clawed at them blindly as they now mixed with blood from the fresh scalp wound, opened by the sharp steel beam that supported the bunk just half a meter above my supine body.

Lice shower!

The realization hit me even before the dream of Danuta completely evaporated.

Lice! The Ukri!

It was a common prank. The *Ukri*, the Ukrainian gang that ruled this netherworld that was the prison ship's hold, had given me one of their infamous lice showers. They collected piles of them, each man contributing hundreds from his own plentiful stock. It took hours, but there was no shortage of time down here, where we eight hundred prisoners had been crammed these past three weeks with no room to even stand, and only limited access to the three on-deck toilets. The *Ukri* would gather them into a rag, sneak up on the unsuspecting victim, and shower them over his sleeping face. The panicked and hungry insects made quickly for any orifice available, invading eyes, ears, mouth and nose with equal vigor, to the uproarious entertainment of the bored spectators.

A revolting experience, by my old standards. Yet in this hell, as a ward of the Soviet NKVD—the People's Commissariat for Internal Affairs—my standards had changed. Rumor had it they were sending me to build a work camp in some frozen wasteland near the Arctic Circle. I had last bathed over two weeks before, in freezing water.

Despite the omnipresent cold, I wore thin cotton pants, a grey rag with arm holes that served as an undershirt, and a threadbare and filthy jacket that would not have even lined the cat's bed back in Warsaw. My feet remained bare, save the rags I'd tied haphazardly around them. I had last eaten off a plate three months previously. This morning, I waited for three hours in a line of prisoners to climb the ladder to the deck, for the privilege of emptying my watery bowels into a hole through which the cold river spray stung my chapped buttocks. On the way back down, I filled my battered tin cup with a grey "soup" in which some unidentifiable vegetables floated like bloated grey corpses.

I ate it with relish. My standards, you see, had changed.

In this leaner, feral version of myself, I recognized the lice shower for what it was: a hazing—a good thing. The *Ukri*, despite my being a Jew, were taking me under their protection, likely because of the prisoner I'd killed.

Oleg, the *Ukri* second-in-command, clapped me on the shoulder as I climbed out of my bunk, blood still streaming from my throbbing head. I slipped in the filth that sloshed back and forth on the floor with the gentle pitching of the ship, and he steadied me with a powerful hand. He smiled, showing a gapped row of blackened teeth. "You're okay. For a *Zhid*, that is."

Despite myself, I smiled back.

If I were to write a scene of how I met Danuta, it would read like this:

> **SETTING:** *A late-night, smoke-filled bar. Around a long rough wooden table, center stage, sit a collection of raggedly clothed intellectuals. Books, cups, and full ashtrays cover the table, conveying a lengthy and intensive discussion. All are arguing, raising a cacophony of voices. Samuel, at the head of the table, stands, and a respectful hush falls.*
>
> **SAMUEL:** *(He speaks with passion and authority, gesturing with his cigarette.)* Yes, Misha, but can you not see that Schulz's ontological issues clearly overshadow the epistemological? "There are no facts," as Nietzsche says, "only interpretations." This was Schulz's view, too. *(He smiles playfully.)* Or perhaps when you're in your

cups, you have trouble grasping the finer implications of this? You see....

As Samuel continues making the motions of his passionate speech, his voice fades, and the audience hears only silence. The stage lights fade too, and two spotlights come up, one gently illuminating the gesticulating Samuel, and the other Danuta.

Danuta is seated halfway down the table, listening raptly to Samuel. His words are clearly moving her deeply. She nods her head and leans forward as if to better engage with his brilliance.

Samuel suddenly stops speaking and looks directly at Danuta. He's intrigued by this new and beautiful face, so intrigued that he loses his chain of thought.

SAMUEL: *(He speaks gently.)* Hello, do I know you?

DANUTA: *(She smiles sweetly.)* Not yet, but you may.

"Not yet, but you may." Yes, this is how I would write the scene. Unfortunately, it would be utterly inaccurate, because no one has ever listened to my words with rapture, nor has my brilliance ever struck anyone dumb. Nor have I ever addressed more than three people at once, except at family dinners, and then only when asking someone to pass the peas.

In fact, I met Danuta under circumstances that were, to say the least, dramatically less flattering — nearly personally injurious.

Warsaw, Poland, November 1937

I left Jacek, whistling to myself as I exited the narrow hallway from which heavy wooden doors led into numerous lecture halls, and came into the building's foyer. The vast chamber sat nearly empty, it being near lunchtime. Only one boisterous group had gathered around one of the long wooden benches that lined the walls of the entranceway. I recognized them from afar as National Democrats — my political nemeses — and would have preferred to avoid being anywhere near them. Unfortunately, there was no other way out of the building.

Does one ever really learn to live with slurs? Does one eventually develop a "thick skin," so epithets "roll off one's back?" Or do the words work themselves slowly into the flesh — like microscopic cacti barbs, innocuous at the initial prick, but building to a critical mass of pain — that must eventually either scratch the soul or erupt violently?

I'd been called every imaginable form, permutation, or slang of "Jew" from childhood. Somewhere along the way, I'd accepted it as a simple fact of life, and today should have been no different.

But it was.

Since the advent of the ghetto bench, I'd been volcanically on edge. I reached critical mass when the egalitarian future my father had dangled before me had been rudely yanked away—with a derisive laugh, at that. This anger, I found, felt liberating and empowering. I no longer feared the bullying, and I welcomed the chance to use my newfound linguistic courage to boldly fling barbs back at my attackers. Reckless? Perhaps, but I didn't care.

When the National Democrat Cro-Magnons started in, I didn't hesitate to answer back with vitriol, perhaps fueled by my humiliation in the lecture hall. What I didn't take into account was the complete emptiness of the building, and my own relative distance from the safety of the exit. Before I'd even finished my opening diatribe about the size of their hooded genitalia being in direct proportion to the size of their clearly miniscule brains, the Cro-Magnons had me surrounded.

They literally backed me into a corner, holding my shoulders and legs tightly with their rough hands. The largest of the group, a brutish-looking fellow whose thick face was partially obscured by a flap of pomaded hair that had broken loose from his Hitler Youth haircut, pulled a closed switchblade knife from his back pocket. He clicked it open with a practiced flourish, its click echoing in the empty, silent hall. He sneered when he spoke, making his already unattractive, simian face even uglier.

I thought it wise not to point this out.

"It seems," he said, "as though you have some phallic issues, my small friend. Let's see if what they say about the size of you Jews is true. If it is, perhaps some trimming is in order—just so you don't overshadow we under-endowed Poles, of course." He nodded at a boy next to him who was not involved in controlling my increasingly violent struggles.

The boy undid my belt, and started to slide my pants down, to the delight of the onlookers, who hooted and jeered.

"What *would* your mothers say?"

The voice that rang out was so powerful in its matronly command that all intuitively stopped—myself included—and turned towards it. We Poles, gentile and Jew alike, shared a sympathetic nervous system that responded with Pavlovian reliability to the voice of any Polish female, especially mothers. This inborn response returned grown men instantly to the worst moment of their boyhood—when they were caught hitting a sibling, conducting a prank, masturbating in the bathroom, or concealing a piece of gristle in a napkin. The response turned knees weak, clenched bowels, froze arm or leg muscles, and created instant subconscious guilt from which only the most powerful could free themselves.

This voice wielded such power.

The hands released me and I caught my pants, which were already halfway to my knees.

The Cro-Magnon with the knife quickly concealed it, then he and rest of the group skulked away from me like chastised kittens from a half-finished saucer of cream. They left the building without another word.

I caught my first glimpse of my savior, like looking directly at the sun. The green-blue image would remain forever seared on my retinas.

The origin of the voice stood in front of me, as I clutched my pants at my waist and fumbled with my belt with as much dignity as I could muster. She stood half a head shorter than me, and two full heads smaller than the largest of my assailants. Her dark brown hair fell below her shoulders loosely, framing a round face with a perfectly even smile that created miraculous dimples in her smooth-skinned cheeks.

I cleared my throat. "Good thing you came along. I was just about to really let them have it."

She pushed an itinerant strand of hair from her eyes, which smiled even as her face grew mockingly serious. "Yes, I could see that. I acted solely in the national interest, to prevent unnecessary Gentile bloodshed. Thank goodness I did so. Are you all right?"

I haphazardly finished arranging my pants, straightened my hair, and gathered the books that had scattered from my fallen bag. After regaining a semblance of composure, I straightened up to my full height and looked her in the eye.

With grave suavity, and using my most ceremonious and deeply baritone voice, I said, "I'm fine, thank you. Poland owes you a debt, madame."

Her smile, returning in earnest this time, lit the foyer.

I began to feel more confident, relaxed, back in control.

This is really happening! This beautiful woman is standing here, and wants to hear what I have to say. She wants my philosophical explanation of the evil that has befallen me.

Images of our future together sped through my head—long conversations into the night over wine, a romantic walk along the Vistula, a candlelit dinner, her lips on my neck, the whiteness of her bare shoulders in the moonlight.

Then she spoke again. "Poland might be even better served by you fastening the buttons on your fly, kind sir. But only after you tuck in your... uh... you know."

Thus, I developed a preference for my own fictional, yet infinitely more egotistically palatable, version of our first meeting.

CHAPTER 3
Samuel: Resonating to the Core

Warsaw, Poland, November 1937

I was either supremely self-confident, supremely stupid, or—more likely—a healthy combination of both., Why? Because I managed to carry on an intelligent conversation with Danuta even after inadvertently exposing myself to her—after my humiliation at the hands of the Cro-Magnons.

I'd been accosted before by bullies, though never to such an extreme. The streets of Warsaw were no longer safe for Jews to wander alone, at any time of the day. President Pilsudski had truly seemed immortal and invincible, but turned out to be neither. Since his death, not only had the economy gone downhill, but our personal safety, too.

Being beaten scars the soul, and there is really no shutting it out. Of course, there are those who would say that the aggressors' souls are equally, if not more, scarred by such violence. Of them I would ask, "How many apex predators do you know who are currently undergoing psychoanalysis?" Bullies and evil people everywhere kill because *they can*, because no one stops them. Evil does no damage to the *souls* of evildoers simply because *they lack them entirely*.

This might have explained the resilience I displayed in my interaction with this magnificent creature who had—now for the first time—come to my rescue. After I'd returned all parts of myself to their rightful places, during which time Danuta demurely and tactfully looked away, I turned back to her and mustered a smile, even as the heat began to fade from my cheeks.

"By all rights, if our acquaintance is to begin on equal footing, I should know something intimate of *you*." I looked straight in her eyes as I said this, softening the audacity of my words with a kind smile.

I tried to ignore her intoxicating yet obstinately casual beauty. Hers was the glow of someone who knew of her beauty, yet regularly discounted her physical attributes. It was a rare external beauty because it was equally mirrored within, as I was already learning.

She was shorter than me, which certainly made her no Nordic god in stature. What she lacked in height she more than compensated for in proportion. Perfect leather-shod feet eased upward via narrow ankles to light-muscled calves, the perfection of which disappeared into a heavy wool skirt, only to emerge into a firmly rounded posterior that I admired surreptitiously and at length the moment she turned to leave.

Moving up, everything was so marvelously apportioned that the adolescent in me couldn't help but rise to the occasion. I shifted uncomfortably, unobtrusively pulling my jacket to cover my erection.

Whether she noticed this, I was not yet sure. In any case, she seemed unfazed by my audacity as she clutched her small stack of notebooks to her chest and turned away. "Perhaps you shall know nothing of me at all, young Samuel Katz."

She flounced away across the foyer, taking my breath with her as she went. She got as far as the door and then—blessedly—turned her head just enough for me to see one eye and a perfect profile. "That is, unless you are to buy me a hot chocolate in the student commons. If you feel you'll be able to sit comfortably with that... you know."

I couldn't get the silly smile off my face for the next hour.

Pechora River, Soviet Union, February 1941

I learned what despair smelled like: the sharp fetidity of suppuration. It smelled like the slow agony of flesh that rotted while still attached to the living body. I smelled it on every frostbitten work detail to which we shuffled, knowing each time that some would not return. Mostly, I saw it... in the eyes of the ones the guards called *chleno rubi*.

The work was impossible. All day we moved iron rails, two men to a rail, from a mountain-like pile next to the end of the rail line, to another pile 200 meters away. None of the guards explained why this was necessary, and none of us prisoners asked. The fact that the rails were frozen solid to each other in their massive pile, the result of freezing rain, complicated the work. We had to break them free by sledgehammer before we could lift them.

At minus 42 degrees, the steel of the rails became carnivorous, devouring the ungloved flesh of our hands. It predatorily sought the warmer parts of our palms and fingertips, keenly calculated the temperature differential, and quietly latched on to these parts only. We didn't realize we were stuck until we dropped the rail, and small strips of flesh tore off our already chilled and sensitive hands. These small wounds accumulated over the course of weeks, until all of our hands looked like so much ground meat.

The *chleno rubi* didn't have these problems. "There are three stages of life, as I see it," Oleg said, as he released his end of the rail. He had again forgotten to warn me before he did this, and it narrowly missed my foot as it crashed to the frozen ground.

I tracked the rail's slow-motion downward progress dumbly, and noticed that the rags wrapped around the tatters of what I loosely called my shoe had again come undone. I stooped to arrange them as Oleg droned on.

"Birth, pain, death. Nothing more to it. But the *chleno rubi* have added a new stage, or at least a sub-stage, which falls somewhere under pain. They added 'rest.' I'm telling you, *Zhid*, they're onto something."

I nodded in agreement, as I always did when Oleg spoke. He was my protector, the head of the *Ukri*. Thus, I agreed with anything he said, as a rule. This made our conversations rather tedious, but I quickly learned that 'yes' was always the best answer when chatting casually to a sociopath. In any case, I didn't bite the hand that quite literally fed me. I remained alive only because I was the Ukrainians' pet Jew. We got the best of the meager rations the Soviets provided. If I had to suffer some poor conversation, it was a small sacrifice.

Ironically, this time I agreed with Oleg. The *chleno rubi* really were onto something. They had become limb-hewers, self-mutilators. The smell of their despair struck even before they purposefully positioned a finger under a rail, the millisecond before it slammed down against another, or before a well-aimed hatchet separated a steaming, filthy toe from its foot after a guard turned his back.

The truth be told, self-mutilation was an excellent strategy for staying alive, especially in the camp-which-was-not-yet-a-camp. Until we completed the rail line, which would facilitate transport of materials for our bunkhouses, we slept outside, heaped in shallow trenches we chiseled into the frozen ground. At night, so desperate for warmth, all set aside their self-consciousness. I huddled with my face pressed to a backside, a stomach, a groin—it was of no concern, as long as it radiated heat.

The merciful Soviets would grant the *chleno rubi* two weeks recovery in the lice-infested "hospital ward" back in the main camp. Two weeks of sleep under a roof. Two precious weeks that enabled the body, and not just the stump of the missing appendage, to recover a little. Of course, the Soviets added an extra month to each self-mutilator's sentence for inflicting grave damage on state property. Nonetheless, while we prisoners slept knowing with certainty that not all of us would wake, the *chleno rubi* could rest assured that they, for the time being, would. Was this not worth the price of a finger or two?

Such misery inevitably caused me to recall Danuta's first touch. It was a touch that never ended. Because throughout this taste of hell, deep beneath the accumulated grime of the ship and the work camp, below the frostbite, above the hunger and mortal fear, that first touch continued to tingle. It continued to resonate to the core of all that I was. It remained within, in a deep place where I alone could reach it, feel it, be rescued by it—even if only for a moment.

Warsaw, Poland, November 1937

Had I been a typical bookworm, I'd have said my fondest and oldest memory was when I first put two letters together and was touched by the Hand of God—a personal Creation of Adam moment. Yet I was not a typical bookworm. I didn't even remember putting C-A-T together for the first time, nor did it carry any relevance to what I had become.

Words were vehicles for stories, nothing more. Individually, they carried meaning, but only as the cup contained the water—only as the vehicle. What moved a thirsty man to raise the cup to his lips was the thought of drinking, the remembrance of past satiation. For me, the words were water—but the story was the long, cool drink.

Only when words coalesced into a story did they come alive.

My story with Danuta began that day, with the steam of her hot chocolate repeatedly fogging the lenses of her round-rimmed glasses. Each time, she would absentmindedly remove them and smear at the fog with the hem of her dress. The din in the bustling student lounge forced us to lean in close to hear each other. With a smile, I challenged her to name her closest confidante.

She shouted her response intimately over the background noise. "Adrianna, my cousin from my mother's side. She lives in Vilnius. She's my best friend, and I share everything with her. Perhaps I shall write her this very evening."

I fired back, mentally kicking myself even as the words left my mouth. "I should very much like to be a fly on the wall above your desk during *that* writing."

She smiled at me and blushed, and I realized with a surge of joy that she was not aloof, as I had first worried. She, the Catholic girl with the angelic face, the body of Aphrodite, and the beautiful soul whose murky depths I longed to plumb, felt shy around me. Realizing this, I backpedaled rapidly.

"I didn't mean to be bold. That is, your private correspondence is certainly your business. I just—"

"Someday, perhaps you shall know." Then she reached out to touch the back of my hand, which was resting on the wood tabletop, lightly with her fingertips. She never let go.

From that day in the commons, Danuta and I spent most of our time together.

She loved that I made her laugh. She loved my hair, my long fingers, the tickle of my light stubble against her cheek. She loved that I could look at the darkening skies closing in on Poland and find humor. She would laugh aloud as she corrected the typos in drafts of my now weekly articles for *Glos Gminy Zydowskiej*. I had turned the column into a satirical faux-advice column titled *In the Land of the Blind*.... In it, I posited possible Jewish responses to the growing anti-Semitism we all suffered, and created an alternate, Jewish-centric reality.

"I'm not sure," Danuta said, "that hoarding Christian children and reselling them on the black market would be the best move for a Jewish businessman, darling." She chuckled and kissed the top of my head as she leaned over my desk. "And neither will instituting a *numerus clausus* quota for Christians buying from Jewish tailors. Frankly, I'm not sure whom that would harm more—the Jews that would go hungry, or the Gentiles who would end up sockless. And must you look down my blouse *every* time I lean over you?"

I wrote with a young man's audacity, cynicism, and utter lack of concern for consequences. I wrote with the passion of the damned and the ferocity of the caged. Not all accepted my humor with good grace. I received outraged letters and blatant threats. Yet we were all staring into the empty-eyed face of imminent, unnamed horror. The angst, though unspoken, remained omnipresent. I believed that my descriptions of a ridiculous upside-down world, wherein Jews arbitrarily ruled, brought a measure of comfort and amusement to my readers.

Then a letter arrived from Warsaw University, cowing me into silence. Even with the looming threat, it was the darkest day I could recall.

Danuta stood fast and firm. "Listen to me. They do not define your worth. They do not define your being. You are a person. I am a person. It's Samuel the *person* I love, not Samuel the student, not Samuel the writer, and certainly not Samuel the Jew. Do you love Danuta the Catholic, Danuta the student, or just me?"

She demanded this of me as I limply clutched the notice informing me that I could no longer continue my studies. As if in direct response to my editorial taunting, Warsaw University had revived the traditional *numerus clausus* quota, which limited the percentage of Jews in Polish universities. From that day, in addition to being friend, lover, confidante, compatriot, and editor, Danuta became my professor, too.

Every afternoon thereafter, she or Jacek—sometimes both together—would come to my parents' recently purchased fifth-floor flat at the corner of Wybrzeze Szczecinskie and Klopotowskiego. The new building, one of the first in the Praga district, had an elevator. We would sit by the large window in the living room, watching the Vistula and Warsaw's Old Town above the riverbank greenery.

I loved the view from that window. In the mornings, seagulls whirled over the Vistula, asking unanswerable questions and not bothering to wait for replies. The slow-moving current kissed the banks in a constant farewell. Beyond, towards Old Town, building-block houses climbed the hill via steep and winding staircases, their massive curving stone foundations reaching deep into the cobblestone-faced earth, as if announcing their refusal to budge. The red-tiled roofs of Warsaw University, directly across the river and now mockingly out of reach, laughed at me.

Jacek or Danuta would relate each lecture from memory, consulting their notes, while I listened and absorbed. I kept up with reading during the day, in vain hope that the madness would somehow blow over and I'd soon be able to continue my studies.

Of course, having Danuta around was not always entirely conducive to contemplation of matters of the higher mind.

Jacek huffed. "Hey, *malpeczko*, you want to get your mind back on Kant, and out of the gutter? The drool is so deep in here that my fucking socks are getting wet!"

He enjoyed catching me when my glazed eyes strayed from his recounting of a lecture to, for example, the magnificent whiteness of Danuta's knee peeking from her skirt as she sat, cat-like, with legs tucked under her.

We made an unlikely couple in the context of that time — *impossible* would be a better word. The repulsive anti-miscegenation laws of the neighboring Third Reich had not yet reached Poland, although many there would have welcomed them. Poland's response to "the Jewish problem" was already blossoming from propaganda into violence, from discriminatory practice into overtly anti-Semitic legislation. Association with Jews became first socially unpopular, then unwise, then dangerous. To the best of our knowledge, Danuta's parents knew nothing of our romance. My parents were aware of the connection for obvious reasons — Danuta was inevitably at our house — and were not against it in principle. Their acceptance, however, grew progressively more conditional: they first urged prudence, then counseled caution, and ultimately demanded absolute secrecy.

Amazingly, no one ever caught us in our many "illicit" liaisons. No one ever publicly accosted us as we walked together — always after dark and always keeping to unlit side streets. No one ever called Danuta a whore, or cursed me for ruining a Catholic girl. We kept to ourselves, insular in my living room, longing for the moment when my mother would leave for the market, at which time we would be drawn together with electromagnetic force, silently and insatiably groping and grinding on the sofa. All the while, one of my ears would listen intently for the sound of my mother's key in the lock, while the other was gloriously filled with Danuta's urgent breathing.

It was wonderful. It was horrible. I wanted it to last forever.

CHAPTER 4
Samuel: Finding the Words

Naryan-Mar, Soviet Union, August 1941

If I'd been in front of a typewriter, I would have been joyously ruminating on the true essence of freedom.

What power the term carries, even though most have never even had a whiff of its fair fruits! How it conquers dreams, moves worlds, yet defies achievement even in the most just of societies.

Yet I was not in front of a typewriter. In fact, my feet would cover thousands more kilometers before I might, if lucky, caress those keys again. What's more, I had little time for rumination at that moment, not just owing to my preoccupation with love or the neglect of justice, but because a wild-eyed, pitchfork-wielding farmer was chasing me through a muddy cabbage field.

I ran like I'd never run before through the field, a clay nightmare just north of Naryan-Mar. I ran as if the devil himself nipped at my heels, all the while tightly clutching the half-rotten head of cabbage I'd just stolen. My lungs burned as I pushed my withered sticks of legs ever faster and my mud-streaked feet sought, as if autonomously, the clearest path to the relative safety of the forest. I hugged the cabbage tighter to my abdomen, and willed my legs to give me one last burst of speed. Six months of *gulag* fare betrayed me, however, and an instant later, my hunger-weakened legs gelatinized.

I slid to a stop facedown in the mud, and raised my head, gasping for air. The heavy-booted splash of footsteps sounded closer. The instant's respite restored me, and I began to scramble for a foothold, prepared to rise and resume my flight. I found hope, and footing, and actually began to believe I had a chance, when I heard the whoosh of the pitchfork in the air above my head, then felt its butt — thankfully not its prongs — strike me just above my ear. Then I felt no more.

When I woke, a warm night breeze sang one of Chopin's *Nocturnes* in my ears. I think it may have been #4. The warmth enveloped me, making me almost forget the sucking mud in which I lay half-submerged. I stared into the star-choked sky, and saw in my mind's eye the rapturous face I'd first seen above me in another field, on another warm summer evening, happily blocking my view of different stars.

I closed my eyes and again felt the whisper of Danuta's velvet hair brushing my cheek, the satin of her belly as it pressed to mine. I felt the spot on the back of my hand that still burned from her first touch. I tasted the very light that she was, and inhaled the powerful delicacy of her scent after we first made love.

I opened my eyes, and smiled, for I recalled that I was free. The Soviets had released me and all the other Polish prisoners from the work camp—just let us go. I learned that over 250,000 of us were now free thanks to Adolf Hitler—who simply couldn't keep his pecker in his pants, as my father used to say. Germany attacked the Soviet Union in June 1941, and among the resulting benefits was the release of all Polish prisoners from Soviet prisons.

Thus, a week previously, a guard had called me from the work detail, to the immense outrage of my *Ukri* companions. "Are you the Polish *Zhid*?" he asked.

When I nodded in affirmation, he marched me, with no further ceremony, straight to the "gate" — which was really just a rectangle of logs lashed rudely together with barbed wire.

Oleg protested loudly behind me. "Why him? What's so special about that scrawny *Zhid*? How about us?"

"Congratulations, *Zhid*, you've been released," the guard said. He stuffed half a cabbage and a flimsy piece of paper with Russian writing on it into my hands, and shoved me out the still-unbuilt work camp with a final curse in Russian.

My clothes were rags, and I was barefoot. I had no money, no papers save the one the guard gave me, and no possessions except the bundle with Danuta's letters, which I'd somehow managed to keep safe over the preceding months. I also had not even a clue as to exactly where I was, or how I could possibly get to where I so desperately needed to be. Thankfully, it was warm by sub-arctic circle standards, but I knew it wouldn't last long.

I also knew that Soviet bureaucracies were fickle beings and decided not to look a gift horse in the mouth. I needed to be as far away as possible from the NKVD, before some bureaucrat belatedly realized that my release—and that of my fellow Poles—had been a mistake. As I would learn during my newfound freedom, freed Poles were supposed to be assigned to work companies, and encouraged to join what became known as Anders Army, officially the Polish Armed Forces in the East, headed by General Wladyslaw Anders. They were decidedly *not* supposed to be summarily shown the door, as I was.

I gauged my direction by the faint sun, tucked the paper into a tattered pocket, and set out southward, munching cabbage as I marched towards *Eretz Yisrael*, towards my brother Aron, towards Danuta.

Over the next week, I worked my way south, following the Pechora River. Its course, I'd learned from a passing glimpse at the maps in the camp office, meandered. Yet it was the most reliable guide I had. I slept in fields, and hid in ditches when hay wagons or troop transports passed. I adapted to life at its most feral. Perhaps this was freedom, but in its elemental state—no possessions, no promise of tomorrow beyond the assurance that the sun would rise. Yet if it *was* freedom, it was empty, for I also lacked any companionship save the birds that woke me and the mosquitoes that sang me *Nocturnes* at night.

Thus, I now fought against the suction of the mud, which threatened to imprison me again. The left side of my head was a swollen, bleeding lump. My left ear rang with a high-pitched whine, but I was alive, and I was on my way.

I sat up and gazed around the now-empty field. I found the half cabbage, which in some passing convulsion of generosity or pity, the farmer had left for me. I chewed it vigorously, savoring the glory of satiation even as I spit out mud out between mouthfuls. I ate every leaf and stalk of that cabbage, including the insects I found among the leaves.

I knew that I would need strength to find Danuta in Tel Aviv. I knew she would be waiting, and I had never been one to break a date.

Vilnius, Independent Lithuania, December 1939

"You couldn't have known. There was no human way you could have known." Insistent and sincere, Danuta pressed tighter to my side.

We huddled on the splintered wooden bench at the tip of Kalnai Park. The confluence of the Neris and Vilnia rivers was already partially covered by mica-thin December ice. The high river embankment sheltered us from the frigid wind, but the cold bit at us all the same. The sky had turned an impending-winter grey. My mood had turned abandonment black.

"I left them," I said. "First Aron left, then I left. What kind of son does that? What kind of person knowingly leaves his parents in danger?"

I'd never made the acquaintance of personal mortal anguish, but I was already the best of chums with the familial brand. I left Warsaw at my parents' urging the night the war began. I slinked through the darkened streets as the German bombers whined like destructive toddlers overhead, clumsily but effectively turning more than a tenth of Warsaw into rubble.

From the window of our darkened flat on Wybrzeze Szczecinskie Street, we could clearly see Old Town across the Vistula. Giant footfalls of explosions tramped across the city, sowing hungry tongues of fire, which licked at buildings that had stood for hundreds of years. An anti-aircraft gun chattered to life on the sandbar in the middle of the river. Even from the relative distance, the rapid succession of *thwocks* produced by the outgoing shells rattled our building, creating a teeth-chattering effect as we struggled to speak.

"Th-th-th-this will be no place for Jews, s-s-s-son. You have no f-f-f-future here." My father's voice hissed as he spoke, his passion vying mightily with a misguided sense of discretion. He tried to keep his voice low even as he struggled to be heard over the din of the guns, so that Mother wouldn't overhear.

It didn't work.

"Your f-f-f-father is right..." she began, entering from the hall, but her words trailed off.

From high above, an unearthly scream arose, coming closer and increasing in intensity, until we instinctively stuffed fingers in our ears to muffle it. We all looked up as if the ceiling could somehow reveal the angel of death that we were sure dove mercilessly towards us.

For the first time in my life, I saw visceral fear in my parents' eyes. I saw them in their helpless frailty. I saw my stalwart mother—who'd never backed away from an argument with a teacher, shopkeeper, or neighbor—cowering.

My father's words, which stood in direct contradiction to all he'd taught me of Polish civic rights and obligations, reverberated deep in my consciousness, momentarily overcoming even the siren's whine: *"You have no future here."*

The scream continued, the ghastly signature of a German Stuka dive bomber. The Nazis had equipped them with Jericho Trumpets, propeller-driven sirens powered by the increased airstream of the plane's bombing dive. They'd designed the sirens specifically for psychological effect, to terrify anyone in the plane's path.

It worked fantastically on us.

The explosion was close enough that we could feel the shock wave roll over and through us. Plaster dust drifted from the ceiling. Our building had neither basement nor even crawl space in which to hide, so we'd moved to the kitchen, the most internal room in the flat. Although the bombers targeted the anti-aircraft gun, we were well within their margin of error.

My mother raised her voice. "Go to Vilnius, just for now. Take Danuta. Her parents approve. We've talked to them. Yes, they know about you two. They're good people. Go! Stay with Danuta's cousin, just until things settle down."

Despite her best attempt at a reassuring parental tone, the tremor in her voice betrayed her clear knowledge that things would *not* settle down.

I tried unsuccessfully to keep the childish pleading out of my voice. "But I want to stay with you. Why can't we stay?"

I hadn't yet come to terms with this sudden about-face regarding my place in the world. I'd grown up knowing that Poland, despite its ills, was our home. It was our future. We would fight for it, embrace it, and steer it like a wayward child back onto the path of justice. This was our mission.

And now it *wasn't*?

We huddled in a corner of the kitchen as another wail began from above.

I changed tack, raising my voice so they could hear me. "What if we *all* go? You come with us? We'll make room for you at Adrianna's. We'll find you your own apartment. We can wait it out together."

The new explosion was closer. Glasses fell from shelves, and an ominous crack appeared in the kitchen ceiling, but I could not persuade them.

They revealed their plan to leave the city, too. My father's elderly parents, the grandparents I barely knew, were alone in their village. They needed caring for. My parents' place was in Poland, no matter what.

My place, *my* future, could not be so.

"Look," my father said. "We'll meet back here. We'll be fine. Go!"

For the next thirty minutes, as the Stukas shrieked and the bombs shook the physical and metaphysical foundations of my childhood, they urged, cajoled, and reassured me.

In the end, I listened. Like some teenager torn between the temptation of a night out with friends and the burden of a family dinner, I convinced myself that what I *wanted* to do was in complete alignment with what I *should* do. With my mother's oversight, I packed a small bag, and the noise outside subsided somewhat. Perhaps the Stukas had finally hit the anti-aircraft emplacement, and moved on to other sections of the city. Acrid smoke drifted thick across the river, obscuring Old Town from our view.

"I'll write you," I said after the formality of our hug.

I was already thinking about seeing Danuta, about the life we'd make for ourselves in Vilnius, about the lascivious possibilities of spending every single night with her in our own bed. God help me, even as the guns began roaring again and I crossed Panienska Street, heading towards her parents' flat, I thought about Danuta's body. I envisioned the way she gasped when my fingers entered her, about the way her tongue would lightly flit to the corner of her mouth when she came. In my mind's eye, I was touching her oh-so-lightly when the wail of a diving Stuka began above me.

The bomb slammed without warning into my parents' building behind me. The shock wave lifted and threw me rudely, and I crumpled into the cement wall of Praski Hospital.

My ears rang, and my mind didn't yet comprehend what had happened, as I raised my head to look in the direction of my home. The dust cleared, and the volume of my own wail drowned out even that of the Stukas.

"You couldn't have known," Danuta repeated gently, still pressed against me on that splintered wooden bench.

I didn't look up. In the month that had passed since our three-day odyssey from Warsaw to Vilnius, the adrenalin had receded. We'd settled into the guest room of Adrianna's flat, and I'd settled into the comfort of heavy silence.

I huddled deeper into my father's overcoat, one of the last things I'd grabbed—at his insistence—on my way out of the flat. Why had I agreed to take it? Had I thought he wouldn't need it?

I slumped lower on the bench, but Danuta grew insistent. She took my face in her gloved hands and raised it to her own. The eyes that, over the past month, had shown me empathy, worry, and even some pity, now flashed unambiguous anger.

"Enough!" She sighed. "Listen to me. Do you trust me? Yes? Then truly listen. More than anything, your parents were committed to your life. That's why they wanted you to leave Warsaw. They were committed to your life. They believed that you were important—not just to them, not just to me, to the world. You believed it, too. Now they're gone, and that's terrible, but I'm here with you, and it's time to share their commitment, Samuel. It's time to pick up your burden. It's time to live. Find the words, and use their power. Write the words that will speak your pain."

As her warm lips met mine, I listened. After the kiss, I took her gloved hands in my own and looked into her face, which now held a mysterious radiance.

"Why are you smiling," I asked? "What could there possibly be to smile about?"

She bent to scrape the snow away from the ground beside the bench, revealing the green fuzziness of the grass below. "I'm smiling at life, my love. You see, it may not always be immediately visible, but its possibility is never too deeply hidden if you take the time to look."

The next day, with a heavy heart but firm resolve, I sat down at Adrianna's typewriter and wrote the first of what would become a weekly column for the newly-founded Polish-language newspaper, *Kurjer Wilenski* — the Vilnius Courier. I called it *This Island of Sanity.*

Vilnius was indeed, for those few months from late 1939 to mid-1940, an island of sanity in a Europe gone mad. Initially occupied by the Soviets, they'd given it over to independent Lithuanian rule in late October 1939. Poles, and especially Polish Jews, flocked to the city, turning it into an overcrowded refuge from the duopoly of Soviet-Nazi terror. A thriving and vociferous Polish-speaking Jewish community emerged, a community ripe for my urgent and no longer humorous calls to reclaim our lost homeland—from both the Nazis and the Soviets.

It was, unfortunately, short-lived sanity. Before I published my twentieth column, in August of 1940, the USSR annexed all of Lithuania, and the NKVD began arresting and deporting "dissidents" who'd had the audacity to speak against the USSR.

One sunny day in late August of 1940, with Kalnai Park redolent with greenery, and Danuta equally so with the perfume I'd bought for her 23rd birthday, the dreaded letter arrived. They "invited" me to the Vilnius municipal building two mornings hence for a "discussion."

Like a good citizen, I went. I kissed Danuta goodbye that morning, and walked out the door of Adrianna's flat.

CHAPTER 5
Aron: A Chance to Do Good

Tel Aviv, Tuesday, September 16, 1940

> To: Samuel Katz
> Lukiskes Prison
> Vilnius, Lithuania

My Dearest Brother,

I received a short note yesterday from Danuta informing me of your incarceration in Vilnius. If I only had your words, I could perhaps better express the heavy angst that has settled in the pit of my stomach since I heard. Alas, you are the writer in the family.

All I can say, Samuel, is that I dearly hope the brotherly embrace of this letter reaches you. I most sincerely pray it finds you in good health and spirits. Despite our distance, you are always in my heart, as you and our parents were since the day I left for Palestine so long ago. If this missive has been sadly uncommunicated by me over the years, it does not, has never, nor will ever alter its veracity.

Danuta mentioned nothing of the circumstances surrounding your arrest, nor when she expects them to release you. All I received was the address to which I now write. If you can perhaps enlighten me as to where you are and what has happened, perhaps I can somehow be of assistance? The Bank does have Lithuanian dealings, and perhaps I could prevail upon my superiors to attempt to use their connections to somehow ease your plight.

My powerlessness to help you, little brother, threatens my sanity. I was a poor sibling to you since long before I left – you then but a child of 13, and I myself barely more adult at 18. Please know that I had only the deepest, most pressingly personal and sincerely ideological reasons for doing so, and don't resent my actions – selfish and misguided though they have turned out to be.

I know so little of your life, nor you of mine — which is my own fault, of course. Since I cannot ask you the questions I'd like, I will share with you something of my own life, here in Tel Aviv. My hands shake even now, almost a week later, as I recollect it.

I still have a copy of Davar from September 9 in front me — a full week ago, which might as well be an eternity! The headline is "Quiet in the Mediterranean won't Last." How right Katzenelson, the editor-in-chief, was! I bought the paper that morning, and by the evening, our quiet Tel Aviv, this island of tranquility in the storm enveloping the world, had changed immeasurably.

It was Tuesday afternoon, and the summer heat had not yet left Tel Aviv. I stood in a line on Bugrashov Street, near the intersection with King George, having left work at the bank early that day. A neighbor had telephoned me in my office to tell me that they were finally distributing kerosene on our street. I'd had none for cooking the whole week previously, so I rushed home to gather my flimsy (what the British call the four-gallon cans we all use for kerosene, since they are so poorly made) and queued up behind the horse-drawn cart. I was chatting amicably to my neighbor, Mrs. Lowenstein, whose affability I have appreciated since I first moved to my flat. How odd it still is to write those words! Me, a homeowner in Tel Aviv. Yet they remain blessedly accurate, despite everything.

I remember thinking how unusual it was to hear any airplane noise, especially given that the British had just closed the Tel Aviv Airport, which was located not far from here, north of the Yarkon River. I saw the five planes come in from the direction of the sea, and noted that they weren't the usual Palestine Airways de Havillands. Their noise faded as they turned north, and I went back to chatting with Mrs. Lowenstein.

I knew something was wrong when I suddenly heard the engines, much closer now, approaching from the East. Before we realized what was happening, they were upon us, huge and moving so quickly. The first swooped down like some prehistoric bird god, and from its belly burst a flood of... paper. Yes, paper! The plane dropped thousands of pieces of paper, which floated gently down from the sky like misshapen snowflakes. The writing was, oddly, in Arabic. I recall feeling relief so immense that I could not help but silently grin in puzzlement to Mrs. Lowenstein and the others in the line. Someone towards the back of the line began translating loudly. All I heard was "...you will recover ownership and freedom of your land with Italian assistance!" I had no time to consider the possible meaning of these words, because the second plane was upon us.

This plane did not drop paper.

What I saw — what I still see now, brother — is something that no one should ever see. I saw Mrs. Lowenstein's legs — which had held her in conversation with me just seconds before. I couldn't understand because they were twitching by the kerosene cart, which had tipped over, whereas she was calling to me from across the street. And I heard a roaring in my head, not through my ears, but actually in my head. When I covered my ears, it only got louder. I didn't hear screaming, but I did see the kerosene cart horse, which lay on top of the kerosene seller, who was moving his mouth as if screaming. I couldn't hear him, and I tried to move, but something was on top of me, and it wasn't a piece of meat. It was the body of the man who was just behind me in the line for kerosene. I knew this because I recognized his red suspenders, but he had no arms. My head was still roaring, and there was SO MUCH BLOOD...

Of course, I never sent this letter. I crumpled it and threw it into the waste bin. Then I retrieved it, smoothed it carefully, and burned it over the sink in my small kitchen.

I did write a letter to Samuel, in which I expressed concern and empathy. The words I wrote were exactly what one might expect a remote — some would say estranged — older brother to write. Correct. Sympathetic. I vaguely offered assistance that both sender and recipient knew I would proffer only in correspondence.

I hated myself for this letter.

I stood with the stamped airmail envelope clutched in one hand, hesitating in front of the red Royal Mail pillar box at the corner of my oddly-named street, Buki Ben Yagli. It was the name of the biblical head of the Dan tribe, but more recently the penname of the Russian-Jewish author Yehuda Katzenelson — no relation to the editor of *Davar*. I'd taken the time to learn this before buying the flat at number 8 three years previously, because I realized this would be more than just a place to rest my head. At the unusually young age of twenty-five, after arriving nearly destitute in British Mandatory Palestine just seven years previously, I was purchasing a home in the very center of what would become the collective home of the entire Jewish people. It was a moment worthy of thorough consideration.

I slipped the tip of the envelope into the mail slot, but kept one edge tightly pinched between forefinger and thumb.

Over the course of a lifetime, everyone embraces and rejects their past in equal measures. Maturity is the acceptance of the past, whereas youth is defined by its rejection.

I was, I feared, still young in this respect. Perhaps I would remain so forever. Yet even as part of me denied connection to my family in the *galut*, the diaspora, I still longed for the comfort of a home built *for* me, not *by* me. Now that I had the latter, the former seemed as precious as it was unobtainable. This, I understood, was why I composed letters to Samuel that I would never send, and instead sent letters that I reviled.

Still not releasing the letter, I looked up Bugrashov Street. Municipal workmen filled in the bomb craters. There had been fifty-six of them—bombs, not craters—according to *Davar*, each weighing 100 kilos. One hundred thirty men, women, and children had died—Arabs, Jews, and one Australian soldier. They'd driven the coffins from the Hadassah Balfour hospital on the backs of trucks, to the Nahalat Yitzchak cemetery, where they would simultaneously inter them in a mass grave. A mutely disbelieving populace—myself included—had lined the streets, silently watching the endless line of vehicles pass by.

Still I stood, unable to let go of the letter that said nothing of what I felt. Like the coffins I'd watched go by, I'd buried my feelings for my family *en masse*—too deeply, I worried, ever to exhume. The farther I reached my hand into the cookie jar of my emotions, the more elusive the crumbs at the bottom became.

On both sides of the street, workmen dotted rickety scaffoldings, busily replacing windows and shutters, and filling in shrapnel pockmarks. The surface of these walls would be smooth, I thought, but their underlying structure would carry the scars of the attack as long as they stood, as would I.

My hearing had improved slightly already. The doctor had told me that the deafness was only temporary, although the high-pitched tinnitus seemed likely to become my permanent auditory companion. Other than a few bruises, I remained otherwise—perhaps miraculously, perhaps unjustifiably—unhurt. I kept asking myself one simple question: *Why?*

Haifa had been bombed just the day before, and London the day before that — the first salvo in what people were already calling the Blitz of London. The Haifa port and the terminus of the Iraq-Haifa pipeline were strategic targets, so they made some sense in all the senselessness. But why Tel Aviv? Why waste bombs on a city with no military value whatsoever?

It was a mistake, or so the quasi-official, ever-reliable Tel Aviv rumor machine reported. The Italian bombers had originally targeted Haifa, but were chased off by British fighters, and rerouted to the Jaffa port. That the Italian pilots didn't manage to find this clear coastline location would be laughable if not for the deadly outcome of their callous incompetence.

A car horn blared behind me, and I started. The envelope — clutched precariously with only the very tips of my fingers — slipped free. It slithered, as if of its own volition, into the letter slot, absolving me of responsibility for its demise.

Samuel will know I meant to write more, I lied to myself. *He'll understand.*

I nodded curtly in inward self-comfort, putting the message to the remnants of my old home behind me, and turning back toward the new.

I'd been out of the office for a week already. It was time to return, yet I stood rigidly in front of the building on the corner of Ben Yehuda and Gordon, long enough to draw curious looks from several co-workers as they streamed in around me.

Two secretaries leaned in conspiratorially, assuming they were out of earshot, and whispered, "He was there, *at the bombing.*"

My eyes were bleary from nights of restless sleep, from which I had frequently awakened, the memories and sweat of nightmares languidly evaporating from my skin with the assistance of my brand new Westinghouse electric fan. I stood on the entrance stairs, closed my eyes again, and tried vainly to rub the sleepiness away. What I saw behind my lids — what I'd been seeing every time I closed my eyes since the bombing — were Mrs. Lowenstein's twitching legs.

I rubbed a hand through my hair, and straightened, feeling the muscles in my back tighten with resolve. *"This is the undertow,"* my father's voice said from somewhere deep within. *"And when you're caught in an undertow, you don't fight. You ride it to wherever it takes you, and keep breathing."*

I had work to do, and one did not maintain the position of youngest resident of the management floor, at the top of the three-story Anglo-Palestine Bank building, by shirking nostalgically.

From the top of the corner staircase, I waved to Sima, the grey-smocked tea attendant, who worked her way down the hallway behind her well-stocked stainless steel cart. As usual, she dispensed as much personal advice as she did over-seeped and greasy tea. This morning, she'd thankfully latched onto another bachelor employee. When she looked in my direction questioningly, I shook my head, smiled regretfully while demonstratively checking my watch, and ducked quickly into my stuffy, windowless office.

I closed the door behind me, and checked the calendar on my desk. Mr. Hoofien, my boss and Chairman of the bank, would arrive at 1 p.m. for an update on the status of our holdings in the Tel Aviv port, which we owned through Otzar Sea Industries. Otzar was my primary responsibility at the bank, or had been until the British nationalized the port last year, when the war broke out. It would be a short meeting with Hoofien, indeed, as I had little to report. Commercial activity in the port, which had opened just three years previously, had ground to a halt after its Greek longshoremen, along with their heavy equipment, were drafted.

I'd just put the finishing touches on a memo when the first *whump!* of an explosion rocked my desk so dramatically that my fountain pen rolled to the floor. It was followed by a second *whump!*, this one close enough to raise the volume of my tinnitus by several decibels. The still-fresh memory of the last bombing turned my bowels to water. For a time — perhaps seconds, perhaps minutes — I was utterly lost in phantasmagoric images that I'd hoped never to revisit.

When my instinct for self-preservation finally overcame, I bolted toward the door and shot out into the empty hall. It was 12:20, and the building was nearly empty. Most employees had already left for the daily afternoon break, observed by most businesses in the city. They would head home for a heavy lunch and a nap, and return at 3 p.m., after the heat diminished somewhat.

I sprinted to the stairwell, heading for the building's basement shelter. A third explosion shook the building as I reached the ground floor. My footsteps echoed loudly as I crossed the high-ceilinged main hall, now breathing hard. I ran past three clerks, who were just getting up from their desks in alarm, and urged them over my shoulder to hurry after me. Another *whump!* rattled the windows facing the street, pushing us all to move faster. I'd just skidded around the corner and into the stairwell leading down to the shelter, the other three close on my heels, when we heard the front door crash open.

I turned, already concealed in the stairwell, as six masked figures came into the bank, all brazenly carrying pistols.

"*Zeh shode!*" the first figure bellowed in Hebrew — this is a robbery!

I'd felt many things over my four years in the Anglo-Palestine Bank building on Ben Yehuda Street. I'd felt immense gratitude at the opportunity of employment so soon after my arrival in Tel Aviv, downtrodden and still feverish from months in the swamps of Kibbutz Mishmar HaSharon, on the recommendation of my father's colleague at Bank Zachodni in Warsaw. I'd felt amazement when singled out and "adopted" by Hoofien, after speaking up about the holding structure of the Tel Aviv port at a mid-level management meeting. I'd felt unabashed pride as I became Hoofien's go-to man for everything related to the port.

Yet I'd never felt the righteous indignation that suddenly swelled my chest at the sound of that single Hebrew phrase.

A robbery? By Jews?

Even as my ears burned with anger, I remained cautious, staying in the safety of the stairwell, out of sight.

The robbers had spotted my three colleagues, and ordered them to halt. The two clerks farthest from the stairwell obeyed immediately, raising their hands in submission and turning toward the robbers. The third man, who was closest to the stairwell, reached behind his back quickly, apparently for a concealed weapon.

A gunshot echoed loudly in the hall, torturing my already-ringing ears, and a rush of air hit me as a bullet ricocheted off the wall behind me.

The third clerk, unharmed, slowly raised his hands above his head.

The lead robber ordered two of his men into position by the door. The remaining three moved quickly to the service desk, smashed open the door to the tellers' positions, and started gathering cash from the tills.

Gun steady, the leader of the thieves calmly approached the clerk who had attempted to draw the weapon. He reached behind the man, took the Webley .38, weighed it appreciatively in his free hand, then viciously whipped the clerk across the face with its handle.

The clerk crumpled to his knees with a loud groan, his hands clutching his face.

"What were you planning on doing, brother?" hissed his assailant. "Shooting me? Why? I'm not the enemy. Your masters at this bank, the ones collaborating with the British... they are our enemy—yours and mine. They are the ones we in the *Irgun* fight. And you want to shoot *me*?"

He was close enough that I could see the throbbing artery that stood out on his forehead, and the sweat that ran in rivulets down the sides of his face, disappearing into the kerchief that concealed his identity.

The clerk stood hunched over, clutching his injured face, but the robber shoved him onto his back with one foot, and leveled the pistol at his midriff. "A gut shot should put you out of our misery, but still give you time to consider the error of your ways." He spat and cocked the weapon with a loud click. "One less Jewish collaborator to impede our progress toward nationhood." His finger slid into the trigger guard.

I'd also felt sheer boyish glee in the Anglo-Palestine Bank building. It was the hot glee of the child who grabbed a whole plate of sweets from the party table before others could partake. It was the glee of an older brother who successfully wrestled a toy from a sibling's small hands. It was the glee of a bloody-muzzled hyena that successfully fought off rivals at the site of a fresh kill.

I'd set it up simply and beautifully. The bank had financed Otzar, and Otzar had built the port. Yet the port either lost money or barely broke even every year, because they'd built it in a sandy, shallow water location that prevented large ships from approaching the small anchorage. This translated into expensive and time-consuming manual offloading that ate into profits. Things improved after I came in, thanks to some creative reporting techniques, for which I discovered I had a true penchant.

I ensured that the bank continued to pump money into Otzar. Otzar, in fair turn, continued to pump money, through several untraceable middlemen, into my personal account in a rival bank. Everyone was happy. Tel Aviv had a source of Zionist pride and joy in which the bank could claim a pivotal role. Otzar could keep operating, despite having no legitimate business *raison d'etre*. And I could, at the age of 25, purchase an apartment on a quirkily-named Tel Aviv street near the bustling center of town.

I felt no glee now, at the audacity of this robbery *by Jews*. I had stolen from the Bank myself, but I had not *robbed*. I was a man of conscience, albeit not one built for denial based thereon. I'd seen an opportunity and taken it, the same way others would have done. I'd hurt no one, threatened no one.

This man, whose finger slid ever closer to the trigger, even as the sweat dried from his forehead and his breathing slowed, represented everything I hated, and everything I secretly feared I had become.

I acted without thinking. I saw the opportunity and grabbed it blindly. "Stop!" I heard myself yell. I stepped suddenly out of the stairwell, my own hands raised.

The thief, startled, swung the pistol toward me and fired a single round, which went thankfully wild. He checked himself when he saw that I was unarmed, and turned the weapon back to the prone figure of the clerk. He hesitated, seeming less certain.

"Stop, brother! Jew!" I repeated.

Emboldened, I took the next move on the real-life chessboard on which I now acted without hesitation. I inched slowly between the gun and the clerk, keeping my hands held high. My voice remained steady, calming, although my heart was racing.

"I don't think you want to kill anyone, brother, but if you need to, kill me. I'm a senior manager at this bank. This man is just a lowly worker."

"We've got it! Let's go! Let's *go!*" The voice of one of the other robbers broke the stillness.

Still the thief wavered, gun pointed at me, his eyes darting to his comrades.

When they next returned to me, I met his gaze. "We are *not* the enemy, brother. Take what you came for and leave."

He returned my stare, and I could see his anger drain away. Without a word, he turned, joined the others, and left the bank.

I turned back to my injured colleague, and with no pride in my reckless yet undeniably selfless actions the moment before, wondered why the chance to do good came along so much less frequently than its opposite. As I bent to help him, I saw the robbers through the front doors. They piled into a single car and tore off down the utterly deserted street.

I later learned that the explosions had been decoys, brilliantly conceived to spook the still-skittish citizens of Tel Aviv, and leave the streets clear for their escape. It had worked. The robbers got away with over 4000 Palestine Pounds — a staggering sum — and only one was caught.

CHAPTER 6
Aron: Wherever You Go

Tel Aviv, September 17, 1940

The spotty shade of the date palm in Dizengoff Square, where I'd ended up after another sleepless night, did little to alleviate the heat of the morning. *Hamsin* dust had crept up on the city in the night, born by southerly winds from Saudi Arabia. It hung heavy in the languid oven of Mediterranean air, clouding vision and impeding breathing. I sat in the grass, fanning myself ineffectually with a flyer for *Argentine Nights*, which was playing in the nearby Allenby Theatre, featuring "the incredible Andrews Sisters!"

Through the haze, I watched the trickle of human activity flow by. Here, a young mother stopped a high-wheeled pram to softly coo to the squealing infant within. There, a businessman sweating in jacket and tie constantly moved his hands, deep in animated conversation with a short-sleeved, sandal-wearing colleague. Beyond them, two British soldiers, clearly off-duty and looking for diversions, smoked and watched the slim young mother with casually lascivious eyes. In front of me, the fountain streamed endless arcs of water. Behind me, automobiles scurried around the traffic circle.

I sat on my figurative rock above this human stream, as it seemed I always had. The effervescence of human joy and the detritus of its malaise flowed by me. In truth, it barely dampened the soles of my shoes, even on my infrequent forays into its current.

It had not always been so. In Warsaw, the stream had nearly engulfed me, the sensitive boy who cried easily. At movies in the Era Cinema on Targowa Street, while trying to maintain concentration over the notorious squeaking of its wooden chairs, I would tear up at the slightest hint of emotional strife. When Stefania died so tragically in Puchalski's version of *Leper*, I literally fell to the floor, and curled under the chair despite the sticky floor, as overcome with grief as if my own love had left me so tragically on the day of our wedding.

I was wholly immersed in this stream of emotion, so deeply that my father called me to his study, wearing the serious look that announced a father-son chat. He gestured for me to sit facing him, he in his wooden-backed, wheeled office chair, I in the overstuffed armchair by the window that overlooked the Vistula. The river shone bright blue in the sunshine. Through the open window, the lemony sweet scent of blooming water lilies wafted in, and I could hear the ducks chasing each other merrily on the muddy banks.

Father looked at me for a pregnant moment, his forehead wrinkled in consternation as if unsure how to begin. Finally, he spoke. "Feelings make us human, son. What we experience in the world *should* make us feel. And feeling things as *intensely* as you do is a blessing. If everyone felt things so strongly, and did not choose to dampen or ignore their feelings, the world would be a much better place. But part of growing up, part of being a man, is learning to control your feelings, sometimes even to conceal them. We can argue whether or not this is healthy or preferable, but it is nonetheless the way society expects us to act. Do you understand what I'm saying to you?"

I thought I did, and I inwardly vowed, in the immemorial filial traditional, to please my father. I set myself to the Herculean task of hiding the waves of anger, sadness, and sometimes even joy that so often threatened to physically double me over.

By the time I was sixteen, I felt in control—an adult, as much the master of my emotional fate as my father. I was ready, in 1929, to face whatever the world would throw at me.

Or so I thought. For even as the Great Depression began to chip away at my father's securely bourgeoisie façade, Josef Warszawski began to dismantle my own emotional dam—pebble by pebble, brick by agonizing brick.

"Got a fag, brother?"

The voice jarred me, but did not completely extract me from the vivid memory into which I had sunk. I reached for my pack of Simon Artz's, ever-present in my shirt pocket, without even looking up. I shook one out mechanically and thrust it in the general direction of the voice, then fished the small box of wooden matches from another pocket and did the same. Only then did I raise my eyes to squint at the figure that loomed above me. The sun, mocking the scant shade the palm strove to provide, lit his face blindingly from behind, obscuring his features. All I could see was his uniform — the blue garb of a Jewish Auxiliary Policeman.

We saw more and more of these in recent months, as the city was plastered with posters encouraging young men to join the British-sanctioned *Notrim*, Auxiliary Police, "to protect people and homeland." Putting past tensions with the Jewish community in Mandatory Palestine behind them in favor of a common cause, the British needed all the local manpower they could find. They were desperate to shift more forces to the North African front, where the name Rommel was being heard in ever more reverent terms on both sides of the lines.

"Hot as shit today, eh, brother?"

I nodded in silent agreement, and looked away. Josef's strong features swam back to me — the stubborn cut of his jawline, the thick swath of black hair that he constantly brushed away from his left eye, the thick-rimmed glasses that gave his gaze a remote intensity. He never looked *at* me so much as *through* me, as if he always saw something of greater significance beyond the horizon.

Josef was the leader of the Warsaw chapter of the Gordonia youth movement. He'd recruited me — more ardent ideologues might say "poached" — as I came out of a meeting of the rival *HaShomer HaTzair* Zionist movement. For a reason I still didn't understand, he'd chosen me, ignoring the rest of the crowd exiting the lecture. Right there on the street, the cobblestones shining after a night rain, his breath fogging in the cool air, he'd begun to speak of redemption through working the land and personal sacrifice.

His words drew me in at first, but I lost all power of verbal comprehension when he grasped my shoulders dramatically with two strong hands. He looked deep into my eyes, and asked me something of undoubtedly profound significance to which I had no choice but to answer "Yes." I had no idea what I'd agreed to, but I found myself walking beside him, my shoulders still tingling where his touch refused to fade.

I carried my silent torch for two long years. Finally, convinced that my feelings for him were reciprocal, even as I inwardly trembled at the finality of broaching the subject, I decided to write him a letter. I agonized for weeks, writing and rewriting, revising and erasing. I'd known of my own feelings — so very different from those of my peers—for years, yet I never dreamed that one day I'd find another with whom to share them. My inner dilemma became so all-encompassing that I nearly forgot its secrecy. It consumed me, as only a yearning teenager could be consumed. The pain of it became as familiar as breathing.

I never sent that letter. Yet, as I hurried out the door to yet another Gordonia lecture eschewing the evils of socialism and lauding the glory of pioneering in *Eretz Yisrael*, the Land of Israel, it remained in an unsealed envelope on my desk.

My mother—who never checked her sweet, well-intentioned curiosity for anything as trivial as respect for her children's privacy— found it.

Josef never reciprocated even a modicum of my feelings.

I discovered this when I finally, after two more agonizing years, professed my love for him in person—the unsent letter by then a distant memory. We sat by a lonely campfire in 1933, guarding the watermelon field near our newly founded Kibbutz, *Mishmar HaSharon*. The mosquitoes buzzed in our ears, and the night closed in around us, shutting out the rest of the world. It was just us and the fire, the perfect setting. It had been building in me for so long, it was almost a physical relief to confess.

Instead of taking me in his strong arms, as I had so fervently yearned, Josef tactfully shook his head at first. When I persisted, he raised his voice, letting the disgust creep in.

I left the Kibbutz on the first bus the next morning, and arrived in the raucous central Tel Aviv bus station that afternoon—sweaty, destitute, heartbroken, and just short of desperate.

I started violently, unconsciously scooting away from the young policeman I'd given a cigarette before vanishing into my reverie, whose resemblance was hauntingly similar to Josef.

"Take it easy, brother. I'm not going to bite." He scrutinized me with a shrewd, street-smart policeman's eye that didn't synch with his new-looking uniform. He lit his cigarette, and we both watched the flame of the small match standing audaciously tall in the absence of any breeze, before he snuffed it out.

As he returned the matches to me, our hands brushed lightly, and I surreptitiously jerked my hand away, as if burned.

He surveyed the square intently, then returned his gaze to me. I saw now that he had a stern Oriental visage—dark hair, olive skin, heavy brows. He was powerfully built, but in a loose and lanky way that radiated graceful, not brutish, power. His deep-throated Hebrew was unaccented, unlike my own, which likely would never lose its immediately recognizable Polish twang.

"You look familiar, brother. Where have I seen you before?"

I vaguely muttered a response about working in a bank, where lots of people come and go. He shook his head, and my stomach dropped in flooding recollection. I scrambled to my feet, claiming to be late for a meeting, and tossed a harried goodbye over my shoulder as I walked briskly away, nearly running into another pair of British soldiers in my haste. I excused myself in broken English, and scurried on.

He *knew* me. Of course, he knew me. From London Square. And I knew him, perhaps better than I would have preferred.

"You can't walk away from who you are, brother," he said, his clear voice pursuing me in the tepid stillness of the morning. "Wherever you go, there you are. Right? *Wherever you go, there you are.*"

He laughed, and his mocking shoved me insistently forward, even as his words bore me back, past the memory of Josef, to another conversation altogether, in which I'd heard those very words. It was the last conversation I ever had with my parents.

I hadn't experienced a lot on this earth, but I'd seen enough not to believe in human nobility in any form.

My father claimed to believe, always an optimistic advocate of the fundamental goodness of the human soul, his own included. This, at least, held true until he was confronted with an actual, not theoretical, moral conundrum. Then, without fail, he would tear away the sheer curtain of his "nobility" and make his choice based on preconception and self-interest, like we all do.

Thus, his reaction in 1931, when I was 18 years old, did not surprise me. On a chilly fall evening, sheets of rain combed the hairy vegetation along the banks of the Vistula, and lashed the dining room windows of my parents' flat. The rivulets running down the glass distorted the usually merry lights of Old Town, visible across the river, creating messy luminescent smears that leered at me until I turned away. I faced the three figures at the table, trying to keep my voice steady. My hands clutched the edge of the tablecloth so tightly that my plate squirmed perceptibly towards the table's edge.

"So, I have some news," I said over the slurping noises coming from Samuel's side of the table. My mother's chicken soup did not lend itself to quiet consumption.

"My Certificate came through," I blurted.

The slurping stopped, and only the violent swishing of the rain was audible. Even Samuel, whom I knew had no idea what a Certificate was, stopped eating and stared.

The shocked silence was broken as my mother's spoon clattered noisily to her plate. She jumped abruptly to her feet and rushed through the swinging door to the kitchen, clutching a napkin to her contorted mouth.

Father also rose from his place at the head of the table. He strode icily from the dining room, leaving Samuel and me alone.

Samuel looked at me, wide-eyed and questioning.

I reminded him that a Certificate was official permission from His Majesty's Government, which had been granted the mandate over Palestine by the League of Nations after the Great War, to immigrate. "I applied nearly a year ago, remember? Now it's happening. I'm leaving for Palestine in three months, together with Josef and the rest of our chapter. We're a *garin* now. We're going to build, with our own hands, a new settlement in the Land of Israel. Can you believe it?"

Samuel sat silent, his 13-year-old brain turning this information over and over, until he finally understood its significance.

I had tried to help him understand and appreciate the tenets of Gordonian Zionism, which I'd embraced wholeheartedly — partly out of genuine ideological conviction, and partly owing to Josef's influence, tutelage, encouragement, and attention. Samuel, however, expressed far more interest in books, the school orchestra, and Walerian Kisielinski's escapades on the soccer field, than in the future of the Jewish people in its ancient homeland. I knew he respected me, even worshipped me. He would truly try to listen as I recounted an evening's lecture, or the details of my summer experiences in the *Kibbutz Kielce* training camp. He would *try*, but his stare would usually go vacant shortly after I began talking. When he drifted away like this, I could either leave the room or commit ritual hari-kari on the spot, with equal lack of impact on his reverie.

Now, however, he *was* paying attention. He looked at me pleadingly, his large brown eyes filled with tears. "But what will I do, when you're gone? *Who will be here with me?*"

His words, perfectly framed as they were by lovable pre-teen narcissism, hit me hard. I had no answer for him. How could I explain that he had not, truly, played even a minor role in my decision to leave? I loved Samuel in an abstract way, much as he listened to my Zionist rantings, but I wasn't fiercely devoted to him in any sense. He was there, and my brother, and that was that. In any case, I didn't have a chance to explain then.

My father's voice rang out across the flat. "Aron, will you please join your mother and me in my study?"

Father sat in his wooden office chair, and I—now an adult—sat in the overstuffed armchair, as I had so many times as a child. Instead of kind-eyed guidance and soft-spoken counsel, however, my father's voice broke as he told me what he'd read in my letter to Josef. The look of anguish on his face was so pronounced that my eyes immediately filled in response to a noxious combination of guilt and empathy.

True to his prudence and perhaps prudishness, he'd waited for the right time to confront me with what he'd read in the letter my mother found. He stayed his hand, until my dramatic dinner table announcement forced it.

"*Wherever you go, there you are,* Aron. You're not going to escape this by leaving for some godforsaken life of certain deprivation, and possible depravity." My father's words bounced off me like stones against armor. "Leave our ideological differences aside for now, Son. This is not about your Zionism or my Integrationism. This is personal. We can try other doctors, other procedures, which could alleviate your... condition. Stay here and let us help you. Don't make a rash decision that you will later regret. *Eretz Yisrael* is not going anywhere."

And thus, it began.

And how does it end? I asked myself while rounding the corner of Bugrashov, sweating and wheezing slightly from the exertion in the dusty air. I turned into my street, and made a beeline for the cool comfort of my flat.

Well, here I am in Tel Aviv, fairly well-off and utterly corrupt. I meet stray policemen in dark parks to alleviate my burning loneliness. Josef, the true reason I became a Zionist and emigrated to Palestine, is dead on the banks of Nahal Alexander.

How does it end?

My parents were dead in Warsaw. I'd received a laconic telegram from Samuel, who was now in Vilnius, to that effect. I'd never exchanged meaningful words with them after the vicious argument that rainy evening. I left home two days thereafter, and moved in with Gordonian friends. I next saw my parents at the train station on Chmielna Street, the morning I departed for the port of Constanta, Romania, from which I was to embark for Palestine. Our goodbye was brief and formal, my mother's face flushed from crying, my father's eyes grim and disappointed.

True, I had begged my father for funds after I left the Kibbutz, and he had acceded, ensuring—after several flea-bitten days in a hostel—that I could live comfortably until finding gainful employment. His introduction to his Tel Aviv banking connections, which had jump-started my meteoric career, had been readily—perhaps guiltily—offered. But I would never have a chance to express my love for them, or to tell my mother how much I admired her determination. I would continue, for the rest of my days, to long for my father's strong arms to enfold me once again into a world of comfort that shut out the pain and complexity of adult life.

How does it end?

My pesky little brother, to whom I'd grown more and more attached as our correspondence continued over the past years, was either freezing in a Soviet *gulag* or already dead. The love of his life, Danuta, a woman I greatly admired based on what little I knew of her, was trapped in Vilnius. She awaited Samuel's unlikely return, but had written to say she was in danger of retribution from the Soviets for consorting with a subversive if she remained there. Yet if she returned home to Warsaw, she could face German wrath for consorting with a Jew.

So, how does it end? What if that still depends on me?

I'd never been able to wallow in desperation, always preferring to dig myself out of a hole rather than languish therein. Whether this trait signified great character or abysmal cowardice, I didn't know, but where others vacillated, I acted. Where others hesitated, I pounced.

Perhaps I could use the skills that served me so well in business to help the one person in the world for whom I still hold fond, if remote, feelings.

I took pen in hand and retrieved a fresh piece of stationery from the top desk drawer.

Now is the only time any of us ever have to do right. Amends are made, not granted.

I wrote with no hesitation, excited to take the first steps on a road to possible redemption.

Dear Danuta....

CHAPTER 7
Danuta: I'll Be Waiting

Vilnius, Lithuania, December 2, 1940

> *My Dearest Samuel,*
>
> *Our spot seems so empty, and so cold, without you. Of course, it is now December, whereas we last sat here in August. While this difference may play a role in the cold that threatens to turn my fingers to icicles, I prefer to think that you took the warmth with you when you left.*
>
> *Despite my shivering, I left Adrianna's flat determined to write you with my news, and to do so with symbolic importance right from our own spot. I intend to fulfill this sacred vow even if it costs me a pinky or two.*
>
> *I'm sitting on our bench, the one into which you carved our entwined initials. I'm smiling, with chattering teeth, at the sudden thought that this act actually precipitated your arrest. Yes, now that I consider it, I'm convinced: the subversive articles you penned be damned — it was your desecration of public property that tipped the scales of Soviet justice against you.*
>
> *In any case, here I sit, where after the thaw the Vilnia River will again gently join the Neris. It will un-become the Vilnia. This is not a suicide, however. It is a coalescence. In joining the Neris, the Vilnia creates an entity more powerful than the sum of its parts, yet does not lose itself. Somewhere in the Neris, the Vilnia still flows. I think of our marriage thus, and my stomach again knots up, missing you. At least once a day, the longing consumes me — momentarily, yet completely, like a passing spasm born of bone-deep cancer. I have come to embrace this pain. It is, after all, what I have of you — for now.*
>
> *But not for long, my darling.*
>
> *I hope to God that the censors let this letter slide by, for I am bursting to tell you all. The rumors say that for several litas, the*

postal clerk will add a letter to the "special bag" — the one that bypasses the censors. Let us hope this is true.

So here it is: I'm leaving Vilnius for Palestine, just as we planned!

Moreover, I regret to inform you that I'm no longer your Danuta. No, I'm not divorcing you — certainly not after all the trouble we went to in order to wed — but your loving wife is now, and for the foreseeable future, known as Lea Rachel Cohen, daughter of Reuven Cohen, the carpet merchant from Okrzeja Street in Warsaw. Yes, I am a Jewess, although my conversion was less conventional than most. Either way, shalom, I'm pleased to make your acquaintance. Baruch Hashem. That's all the Hebrew I've managed to learn so far, but fear not! Your wife Lea will be a star Hebrew pupil, for not only has she changed her name and identity, she is leaving this frozen wasteland for the warmth of Palestine next week! She — that is, I — has received a magical Certificate of Immigration from the British!

Now, please hold this letter up to your face while you read, so I can more clearly observe your utter disbelief. Because I'm sure you'll be even more incredulous to know that this is all thanks to your brother. Yes, the very brother you haven't stopped disparaging for a moment since the day of our first hot chocolate in Warsaw University. The one who's "desertion" to Palestine caused you such distress. Well, after I notified Aron of your incarceration — I do hope this was acceptable, as he is your only living family — we began a short correspondence. I wrote him of my fears about returning to Warsaw, and also of remaining here. Being the known consort of the notorious park bench desecrater, Samuel Katz, is potentially dangerous, after all. It took a number of months, but Aron used his new contacts in the Hagana — that's the Jewish underground in Palestine, as you certainly know — to arrange and pay for new papers for me, and passage to Haifa.

Yes, while the Jews of Europe scramble to hide or convert, your wife is swimming against the current. Who would guess that anyone would want to become a Jew these days?

And here's more to fuel your incredulity: your brother, the self-interested capitalist who excelled for years at preserving his own interests over all others, has left his job at the bank, and now devotes his time and considerable financial resources to the greater good of the Jewish community in Palestine, the Yishuv. (Oh, here's another Hebrew word I know! I'd forgotten. That's four now!) It seems his financial skills, not to mention his generous donations, were welcomed at the highest levels of the Hagana organization. He's now rubbing shoulders with some of the most influential men in Palestine.

So there you have it. I'll be meeting you in Tel Aviv when you're released. I'll be waiting for you, my darling, and as you know, I despise being kept waiting. It was quite rude of you, leaving me alone in this awful city, so let's put things to right, shall we?

In other news, Adrianna has given up cigarettes, and the Soviets have declared all land in Lithuania to be publicly owned. It's still not clear which of these decisions will ultimately have greater impact on the fabric of Lithuanian life. You know how attached A is to her fags.

All jesting aside, I long to be free of this god-awful city, and I will be, first thing next week. I have a travel visa to Turkey, and will be catching the morning train to Sventoji next Monday. From there, it's just a hop, skip and jump to Istanbul, where I'll meet the Jewish Agency representative whose address your brother provided. Then, a small jaunt to Haifa, and I will be installed in Aron's flat in Tel Aviv by February, making myself pretty for your arrival.

I believe you will arrive, Samuel Katz, just as I believe that this letter will reach you. For it must, you see. I've heard how terribly they limit correspondence to the prison camps, and I've heard rumors of the terrible conditions you must be facing. Please do not take the flippant or joking tone of this letter, which I now continue from the warmth of Adrianna's flat, as anything but what it is: utter concern for your wellbeing, and a sincere effort to lighten what I can only imagine must be a dire mood.

Now, hold this letter up one last time, so that I may see whether the reality of your surroundings matches my imagination. I know that I will see suffering, and I know that I will see loss. I also expect to see no small amount of desperation on the faces of your fellow prisoners, but look around at them, my darling, and remember one thing: you are not them; you have me. I do not give my heart without great expectations. I have no doubt that we'll be together again soon in Palestine, and you should share this certainty. Share it, and act on it.

I'm kissing this sheet of paper so ardently that I fear it will dissolve. Please keep yourself safe. Keep yourself warm. Keep yourself alive and intact. And come back to me. I'll be waiting.
All my love,
Your Lea (formerly Danuta)

CHAPTER 8
Aron: Will You Remember?

Tel Aviv, February 5, 1941

> *My Dearest Brother,*
> *If this is a difficult letter for me to write, I can only imagine the agony of its receipt.*
> *There is no easy way to convey this...*

"You can't possibly send that, you realize." Sean lay on my bed, his golden curls propped on one bare arm.

The winter sunlight peeked meekly through the slatted blinds, lacking the brazenness of its summer compatriot. Given the chilly air, the heater would have been comforting, but it was difficult to find kerosene, so it remained unlit.

Sean padded over to me, barefoot and shivering slightly in the morning chill. He gently removed the pen from my hand, crumpled the letter into a tight ball, and threw it into the bin. He put his arms around me and kissed the back of my neck lightly.

"You don't *know* anything yet," he said. "You only *suspect*. By the time this letter reaches Samuel — if it ever even *does* reach him — Danuta may be sitting in this very room, writing her own letter to him. Let this resolve itself, *before* you intervene." As his voice became more insistent, his Aussie twang became more grating than endearing.

I sat silently, hunched over my writing desk.

Sean reached for his uniform. "I need to get to work. His Majesty's Mandatory Government in Palestine, as you know, grinds to a halt in my absence. And yes, I won't forget to leave through the back. We can't have the neighbors talking — nor the *Hagana* leadership, for that matter. Consorting with the Mandate... what *would* they say?" He laughed lightly at this and kissed the back of my neck again, then asked if we could meet again that evening for drinks in the Armon Hotel bar, our usual spot.

I nodded vaguely.

Now smartly dressed in his khaki uniform, he came back across the room and took my face in his broad hands. "Tell me the truth." He looked deep into my eyes, with just a hint of a twinkle in his own. "When you're a senior minister-of-financial-drivel in the first independent Jewish State in 2000 years, in between finding funding to house droves of refugees and single-handedly holding off Arab hoards, will you still let me do that...."

He bent to whisper in my ear naughtily, and I couldn't help smiling.

It had been four months since we met, and he seemed to know me well. He was good-natured and gentle, beautiful, and wiser than me in many ways. He was also an officer in the British Army Recruitment Office in Jaffa, and a closet Zionist unafraid of bending the rules to help our cause.

As the door clicked closed behind him, I turned back to my desk and took out another sheet of paper to write to Samuel. I resolved to tell him what I knew, and then decide later whether to add the letter to the growing pile of unsent letters next to my desk, or actually to post this one.

And what *did* I know, exactly? News came to me secondhand, conveyed by Moshe, who'd settled in a small flat I arranged for him and worked in the Carmel market carrying crates of vegetables. He was part of the group of Polish Jews who'd traveled together from Soviet Lithuania to Palestine, by way of Istanbul.

Two days ago, as planned, I met the *Bella-Chita*, which arrived on time from Istanbul at the Haifa port.

It was a miserable, rainy day. Heavy clouds shrouded the grey Mediterranean, which had dropped its summer guise of friendly warmth and bared foam-flecked winter teeth. Waves smacked the concrete pier. The spray slowly soaked through my trousers, socks, and shoes as I watched the passengers disembark onto the rain-slick dock for over an hour, freezing under my wind-whipped umbrella.

Danuta was not among them. Fighting panic, I worked my way through the line of passengers, all Poles, questioning each until I found Moshe and his young son Daniel. They had been on the *Vatan*, the ship on which I'd booked Danuta from Sventoji, Lithuania to Istanbul. They had been witnesses to — and nearly the victims of — the treachery.

Not bothering to introduce myself, I drew them out of the long Jewish Agency processing line, promising to assist with all their bureaucratic details.

Moshe seemed convinced by my fluent Polish and Hebrew. When he read the name on my Palestine Police Force credentials, he gasped. "*You* are Aron Katz? Do you live at 8 Buki Ben Yagli Street, in Tel Aviv?"

We sat in the cramped conference room of the small Jewish Agency Haifa Port office. Three cups of tea steamed in glass cups between us. Moshe had a long equine face, topped by sad eyes that remained largely downcast when he spoke, as if either too travel-weary or ashamed to meet my own. He was traveling alone with his son, he said, and made no mention of the fate of his wife. He said they'd met Danuta in the Vilnius Central Train Station.

She had found them, in fact, approaching them unabashedly as they stood next to the information window in the crowded station, as instructed. "Are you my brave traveling companions to Palestine, then?" she chirped. She smiled at Moshe, introduced herself as Lea, and then bent to warmly shake Daniel's hand and cup his smooth cheek with a chilly but tender hand.

The child had basked in the sudden feminine attention, smiling shyly yet sincerely.

It was just the three of them departing Vilnius that day, but they'd be joining a large group of Jewish emigrants in Kaunas. It was 8:30 a.m. and the train to Kaunas was scheduled for 9:05 a.m. By the time they settled into their hard-benched third class seats, Moshe conveyed with some joy, Daniel was deep in animated conversation with his new-found friend. Moshe watched incredulously as this gregarious boy, whom he had not seen for many months, miraculously emerged from his cocoon of grief. He'd smiled gratefully at Danuta over the boy's head, and helped her with her bags when they arrived in Kaunas.

They found the Jewish Agency representative in Kaunas, a small man determinedly holding a discrete Star of David sign, around noon. At least a hundred other travelers had crowded around him, all asking questions at once, as he raised his hands for silence. Daniel clutched Danuta's hand tightly in the crush, and Moshe rested one hand on the boy's shoulder protectively. The Jewish Agency representative explained that their train to Sventoji would leave late that afternoon, and that they would arrive the following morning, just in time to embark on the small Turkish freighter on which they would spend the coming weeks *en route* to Istanbul.

Moshe fell into the full story.

"Ladies and gentlemen," the agency representative began, his small voice rising above the din of the station hall. "Ladies and gentlemen, please understand that our accommodations on the ship, as well as this evening's train trip, are not exactly first class. I don't have to explain to you that there is a war on, and that conditions—"

The man's speech was abruptly cut off by a large apple core that flew from nowhere and struck him squarely between the eyes. A cheer arose from the group of young Lithuanian men just across the station hall. Calls of "Well done!" and "Serves the Jewish Communist right!" echoed among the group. A tense hush fell over the station.

A blue-uniformed policeman looked up from his newspaper, smiled conspiratorially, and turned ostentatiously away to study the cars pulling up to the curb.

"Why would we Jews *ever* want to leave Lithuania?" a lone female voice resounded across the station, filling the silence. It was, of course, Danuta's. "Why indeed, when we are so clearly welcome here? But fear not, good people of Lithuania! Sleep soundly in your beds! For in our absence, your valiant youth—like the young heroes over there—will bravely defend you with discarded fruit if you are ever again threatened by vicious, unarmed women and children!"

The shocked silence that ensued was finally broken by a guffaw from the ticket seller's window. Another laugh sounded from a woman with a baby carriage, followed by a nasal snort from a man sitting in the shoeshine stand. Within seconds, the entire hall was roaring derisively and pointing at the young perpetrators as they slunk away, with the policeman following close on their heels.

Two long days later, Moshe, Daniel, and Danuta lay ensconced deep in the rusting belly of the *Vatan*, a 4000-ton Turkish freighter hastily converted for passengers, and chartered by the Jewish Agency to convey the Kaunas refugees to Istanbul. Four hundred and seven Polish Jews crowded the cargo hold in narrow, three-tiered bunks, and the surly captain had initially confined them below decks. Following tough negotiations with him, though, and a sizable bribe collected from the passengers themselves, he grudgingly allowed them to roam the deck for six hours a day, weather permitting.

The sea was blessedly smooth. A freezing diesel-tinged wind clawed at the faces of the three travelers—who had been inseparable since their initial meeting in Vilnius—the moment they summited the winding spiral stairway that led up and out of the hold. Fighting this invisible tyranny, they pushed their way to the rail. Their gloved fingers clutched the corroded metal, and they marveled at the moonlight's sparkling path to infinity, which spread below them on the flat sea. The thrum of the engines below created an illusion of warmth that traveled upward from the soles of their feet, but was arrested below knee-level by the reality of the December cold.

"Where does the path lead? The moon path?" Daniel's small voice battled the wind and reached Danuta's reddening ears only after a short delay.

She bent to share the child's perspective. Her small hands covered his, and she marveled at how different it was to peek *through* the rail, instead of looking over it. "A child's view of the world," Moshe heard her whisper to herself, "so drastically confined, yet so incredibly focused because of it. Adults see so much more, yet are in wonder of so much less."

She turned to the boy. "I think a moon path leads everyone to a different place, Daniel. That's what's so magic about them. They always take you exactly where you most need to go."

The boy pondered this for a moment. "And where do *you* need to go, Lea?"

She smiled and ruffled his hair. "Well, I *want* to go with you, to Pales—"

A hoarse shout in Turkish sliced the icy air, cutting her off mid-sentence. In seconds, the vibration of the engines ceased, taking the illusory warmth in their feet with it. The eerie silence that ensued was broken with growing frequency and increasing urgency by whispers among the passengers. Long and tense minutes passed as the wind grew stronger, pulling more insistently at scarves and hats and whistling in ears.

A dark shadow crossed the moon path, dissecting their lifeline to the infinite.

Over the wind, a remote thrumming became audible, quickly growing closer. The ship appeared so quickly, and its searchlights flipped on with such cruel suddenness, that Moshe thought perhaps it had always been there, just waiting for the chance to show itself.

"This is the Captain of the *Emden* of the *Kriegsmarine*. Prepare to be boarded. *Heil Hitler!*" The harsh tone of the voice left little room for doubt even among those who didn't understand German.

The passengers at the rail gasped collectively, blinded by the eye-searing searchlight and paralyzed with fear.

Danuta grabbed Daniel's hand, shook Moshe's shoulder roughly, and whispered to him urgently. "We need to hide. Now! And *quietly.*"

Moshe nodded. She led them quickly and inconspicuously away from the rail, away from the knot of passengers that now thronged the deck, away from the cloud of dread that hung so heavily over all their heads as to be nearly visible. They made their way toward the stern, and entered the first port they encountered.

Behind them, a voice in Turkish-accented English protested over a loudspeaker. "This is the *Vatan*. We fly the flag of Turkey, a neutral and non-belligerent nation. You have no legal right to—"

A deep *whump-whump-whump* cut him off.

The gun's roar made the three of them jump in such perfect synchronization that Danuta choked back a laugh. She turned to smile at Daniel. "We could go into the circus with an act like that, could we not?"

The boy smiled back warily.

They followed her ever deeper into the ship's bowels, even as the clang of grappling hooks resonated through the hull above. They neared the engine room, and the temperature rose noticeably. Danuta took off her heavy winter coat, and Moshe took it from her in a gentlemanly gesture so incongruous with their dank surroundings that Danuta again nearly laughed. Finally, she found a small room, packed nearly to bursting with burlap sacks full of something vaguely leafy.

They squeezed past the sacks, which were thankfully easy to move, and Moshe closed the door behind them. They built a small hollow and moved the bags in front of them to block the entrance.

Then, they sat. A sliver of light made its way from the hall, through the door's ventilation slats, and through a tiny gap that they'd left between the sacks. Moshe watched the dust dancing in it. It was their own private moon path, leading... to where? What hope would they find at its end—in the hall beyond this room, on the deck above, in the pulsating sea below?

As their eyes adjusted to the darkness, Danuta and Moshe could see the outlines of each other's fear.

"Now," she said, "we must all be as quiet as possible for a little while. Can you do that, little mouse?"

Danuta's voice visibly soothed Daniel, who trembled as the adrenalin of their flight continued to course through his small body. He nodded weakly, shuddered, and laid his head back against Moshe's shoulder.

Moshe smiled at her with gratitude.

No sounds from the deck above penetrated their fortress. Neither had a watch, and there was no way to tell how much time had gone by. An hour passed, perhaps two. They slept, woke, slept again. They began to feel faint hope. Perhaps the Germans had left the ship. Perhaps the engines would restart any moment, and they could rejoin the other passengers watching the moon path from the cold rail. Perhaps the danger had passed.

Danuta had just started to whisper a story she recalled from *King Matt the First* when the footsteps sounded, loud on the metal floor, moving closer.

The voice came not far behind. *"Raus!* There is no point in hiding. We shall find you. *Raus!"*

Danuta held her finger gently to her lips, and Daniel nodded in understanding, his eyes wide with fear.

From the hall, the sounds of a door being opened roughly, and objects crashing to the floor, made them cringe. They pressed themselves more tightly against the metal wall behind them, as if willing it to swallow them. Another door opened, followed by more crashing and a single voice cursing in German.

Daniel drew his knees up against his chest. His buried his face in Danuta's bosom, and she held him tightly. Another door opened, this one right across the hall from their own, by the sound of it. More cursing ensued, followed by the sounds of something being viciously kicked, as if in growing frustration.

After releasing a long and quiet sigh, Danuta gently but rapidly disengaged herself from Daniel, and passed him quietly to Moshe. She removed her shoes, touched Moshe lightly on the head and Daniel lovingly on the cheek, and stood. She straightened her skirt, smoothed her hair, and unbuttoned the two top buttons of her blouse.

She turned to Moshe. "Aron Katz, 8 Buki Ben Yagli Street, Tel Aviv. Tell him. Will you remember?"

Moshe nodded, and she nodded back. Then, wordlessly and without looking back, she pushed through the sacks, closing the gap behind her as she made her way to the door.

Moshe heard the door open, and her voice call out in German. "I'm here. You have found me. I'm all alone, and now we are all alone together, are we not? My goodness, you are quite tall, are you not?"

Her laugh sounded nearly genuine, her breathy voice convincingly seductive, but Moshe could hear the fear just beneath its surface.

The footsteps sounded louder. He heard a gruff grunt of surprise, and the door to their room slammed brutally closed. This time, it left them without the hope of a private moon path to an infinitely better future.

Moshe and Daniel stayed hidden in their sack haven for two full days, long after the engines had restarted their rhythmic thrumming. They emerged ashen, thirsty, and blinking, and made their way to the passenger hold. It was significantly less crowded.

The savvy captain, it turned out, had traded half the refugees, plus a select part of his cargo, to the Germans in exchange for safe passage. The Germans had insisted on searching the ship in any case, turning up a number of hidden Jews. All of these had been taken, along with the others. No one knew anything of their fate.

Their tea had long ago cooled. Daniel took a tentative sip, smiled at the sweetness, and looked up at Aron with innocent eyes. "Do you know Lea? Are you her friend?"

"I am her friend, little man," he answered sincerely. "And I only hope that I know her well enough...."

CHAPTER 9
Samuel: The Doghouse

Chelyabinsk, Soviet Union, January 1942

It smelled like farts in our doghouse.

When Aron and I were little, farts were our thing, our ritual—a less subtle precursor of the aching sibling torture to follow. Whenever we felt one coming on, the perpetrator would run immediately to the victim's room in order to release his foul gift. Ideally, this release would occur while the perpetrator was sitting on the victim's pillow. On rare occasions, the perpetrator could compound the damage of pillow farting by pulling down his pants, but this required pinpoint timing and accuracy.

This "game" went on long past the age at which propriety dictated it should stop, and even longer past the time at which it ceased to amuse me, its primary victim. Aron's filial cruelty was of the offhand variety, and all the more hurtful for its lack of recognition of its victim. My brother never stopped seeing me as a conveniently proximate target for insults and pranks, rather than a real person living and interacting with the world.

Then he'd left.

It had been a long, long path between the Pechora River *gulag* and my fart-infested doghouse in Chelyabinsk. I would summarize it in one word: *misery*. After the agony of winter in the *gulag*, during which I came to truly envy the hard-won leisure of the self-mutilators, it surprised me to discover that my situation could, in fact, deteriorate further. From the wet and muddy August nights near Naryan-Mar, right after the hope-filled day of my accidental release, things had gotten progressively worse.

Over the course of the following two months, I walked, stowed away, hitched, and train-hopped nearly 2300 kilometers. I learned to survive in this brutally feral state of freedom. I learned where to find remnants of crops that farmers didn't want, and that cow blood provided protein. I learned where one could and could not sleep, and why. One *could* sleep in haystacks and under bridges, for example, but the prudent traveler kept in mind that shelter sought by humans might just as likely be sought by fellow travelers—of the crawling, creeping, and slithering variety. A midnight wakeup call from a nest of snakes somewhere south of Ust-Tsilma had helped reinforce this principle.

I traveled unburdened by food, shelter, or even shoes at first. Rags tied around my feet protected them until I earned enough to buy a secondhand pair. I carried nothing, for I *had* nothing, save the papers I'd received on my release and the hope of another Palestine-postmarked letter waiting for me at the next town, to add to the small pile I'd already received. In Naryan-Mar, right after my release, upon hearing of the Soviet takeover of Vilnius, I wrote to Danuta care of her cousin Adrianna. I informed her that I was on my way to Palestine, and sent a copy care of Aron in Tel Aviv, in the event that she'd already left for Palestine. In this letter, scrawled in my most space-saving handwriting over the front and back of the thin sheet of airmail paper, I mapped out the best guess of my southerly route. I told her to send me letters *poste restante* to each major stop along the way. Thus far, it had worked perfectly. I received letters, all of which she forwarded through Aron in Tel Aviv, held for me at the General Delivery window of the post offices in Ust-Tsilma, Ukhta, Syktyvkar, Kirov, and here in Chelyabinsk.

These letters brought pure sunshine to the endless winter I was living. Indeed, by the time I staggered up to the guard at the Chelyabinsk train station in mid-November, sunshine was already in short supply. Temperatures dropped to -20 Celsius on the bad nights. No amount of blankets—which was exactly the quantity I had—would warm me without a roof and walls. The time had come to find a winter haven.

From the moment I climbed out of my freezing, grease-caked hiding place just above the boxcar axle, all I saw for the five months I was in Chelyabinsk was black-and-white. The soot-filled sky, the ash-tainted earth, the smeared charcoal and grease on tired and underfed faces—all were as if forged by an antique printer's press rather than by the full-color hand of Creation.

At the internal immigration checkpoint, I confidently handed the soldier my excellently forged papers. They'd cost me two weeks of mucking out stables in Kirov, and I was quite proud of them.

The dull-looking fellow with flaccid eyes had an upper lip that drooped so dramatically, an icicle of drool had formed between the corner of his mouth and the topmost curls of his heavy beard.

I smiled politely, as one does when interacting with the mentally deficient. As he thumbed ploddingly through the papers in their new-looking leather folio, I whistled cheerfully to myself. I smoothly slipped him a coin I'd earned emptying chamber pots in a boardinghouse halfway between Kirov and here, three days ago, and asked where I could find accommodations.

The soldier finished reviewing my fake papers and pocketed my proffered coin. Then he raised an eyelid to reveal a dull spark of interest, and arrested me on the spot.

They locked me in a grimy cell not more than ten meters square, which stood in the center of a large, high-ceilinged rotunda. The Chelyabinsk police station had been, in more pious days, a small church. Grey daylight filtered from the dusty windows that studded the dome above. This light mixed with the fetid luminescence of several ancient bulbs suspended from dust-caked wires, creating a miasma of sickly illumination that was not quite bright enough to clarify, yet not dim enough to conceal.

Surrounding my freestanding cell on all sides were the paper-cluttered desks that comprised the frontlines of the Soviet Internal Security bureaucracy. Haphazard piles of bulging manila folders struggled to contain the myriad details of lives already ruined, in the process of being ruined, or ruined then abruptly ended. Grey-skinned, grey-clothed figures sat shuffling grey papers at grey desks, as weak tendrils of rotunda-bound grey smoke rose from their lopsided, hand-rolled cigarettes.

Two drunks shared my cell, both sleeping—one slouched against the bars, and one whose head rested placidly in what appeared to be a congealed pool of his own, or someone else's, vomit.

The hall, despite its size and the number of bureaucrats populating it, was nearly silent.

"I did *not!*" A deep voice abruptly broke the silence, reverberating through the rotunda. It was simultaneously large and small—mature in tone yet with a clearly childlike timber.

"Yes you *did*, you turd-wad. You just never admitted it to Mom, which makes you a double-buttface-liar." The second voice, also speaking Russian, sounded similarly large, and similarly small. "*You're* a double-liar, and I'm going to smash your lying dick-breath head!"

Scuffling came from the direction of the voices, and chairs screeched as they were pushed roughly across the floor. Papers slid in graceful cataracts to the floor, and pencils rolled into irretrievable purgatories under desks. Through the narrow view afforded by the tight bars and the dim light, I saw two groups emerge from the shadows. At the center of each group walked a giant. From each giant, a small group of uniformed policemen hung. The giants bellowed epithets and struggled to reach each other. I managed to make out "dodo head," "poop breath," "penis face," and a few others more suited to nine-year-olds than to these huge men struggling with the police.

The policemen slowly overcame their massive foes, dragged them step-by-step toward our cage, and ultimately succeeded in throwing both in and slamming the barred door.

This, of course, made the gargantuan rivals madly happy. They immediately set upon each other—pummeling, pulling hair, gouging eyes, and rolling so violently around the cell that I only just managed to save the unconscious drunk from a sure broken neck, pulling him to safety before the avalanche of man-boy flesh fell on him.

Once they'd confined the giants in the cage, the police lost interest. What was one more squashed drunk?

After leaping out of the way for the third time, and slipping in the puddle of vomit in the process, I'd had enough. Recalling Danuta's battle with the Cro-Magnons in Warsaw University, I summoned all the quasi-parental outrage I could muster, took a deep breath, and yelled authoritatively in my best Russian, "Boys! Shame on you! What would your mother say? Stop this instant!"

To my shock, it worked.

It turned out that the Russian response to parental reprimand, much like that of the Pole, was deeply ingrained. As I cleared my throat, raw from the sudden exertion, they separated, shuffled resignedly to opposite sides of the cell, and with downcast eyes, nearly simultaneously muttered, "Well, *he* started it!"

As peace returned to our cage, I assessed the giants. Both stood at least two meters tall, built like pitbulls. Neither possessed a discernible neck. Their shoulders simply paused slightly before merging directly into snowman-shaped heads, topped by raggedly cut hair. Their shirts were filthy rags that barely covered their massive arms, which ended abruptly in meat hook hands with ragged nails. Their leather boots were split on the sides, revealing grey cloth that may once have been socks. They smelled like a foul combination of unwashed llama and rotting vegetables.

Self-satisfied, I looked up to meet the gaze of a higher-ranking policeman seated at a nearby desk.

He'd been calmly observing the scene, and seemed relieved that silence had returned to the rotunda. His face showed admiration, and a glint of an idea shone in his eyes. He rose, approached the cell, and motioned that I should move toward him.

His breath reeked of alcohol. "Listen, prisoner, these boys have been driving my men crazy for weeks. They're twin brothers, and they work like horses in the munitions factory for my cousin, who's their foreman. I'd hate for him to lose them. The problem is that, once a week or so, they get drunk, and it takes a platoon to subdue them. You seem to have a talent for it. If you can do it again, I may have a proposition for you. Can you?"

Smelling opportunity, I nodded vigorously, and again summoned paternal energy from a reservoir I'd never known I possessed. I called on the giants to apologize to each other, and they did so, grudgingly yet obediently. I had them shake hands to seal the pact.

The policeman nodded in appreciation.

Thus, I negotiated accommodations, two charges, and a deal with the police. As long as Igor and Viktor showed up for work at the police officer's cousin's factory, and stopped reigning terror on the local bars, the police would overlook the "discrepancies" in my paperwork. To sweeten the deal, the officer gave us a note for the housing authorities, and arranged for us to be assigned joint living quarters.

Thus, I came to reside in a doghouse with two farting giants.

It really *was* a doghouse. Our shack had once housed the hounds of a minor nobleman. While the nobleman was long dead, the smell of his dogs seemed eternal. As befits a doghouse, the door was dog-sized, and the room was so narrow, the roof so low, that we had to crawl across each other's beds to get to our own. Once the temperature dropped permanently below zero, the cracks through which freezing rain dripped during the pre-winter weeks froze closed — small blessings. We had no windows, no source of light excepting an occasional candle, nor any source of heat save our collective warmth and the oppressive heat of the Vapor Twins' anal exhalations.

Our only living companions in the doghouse were a population of bedbugs so massive, their ultimate organization into complex societal units seemed inevitable. I imagined a bicameral bedbug parliament, a free bedbug press, and bedbug *maître d's* who decided nightly exactly where to seat each diner on Viktor, Igor, or me.

My bed, a slab of rough-hewn wood about a meter shorter than my body, had no mattress. Splinters poked me through the rough wool blanket in which I remained constantly wrapped, no matter how many hours I spent trying to work them loose. It was as if they spontaneously regenerated each day while I worked my 14-hour shifts in Salzman's office. On either side of me lay two other slabs, for Igor and Viktor.

Despite the bickering and farting, our doghouse felt like *heaven*. I'd vowed to never take a roof—*any* roof—for granted again. In the boomtown known as Chelyabinsk, we were lucky to have it.

Chelyabinsk had been a sleepy industrial town until Joseph Stalin decided it would be prudent to move Red Army munitions and armor production eastward, out of the way of the advancing Nazi army. From late 1941 until the end of the war, they produced some 18,000 tanks, 48,500 tank engines, and more than 17 million units of ammunition in what quickly became known as "Tankograd."

When I arrived in Chelyabinsk, they were still in the final stages of moving production from Leningrad, which was already under siege. Hundreds of thousands of workers and refugees flooded the city looking for food, shelter, and work. Thousands more, deportees to the Siberian *gulags,* passed through monthly. It was chaotic, overcrowded, and dangerous. Having two over-sized bodyguards, who were obligated by the local authorities to remain with me, provided a distinct advantage for someone of my size and physical prowess.

We settled into a doghouse routine. I would ensure they were up and out to their factory jobs by 8:00 a.m., that they had a hot meal at the pub in the evenings, and that they kept their drinking in check. They seemed to appreciate my concern, and we quickly moved beyond a strictly custodial relationship. We became, to my surprise, friends.

Viktor and Igor were fraternal twins. Just after their 22nd birthdays, in the late summer of 1941, they fled their home city of Leningrad along with some 300,000 others. As I made my way south from the Pechora River *gulag,* they said a teary goodbye to their small working-class home and beloved parents. Owing to their size, the military had exempted them from service, and authorities assigned them to some of the most dangerous and strenuous work in the Chelyabinsk munitions plant.

Despite my initial assessment, they were neither ignorant nor mentally impaired in any way. They were grade school educated, literate, and highly intelligent. Their frequent sibling skirmishes always degenerated into pre-adolescent name-calling, if not blows. This, I learned, was simply a result of the primal ferocity of their fraternal connection. As brothers who'd shared a womb, any sort of confrontation touched a deep place in them, bringing them immediately back to the emotionally rich state of childhood. In this they were, I felt, lucky. For most of us, the majestic intensity of childhood emotions dulled to pewter with age. In this sense, Viktor and Igor remained happily and eternally young.

Neither were the brothers of uniform disposition. Igor was a dreamer whose feet occasionally touched ground to deliver such deadpan and hilarious assessments of the human condition, I once literally fell off a pub chair laughing. Viktor was sharp and cynical, a quick thinker whose conscience and realism kept the two on a straight moral track from which only alcohol could cause them to deviate.

In a dangerous time, in a dangerous place, trust was a scarce commodity. By Christmas of 1941, Viktor, Igor, and I trusted each other. We learned to rely on each other in an environment where comfort— and indeed, survival itself—was not a given. It was a trust that I, in my shortsighted hubris, would ultimately abuse. This trust would lead to consequences for which I would never forgive myself.

CHAPTER 10
Samuel: Lost

Chelyabinsk, Soviet Union, March 1942

I believed in second chances. My brother Aron did not. He seemed to cognitively recognize the frailty of human fallibility. Yet it seemed that each expression of it—when it affected him directly—indelibly and painfully scratched his soul. I spent much of my life trying to buff one scratch, only to find myself the cause of another. I could never please him. Each of my wrongs was a grain of sand that imperceptibly tipped his invisible scale away from me, added to a load that could never be offset, no matter how I tried.

I lost my older brother when I was thirteen, and I'd never been able to shake the feeling—irrational though it may have been—that it was partly due to the insufferable burden of my imperfection. Then again, he too lost me—once when he left for Palestine in 1931, and once before in the summer of 1927.

I was nine, and Aron was fourteen. The twin wooden pyramids that topped the concession stand at the Kozlowski Brothers' beach bore the brunt of the sweltering July sun, high above us. I watched, sweating, as Aron carefully paid the attendant 5 *groszy*. This left us 15 *groszy* of the 20 Mother had given us to spend on candy, I calculated out loud with pride.

Aron either did not hear me over the din, or—more likely—he simply ignored me. He was angry, and I knew why.

"You can go, *if* you take Samuel," Mother had called from her workroom as she caught up on home accounts and TOZ correspondence. She was the head of the Praga district chapter of the Society for Safeguarding the Health of the Jewish Population in Poland—more palatably referred to by its Polish initials, "TOZ." She frequently spent her evenings and Saturdays, not to mention numerous days during the week, "TOZing," as she called it.

I was proud of her, of course, just as I was of my father's important position at the bank. Everyone knew someone who had been treated at a TOZ emergency clinic, just as everyone — it seemed — knew my father. Only later would I learn to regret the frequent absences from home life that accompanied my parents' professional success. At age nine, dinner served by the cook, alone with my brother in the kitchen, seemed the most natural thing in the world.

I was pleased and proud to be in my older brother's company, however the accompaniment had come about. Even in the heavy silence he maintained during the entire walk along the dirt path by the river's edge, on our way to the beach, I felt confident, protected, and secure in his presence.

Our 5 *groszy* entitled us to access the fine sand of the wildly popular riverside beach. All of Praga seemed to have congregated on the Vistula that summer Saturday morning. From hidden loudspeakers, Al Jolson sang *Toot Toot Tootsie Goodbye* – a song I knew well, since Aron listened to it over and over on our Victrola that summer, ever since he'd seen *The Jazz Singer* at the Era Cinema. I gaped from the stairs of the concession stand at the sea of bathers spread out before me: some lounged in wooden-framed cloth beach chairs, some splashed safely in the tepid river backflow, some braved a swim in the slow moving, chilly eddies of the Vistula itself.

I was still squinting in the bright sunlight at the throngs of white-skinned shirtless men and chubby-legged, shorts-clad women when I noticed I was alone. The reluctant clasp of Aron's hand had vanished. As the crowd closed around me, Aron's blue-and-white striped bathing trunks were nowhere to be seen. The friendly, inviting, and festive atmosphere began to subtly turn hostile and foreign. The world yawed enormous around me, threatening to sweep me into its vastness without the anchor of my brother's hand.

I started to cry.

It could have been five hours or five minutes until the kindly lady with the straw hat bent down and asked me in a strange singsong language if I was lost. She repeated herself, this time haltingly in a language I could understand, and offered her hand. She led me to the concession stand, and spoke briefly to the man in charge.

I could hear only snatches of their conversation: "lost boy... doesn't speak Yiddish... I don't know who he is... your responsibility, no?"

The lady bent to me again, smiled, and explained in her clumsy Polish that the man would help me, that I just needed to tell him my name.

I nodded, and she was swallowed back up by the crowd.

Henryk Gold's Orchestra played *Foxtrot Ali Baba*, another song I knew from Aron's never-ending home Victrola concerts. From the loudspeakers high above, the rip of needle parting from vinyl echoed, and on came the lost child announcement that mentioned my name. Hundreds of heads turned silently in my direction, yet no one responded. I heard my name echo again across the beach—reaching, I imagined, out over the Vistula and into the heart of the city itself on the far banks. Then again.

Finally, thousands of eyes turned to follow Aron's blue-and-white clad form, as he picked his way through the crowd toward me.

The world spun more slowly, and I cried again, this time with relief. Aron reached me, his face red with what I took to be shame and worry. I snuffled and explained that I was fine, that he needn't be so concerned.

He apologized and thanked the man who made the announcement, then gripped my hand tightly. Henryk Gold's Orchestra resumed its song, and Aron led me out of the crowd, to a secluded corner near the exit.

I looked up gratefully at my brother, seeking reassurance after my ordeal, but his face remained beet-red with fury and shame. His slap came before I knew it, followed by a yank on my hand that nearly dislocated my shoulder. Through the ringing of my ear and the stinging of my cheek, I heard his muttered words, thrown haphazardly at me over his shoulder, as we passed through the turnstile and onto the sidewalk outside the beach. The words were, I would come to believe, the glue that kept this memory stuck so firmly in my brain, even to this day.

"...would've been better if you'd fucking drowned!"

He lost me that day, literally and figuratively. I understood then, even if my still-youthful powers of expression could not yet give my understanding voice, my true place in his consciousness. I was a burden to be borne, and when possible avoided—nothing more. In any case, the modicum of trust that I still held in my older brother would be violently swept away several years later, by the same waters of the Vistula. Then he left for Palestine, and his presence—malevolent, indulgent, or otherwise—became irrelevant.

Aron had left his own indelible scratch on my soul, yet I still believe in second chances. Perhaps this was good, because in my own irrefutable hubris, I literally lost my best friend in Chelyabinsk.

Without second chances, where would I be?

Three months had passed since I arrived in Chelyabinsk, and I could feel my literary talent slipping away from me. I was doomed to a twisted version of playwright purgatory wherein all on-stage dialogue sounded like my twice daily — morning and evening — dose of titillating brotherly colloquy:

> Igor: "Where are my socks? You took them!"
> Viktor: "Did not, dick eater!"
> Igor: "Did too, toilet face!"
> Me: "Shut up!"
> Viktor: "Yeah, shut up, fart breath!"
> Igor: "No, *you* shut up, pimple butt!"

If writing memos in Zaltzman's office day in and day out had dealt my literary senses a vicious kick to the groin, living and interacting with Viktor and Igor had proven the knockout uppercut. My words, I felt, were escaping me.

I tried to keep them alive in my frequent letters to Danuta, which I now sent regularly care of Aron in Tel Aviv. Her regular replies were oxygen in the emotional hyperbaric chamber called Chelyabinsk. I tried to resuscitate my words in cleverly worded inter-departmental memos, until Zaltzman told me with little sentimentality that I should keep my literary aspirations to myself, and just get the goddamn tank treads delivered already, unless I wanted to go back to working on the goddamn assembly line.

Zaltzman was Major General Isaak Moiseevich Zaltzman, personally appointed by Josef Stalin to oversee production of the Kliment Voroshilov tanks so desperately needed by the Red Army. He was one of the most powerful men in Chelyabinsk at that time, and a fellow Jew. He'd pulled me from the assembly line almost randomly. One day, as I tried to force my numb fingers to screw on and tighten nut number 45,324 — I kept track to alleviate boredom — a voice rose above the screech of the assembly line conveyor belt.

"Who here speaks and writes Polish, and can type?"

Unhesitant, like a weary pilgrim answering a suddenly revealed savior, I called out, "I can!"

Zaltzman needed someone to help correspond with suppliers in Soviet-controlled Poland, and for the price of a heated work environment and the daily hot lunch that his office staff received at a nearby pub, I was all too happy to oblige.

I was on my way back from one such lunch on a Wednesday, licking my fingers clean from Ludmilla's *Pelmeni* with *Smetana* and trying not to think about the possibly canine origin of the dumplings' allegedly beef filling. I sauntered past a line of grey and hunched figures in ragged clothing, who were being led along the frigid street by two high-booted NKVD guards.

Admittedly, these had been good days for me in Chelyabinsk. Hundreds of thousands flowed into the city, only to find no work, no services, and even less sympathy. Whereas I had a roof, at least one hot meal a day, a little money in my pocket, and access to the highest levels of decision-making. Like some beggar triumphantly brandishing a hard-won scrap of bread, only to have it snatched from him by a bigger and stronger beggar, I was guilty of the sin of overestimated self-importance.

A group of prisoners in the streets of Chelyabinsk was a common sight. In the city, now a major transit point for NKVD prisoners bound for the Siberian *gulags*, I saw such groups almost daily. The year in Pechora remained fresh in my memory, and I'd established a personal custom whenever I encountered such a line of misery incarnate.

Walking quickly, I would pass the group until the crowd closed in behind me. Then, clutching at a pocket as if I'd forgotten something, I'd turn on my heel just in time to collide with the lead NKVD guard. After apologizing, I would continue walking back the way I'd come. The guard I ran into would inevitably turn to his colleague and have a joint chuckle about the clumsiness and stupidity of the locals. Thus, with both guards momentarily distracted, I could press, one by one, whatever coins I had in my pocket into the randomly outstretched hands of the prisoners passing nearest me.

This practice was not only ultimately ineffectual, but also outright dangerous were I to be caught. Yet my sense of justice, I believed — ignoring the glimmer of inner glee I still felt at *not being* one of these wretches — drove me onward. I reviled the *gulag* system, and everything it stood for. This was my small way of rebelling.

In this group, several prisoners mumbled their thanks. Most just pocketed the coins, and continued to shuffle along, the constraints of politeness having long ago been stamped out by hunger, cold, and fear. One man, however, looked up as our hands touched and the coin slid from my palm. He met my eyes with an inquisitive look, clearly surprised by the unfamiliar gesture of kindness. He had dirt-streaked, gaunt cheeks, and sunken eyes hidden deep beneath a heavy brow. As he looked up at me, a lock of greasy dark hair fell from the depths of his ragged cap to partially obscure his eyes. He reached unconsciously to push it away, and lowered his head, having apparently discovered no explanation for the kindness.

I gasped at the familiar gesture, struck by sudden realization, and stopped dead in the street as he continued past me.

"*Wiewiorka*?" The nickname slipped out of my mouth unconsciously.

The figure raised his head with a jerk. "*Malpeczko*?"

Astounded, I trotted to catch up with the slowly moving line. Five seconds later, I hugged the filthy and thin frame of my best friend, Jacek. It was an embrace that lasted the length of my desperate longing for home—forever and fleeting. Ten seconds later, the NKVD guards pulled me roughly away from him, and one threatened me with his truncheon. The line marched on, pushing Jacek farther and farther from me.

"I'll find you! I'll help you!" I called in his direction with a desperate loneliness I hadn't realized I felt until that moment. He represented the temporary embodiment of all that I'd lost—home, family, Danuta. I could not allow him to slip away just like that.

I found Jacek in short order, thanks to the ready access to all personnel files that working in Zalzman's office afforded me. They'd assigned him to work in the munitions factory, pending his transfer to whatever *gulag* was next available. There being at this time far more prisoners than camps, prisoners often spent months in Chelyabinsk. And the Soviet state had proven expert at extracting compensation for the courtesy of feeding and housing its wards.

In March, temperatures had started rising above zero during the day. Spring was now a hope less distant, no longer utterly clouded by winter's grey veil. They'd set Jacek to priming 122 mm artillery shells—a job that should not have logically existed. Priming shells was traditionally done in the field, since transporting primed ammunition was far more dangerous. Yet some nameless bureaucrat had dictated this practice in the name of wartime expediency. They reserved priming, the most dangerous job in a notoriously dangerous factory, for the lowest of the low on the scale of importance to the State. I had watched these Primers in action, from afar, on my occasional working visits to the munitions factory. Each Primer sat separately, his workspace shielded by sandbags to minimize the collateral damage from accidents, which were frequent owing to the rushed nature of the assembly and the low quality of the propellant used in the shells. Luckily, for production quotas, the factory suffered no shortage of replacements following these accidents. After a quick cleanup of whatever remained of the victim in the sandbagged emplacement, work resumed with a fresh — and still intact — set of trembling hands.

The moment I learned of Jacek's assignment, I began forming a plan to help him escape. I had two trump cards: Igor and Viktor, both of whom worked in the same section of the munitions factory. They were responsible for delivering the huge and crushingly heavy wooden crates of unprimed shells to the Primers, and removing the crates containing the primed, and sometimes dangerously unstable, shells. Each crate held eight shells, each weighing around 25 kilograms. Most importantly, given the significant amount of packing material surrounding the primed shells, *each crate was large enough to hold a man.*

The idea was beautiful in its simplicity. The NKVD didn't care about names, only bodies. A prisoner was relevant only in so far as they could account for him — alive or dead. When a Primer got blown to bits, the NKVD officer in charge would check a number off his list, and bring in another prisoner. End of story.

All we needed was for Jacek to die, and he'd be free.

I presented the idea to Igor and Viktor that evening, in the quiet chill of our doghouse. Shifting to raise myself on one elbow, I told them about my encounter with Jacek. They nodded with empathy as I told them the story of our long acquaintance, then listened intently while I explained my plan to save him.

When I finished, the brothers consulted in initially hushed yet increasingly belligerent tones. I feared I would need to break up another name-calling session, but in the end, Viktor pushed his brother gently back onto his own bunk, and turned to speak to me.

"I swore to our mother that I would take care of Igor. This plan could easily get us all killed, or worse."

"Yes, but —"

Viktor held up a hand. "I can't let Igor be a part of this. I'm sorry. But I will help you, by myself. I hope one of us will be sufficient?"

I nodded effusively and gushed gratitude. We were going to save Jacek!

Obviously, I had no intention of killing Jacek, but in order to free him, the NKVD needed a body, preferably an unidentifiable one in poor repair following a propellant explosion and fire. Luckily—for us, in any case—in Chelyabinsk in the spring of 1942, bodies were not in short supply. Authorities carried the numerous dead out of makeshift medical huts, or work details picked them up from the streets, and dumped them unceremoniously into pits on the outskirts of town.

We needed just one.

On a clear night, as the March moon shone starkly in a cloudless sky, Igor stayed behind in the doghouse, and I wore his heavy coat over my own. Viktor and I staggered, feigning drunkenness, and sang loudly as we walked the empty streets towards the burial pits. Minutes after we left the town's last building, and our off-key songs, behind us, the unguarded open pits came into view.

I was not a callous man. Until the Pechora River transport ship, I'd never even seen, let alone touched, a corpse. In my soft urban upbringing, death had been detached from the living, separated by the lacy veil of society. Others handled the dead. We mourned lost loved ones, but remained physically distanced from the messy reality of human mortality. In Chelyabinsk, and indeed during all the months that preceded and followed, death had become an immediate and a day-to-day companion. In my daily comings and goings, I routinely looked past corpses on the street, concentrating on whatever task was at hand. Thus, the tens of bodies facing Viktor and I as we stood on the edge of the open pit held for me none of the abject horror they once would have. Rather, they represented simply a means to a just end.

We chose a fairly fresh gentleman, only partially frozen, and disentangled him with some difficulty from the top of the pile. After we pulled him free, Viktor bent over to get a better look at his face. Unlike many of the others, this face was not contorted, but looked almost placid—as if the man had died peacefully at home, surrounded by loved ones, rather than on the street of a wartime industrial nightmare. Viktor's forehead wrinkled and his brow furrowed in concentration as he tipped his large head to look at the man's face from either side.

"He looks like a Sasha," he pronounced wisely, straightening up.

We thus dubbed the man Sasha.

Viktor dressed Sasha in Igor's coat, and managed to wrench both of his arms free of their rigor mortis-induced rigidity to allow us to support him — as our drunken comrade — between us. In this pose, with Sasha's freezing fingers simultaneously tickling and chilling the nape of my neck, we headed back into town.

As we passed the first outbuildings, we again staggered noticeably and sang loudly, continuing right up to the doorstep of our doghouse.

Getting Sasha in the low door required a few well-placed kicks on Viktor's part. The muted sound of cracking bones resounded in the midnight silence, and several more cracks echoed as the twins fitted Sasha into the ammunition crate they'd filched. They pounded several discrete holes in the sides of the crate to enable Jacek to breathe, then nailed the lid closed and shoved the crate out the door. Sasha would likely not mind the accommodations, we joked, and would wait patiently for the morning.

With a gentle rain falling the next morning, we found Sasha's crate covered in a thin layer of ice that sparkled dimly in the grey morning light. Hefting the slippery box, Viktor returned it to the factory with the pretext of having borrowed it the previous evening to transport some supplies — not entirely false. Careful to keep Sasha's crate separate, he began his workday, lifting the first of countless 200-kilo crates and lugging each to the next Primer in line.

When it was Jacek's turn, Viktor took Sasha's crate, pretending to stagger under a heavy load. "This is a present from Samuel Katz," Viktor told an astounded Jacek, as he pried open the crate to reveal not eight shiny shells ready for priming, but rather a grossly contorted corpse folded inside. "If you want to live, do exactly as I say, and quickly."

The explosion that rocked Jacek's emplacement sent the other workers scurrying out of the building, leaving tools and unprimed shells behind. Fire crews grabbed pre-filled buckets of water and dirt and sprang into action.

"Sorry about that, Sasha," mumbled Viktor

He unobtrusively worked his way toward the far end of the factory compound, heading for the vast warehouse, with Jacek's crate balanced on one massive shoulder. The warehouse was partially full of identical crates.

Viktor whispered to the crate as he gently lowered it in an empty and darkened corner. "I'm going to leave you here until my shift is over, then I'll come get you and take you to Samuel. He's already arranged fake papers, and the NKVD won't even be looking for you. Keep quiet and still. Okay?"

Jacek's muffled affirmative reply came through the heavy crate.

Viktor turned and rushed to help fight the fire which had now scorched Jacek's emplacement, and more importantly Sasha, beyond any hope of recognition. He smiled to himself, as Jacek had been successfully killed.

The cleanup from the fire proceeded quickly, and work resumed at its normal backbreaking pace. Darkness had descended by the time the factory bell rang to signal the end of the day shift, And the temperature had already dropped well below zero, and would drop far lower owing to the now-clear night skies.

Viktor nodded to Igor, and worked his way casually to the warehouse to "borrow" Jacek's crate for the evening. He pulled his heavy coat tighter around him, shutting out the evening cold. His footsteps echoed in the empty hall as he turned a corner to the warehouse door.

His jaw dropped and he stopped dead in his tracks.

What had previously been a nearly empty warehouse was now filled to bursting with tens of thousands of ammunition crates, all completely identical to Jacek's. They were stacked high to the ceiling, and spilled out the doors into the hall.

"A whole trainload of shells were returned," explained a passing worker whom Viktor urgently accosted. The man shook himself free from the giant's vice-like grip. "Get off of me! Something about defective propellant. We need to take them all apart—it could take *weeks*."

And thus, I lost—literally *lost*—my best friend.

Following Viktor's urging and throwing caution to the wind, I made it to the warehouse in just minutes, to see with my own eyes. He was right; it was utterly futile. Even if we could somehow move the tens of thousands of crates, each—except for Jacek's—weighing 200 kilos, how could we explain this activity to the NKVD? And could we complete it in time to save Jacek from freezing to death, or suffocating in the densely-packed piles?

We could do absolutely nothing, except wait for someone to find Jacek's body in the coming weeks, if ever. The NKVD had accounted for all their prisoners, and Jacek would raise a passing eyebrow if found, but nothing more. There was no chance his body could be linked to us, no chance for any repercussions whatsoever for my folly.

No repercussions, that is, save those of conscience.

I am an admitted misanthrope. I trust and care for a select few people, and to these I am devoted to a fault. I am occasionally surprised and pleased when a spark of brilliance or altruism flies from a fellow human's sphere of self-interest and lands, as if scorching, on my own. Yet most of humanity I find predictable, petty, boring, and consistently disappointing.

Jacek was among my select few. I still carry him with me, and will never forget the lesson of humility his death taught me. This is the second chance I give myself. This is second chance I'm still not convinced I deserve.

CHAPTER 11
Danuta: Stop What You're Doing

Tel Aviv, Friday, May 29, 1942

>*My Dearest Samuel,*
>
>*Stop what you're doing, and hold up your hand. Look at your fingers, and close your eyes. See my hand? My fingers are curling through yours. Their wispy gentleness, tickling the valleys between your own, is a prelude to the tightening squeeze to follow. Now our palms are snug together. Your hand is cold and calloused. Mine is warm and suntanned. My thumb caresses the back of your hand. You look down into my eyes, and I gasp as the world and all its fullness is revealed. It is the beauty of the infinite, the sunburst thrust at me from the depths of your soul, which takes my breath away. It is our love, made luminescent and visible.*
>
>*I can see this. Can you? It is both our past and our future. It is an anomaly of time and space – simultaneously there, wherever you're reading this, and here, in Tel Aviv.*
>
>*For here, in Tel Aviv – finally – I am! I arrived in Haifa three days ago, after almost a month stuck in Gdansk after those German pigs took me off the Vatan. They only let me go after I proved that I was actually Catholic – thank goodness I memorized the Rosary! – and explained that I had taken a Jewish identity because of the Soviets' rabid anti-Christianity. The Nazis loved hearing that. Afterwards, I was in Malta, and then another three months waiting in Istanbul for the British to approve my paperwork to come to Palestine. Three months working in that stuffy office, with the randy Mr. Bayar whose hands never seemed to stay where they should! But all this you should already know, my love, if you received the letters I sent via Aron – our personal Palestine post office!*
>
>*The trip from Istanbul was awful, as I knew it would be. No, I did not bend to kiss the ground when disembarking, as so many*

*of my fellow travelers did. My lips are reserved for you, darling —
let Eretz Yisrael be jealous! Nonetheless, I was elated as I stepped
off the ship and onto the dock at Haifa. For I had one thought: the
next time I encounter a ship (for I sincerely hope I may never have
to board one again) may be when you arrive.*

*Aron is a darling, as I knew he would be. He helped me clear
the customs officer's endless questions fairly quickly. In fact,
everyone seems to know and respect your brother. As it was too
late to make the trip back to Tel Aviv, he took me in a cab to a
lovely little hotel in the Hadar neighborhood. On Herzl Street, we
watched falafel stand owners compete for customers with shouts
and "falafel acrobatics," as Aron called them – tossing up the
crispy balls and catching them artfully in the pita bread. After a
wash, he took me to dinner, and then to see Waterloo Bridge at the
Armon Theatre. Vivian Leigh is, as you know, one of my favorites.
I was pleased to show off my English to Samuel. At least
something came of being stuck in Malta all those months,
waitressing for British sailors near the port! But the movie was
hard to see through the fog of cigarette smoke. And the sunflower
seeds! It was like sitting in the midst of a squirrel convention,
with the incessant rustle of paper bags, loud cracking, and piles of
shells littering the floor.*

*I slept like a rock my first night in Palestine, a sweet
dreamless sleep. Until, that is, I was woken by a god-awful
screeching at the crack of dawn. I couldn't recognize the language,
but there was no doubt in my mind as to the content: German
bombers, Nazi Stormtroopers, or perhaps the devil himself was on
the way, and we needed to take cover. I flung myself out of bed
and, still in my nightgown, raced into the hall. I pounded on
Aron's door like a madwoman, and must have scared him silly, as
wild-eyed and disheveled as I was. After calming me, he explained
to me patiently about the muezzin, who was calling Muslims in
the lower city of Haifa to prayer. He sent me gently back to my
room, but there was no more sleep for me. This place, I suddenly
realized with my head still spinning, has but a veneer of Europe
painted over it, and it is mica-thin. Peel it back and the Levant is
revealed – glorious in its wildness and terrifying in its barbaric
potential.*

*In Tel Aviv, which we reached the following morning after a
bumpy bus ride, the patina of Europe is far thicker. Aron's
apartment is lovely and homey, located on a small, quiet, and*

shady dead-end street. I'm writing this at a small table in the guest room, in which Aron has installed me, and from which I will await you, my darling, for as long as it takes. I woke not long ago from a sleep blessedly uninterrupted by morning prayers of any variety. Through the wooden trisim (my new Hebrew word for the morning!) that shade my windows, I can hear the Friday-morning rattle of cars and horse-drawn carts on Bugrashov Street, and the whistle of the policeman directing traffic above the deeper rumble of the Egged buses climbing King George toward Allenby. This city lives and breathes. Tel Aviv, just as I imagined it.

Yet in the three days I've been here, I've learned that there are actually two cities here. There is the day-to-day Tel Aviv, with its kerosene vendors and crowded outdoor coffee shops, its markets and placid shaded boulevards. But there is a dark veil hiding another city — perhaps "shrouding" would be a more apt word. This is the city of anxiety, of fear bordering on desperation. This is the city where pharmacies quietly sell out their stocks of family-size packages of cyanide tablets, even as more arrive. This is the city where no young men are seen — all have gone off to volunteer for the British army, or for the Hagana, the semi-legal Jewish defense forces. I've told you that Aron now works for them — although he told me to use the name of his nominal employer, Kofer HaYishuv, which is a fund set up to finance the Hagana's activities.

There's no need to look further than today's headlines in Davar, which Aron translated for me, to find the source of the angst among the Jews of Palestine: Rommel's advances in Libya. The Axis is pushing for Tobruk, a major Allied port, and the fear here is palpable. If Tobruk falls, the Germans' road to Palestine becomes that much shorter, as do their supply lines.

What is not in the papers, but what everyone nonetheless knows, is that the British are now preparing to implement the not-so-secret plan they call Palestine Final Fortress. If Rommel reaches Egypt, the British will pull out all forces from Palestine ahead of the inevitable German invasion.

If this happens, the half million Jews of the Yishuv — the Jewish community of Palestine — will be at the mercy of the local Arabs, who have made no secret of their support for the Nazis, and who have proven how vicious they can be when unfettered by British soldiers. And after the Arabs have their way, the Nazis themselves will get what's left of us. My love, the stories we've heard of what the Nazis are doing to Jews in Europe are true. The rumors I heard from every fellow refugee from Vilna to Tel Aviv are true – despite the Allies' convenient, and perhaps willful, ignorance of their veracity. Aron claims that the Yishuv leadership has undeniable proof of the systematic murder of the Jews of Europe. Thus, there's good cause to assume that this is what awaits us all if Rommel succeeds. This, then, is the shroud that dims even the optimistic brightness of our Tel Aviv sun. This is the winter night to our lovely spring days, the dark to our light.

Yes, "our." Have you ever noticed how authors use "we," when their actual meaning is "you"? It's as though they attempt to make opinions – criticism or praise – more palatable through self-inclusiveness. As a writer, you will perhaps doubt the sincerity of my newfound affinity for your – now our – people, these Jews I've been living with for nearly two years. I know your feelings toward Zionism, or nationalism in general, darling. One can't expect your father's Universalism to have passed you over entirely, despite it having done exactly so with your brother! Yet given what we now know about the fate of European Jewry, together with our simple understanding of the way the world works in the age of the nation-state, can you truly argue against the logic of Jewish sovereignty? And given what you know of me, is it really so hard to believe that I include myself in this "we"?

There is an incredible resilience to these, my new people. Whether born of desperation, sublimity, or some miasmatic combination thereof, their power, like my awe of it, remains undiminished. Over the past weeks, the Yishuv leadership, Aron tells me, vigorously debated the option of evacuating the Jewish population en masse, if the British pull out. Some suggested that just the leadership should leave, setting up a government in exile ala Poland. Some advocated that only women and children evacuate. Yet the incredibly brave and sadly salient decision was that there is nowhere left to run. That is why the leadership has endorsed their own part of the Palestine Final Fortress, a plan they're calling the "Northern Plan" on good days, or "Masada on the Carmel" on more desperate ones.

Your brother is working frantically, day and night, to bring this plan to fruition, and I hope soon to help him. The Zionist leadership is organizing the evacuation of the entire Jewish population of Palestine north of the Carmel mountain range, and the Hagana has already begun fortifying it as a final line of *defense. The Carmel, Aron explained, is the only natural physical barrier between Palestine and Egypt. Rommel's tanks can roll right over the coastal plains in a matter of weeks with no large-scale British resistance, but there's at least a chance of slowing them with the Hagana's small guerilla forces in the mountain passes. It is a plan audacious in its nobility and heartrending in its desperation.*

So, I now say "we," but without the author's faux inclusiveness. The tribulations I thought ended when I arrived in Haifa may have just begun, but I will face them together with my newfound people. Yet it would be so much easier to face them with you! I know, my love, that I am a selfish, selfish woman, having wasted an entire letter complaining to you. I have been strong these past 21 months, truly, and I know that my experiences have certainly paled in comparison with your own. But this does not stop the tears that come unbidden when I put out a hand towards your side of the bed and find it cold. It does not change the way my stomach drops when I instinctively turn to share some discovery or revelation with you, only to discover your absence each time anew.

Now, stop what you're doing, my darling, and look to the west. Do you see me? I'm standing here now, on Aron's porch in Tel Aviv, waving, waiting. Do you see the longing in my face? Do you see the tears tracking my cheeks? You've never stood up a date with me yet. I'm expecting you to keep your promise.

I love you with all my heart,
Danuta/Lea

CHAPTER 12
Aron: Tobruk Has Fallen

Tel Aviv, Monday, June 22, 1942

"Tobruk has fallen. It's all over," Sean said.

"What? Oh, bloody fucking bollocks!" I called in English from the kitchen, over the hissing of the kettle and the rattling of pans. While I'd been planning breakfast, one of the precious eggs Sean had haggled for at the Carmel market took a suicide roll off the counter, apparently preferring obliteration to cooperation in my omelet project.

Morning sun squinted through the wooden slats of the *trisim*, painting the kitchen floor tiles in yellow and black stripes. I bent to gather what I could recover of the egg into a bowl, and silently vowed not to mention the mishap when serving breakfast. The sounds of Tel Aviv waking up flowed in through the open windows, along with the glorious smells of early summer: dust, jasmine, wood and diesel smoke.

"What's happened, then?" I came into the dining nook, where Sean rested his forehead dramatically on the Palestine Post, and stretched to see past the blond curls covering the top half of the front page. "Are you devastated about... air operations in the Aleutians, then? Eh, mate?" I affected my best Aussie accent, which Sean never tired of mocking. He claimed I sounded like a "ghetto jackaroo with a head cold."

Then he lifted his head, and I saw his face... and the headline it had been hiding. The Germans were claiming that Tobruk had fallen to Field Marshall Erwin Rommel's Panzers. We both knew what it meant, and what came next.

I set the pan I'd been holding down roughly on the table, and sat gently on the chair next to him.

"There were more than 50,000 men defending Tobruk," he said softly.

I touched his hand, and he did not pull it away. I knew of Tobruk's legendary defenses, and that Sean's younger brother Adam was among the ranks of its defenders. Tobruk, the only deep-water port between Benghazi, Libya, and Alexandria, Egypt, had been wrested from the

Axis in an eight-month siege the previous year, and massively fortified by the British. In capturing the port, Rommel had gained a crucial strategic asset on his eastward push, in addition to taking a large part of the British forces out of the equation. This meant the Desert Fox could dramatically shorten his supply lines and redouble his efforts to push towards Palestine.

"Rommel's men are known to treat prisoners fairly," I said softly. This, too, was true—although I was not at all sure it was what Sean needed to hear. He had just found out he may have lost his little brother, and now faced the very real possibility of losing me.

He roused himself from the table and straightened his uniform. The shadows of three diamonds—recently replaced by the single crown of a Major—still showed on the faded cloth of his epaulets. He ignored the food I'd set in front of him, and shrugged off my further attempt at comfort—which was only slightly less clumsy than my handling of the eggs.

"I need to get to the office," he said. "It's the end of days, my love, and I'm one of the four horsemen. Unfortunately, I'm on the black horse. I may not be able to meet you this evening. I'll ring you." He strapped on his pistol holster and breezed out of my flat, blowing a distracted kiss over his shoulder.

The door slammed behind him with a finality that chilled me. Tobruk, I knew, had been pre-defined as the first domino in the line. With its fall, the British Army would immediately put the plan to evacuate Palestine into action. With a sinking feeling in my stomach, I looked around the silent flat, in which the ghostly presence of this man—*this man I loved*, I reminded myself—lingered. Through the door to my room, I could see the crumpled bedclothes, still redolent with his scent. The wine goblet his lips had caressed just last night still stood at attention on the coffee table. In the empty guest room, his spare shirts still moped in the closet. Every part of this flat, and my life, retained and radiated Sean's touch and caress. Yet with him overseeing the group administering the British retreat, and I myself deeply involved in implementing the Northern Plan—which would shortly come to be called *Haifa-Tobruk*—it was highly likely that I would never see him again.

Late the night before, not knowing that at that moment the last of Tobruk's defenders were fighting, dying, or contemplating capture, I walked along Gordon Beach alone before heading over to the Armon Hotel Bar to meet Sean. I stared at the First Quarter moon, already sinking toward the western horizon. My eyes traced the glittering arc of the moon path on the flat sea as it shimmered into the distance.

It was not the same path about which Danuta had whispered to Daniel on the Baltic Sea. It was not the same path that Samuel, perhaps, watched that very moment somewhere far away. It was not the same path, nor did it point in the same direction, yet it had the same source. I kicked at the sand with a bare toe and wondered if all our paths were of common origin. Did we all seek the same thing, driven by core desires deeper than knowledge? Did not all human paths — meanderingly individual as they were — inevitably converge?

Yet my path did not appear to be converging with anything. It so dramatically diverged from that which my father had imagined for me as to make it unrecognizable. So had my brother's, of course, but his divergence was not entirely of his own choosing. Mine, Father would have said, was one of free will — *willfulness*, my mother would have added. I smiled at the memory of my father's face, then frowned, as the harsh words we'd exchanged before I left Warsaw came back to me.

"Nationalism is destroying society, son, not furthering it. Can't you see the inherent artificiality of the nation-state? Can't you recognize that division is just that — divisive? We need to work for inclusion, *and slowly broaden its scope until it overcomes these illusory national borders we erect."*

Suddenly, just behind me, an air raid siren took an audible breath and its familiar yet terrifying banshee wail began to rise and fall. Automatically, my stomach dropped and my heart skipped a beat. *That sound!* That cursed sound carried such power — the power to turn me from a proud, thoughtful man into a rabbit discovered munching lettuce in a garden — that it instinctively and frantically sent me scrambling to hide. Furious and terrified in equal measure, I began to run across the empty beach.

Then the siren stopped. Seconds later, it began again, a single, static cry. *All clear.* A false alarm. I stopped running, pulse racing and head pounding, and sat down hard in the sand.

Forcing my thoughts out of rabbit-mode slowed my heart. Illusory national borders, my father had said. *Illusory.* To me, my father's path had been illusory — willful assimilation into a society that never missed an opportunity to express its collective rejection of him. He truly believed, perhaps right up to the moment when the German bomb took him and my mother, that integration of the diverse and antagonistic segments of Poland was possible. He truly believed in the essential goodness of humanity. I still admired his naiveté—if only because it represented true faith, of which I was incapable.

I had no black and white; everything shimmered in shades of grey. Any hope of faith in my father's Universalist prattle died in me when the semi-frozen saliva of the Polish policeman had hit the back of my neck. I wonder now if he—wherever he was today—had any idea of the life-changing power his bodily fluids had possessed.

I walked home from school on a winter afternoon in late 1929, a troubled sixteen-year-old. In class we'd discussed the recent destruction of the ancient Jewish community of Hebron, in Palestine. My mind still reeled from the descriptions of that massacre.

I pulled my cap down over my frozen ears. Samuel, who tagged along behind me as he did every day on the way home, did the same— less from cold than from adulation, I knew. He was unusually chatty that afternoon, prattling on and on about some convoluted classroom intrigue, until finally the babble got the better of me.

I stopped, turned abruptly, bent down to his level, and looked him the eye. "I really, truly, and honestly do not give a shit. Would you please just shut up!"

Even in my frustrated state, the look of hurt in his eyes affected me... quietly.

Fifty or so souls had shown up to the Nationalist Party demonstration on the corner of Szeroka and Petersburska streets, across from the grand round synagogue building in which I'd never set foot. They wore their signature black berets and matching armbands, and carried typically belligerent signs.

Jews Out! Catholic Polish State NOW!

Catholicism and Nationalism - True Polish Brothers

I took Samuel's hand and led him hurriedly into the slushy street. Skirting behind a passing streetcar and avoiding a spindly-tired Model T, we moved away from the vociferous group and past the bemused and bored-looking policeman who'd apparently been assigned to watch them.

This policeman's face was a familiar sight on the streets between our house and school. As children, we'd surreptitiously watched him polish the shiny brass buttons on his tunic. He would rub with such vigor and concentration that his brimmed hat would inevitably slip down over his eyes, causing him to start and us to flee, laughing. He looked up with vague recognition as we approached.

I nodded in greeting, seeking a measure of empathy from someone so long a fixture of authority in the predominantly Jewish Praga neighborhood where we lived.

He straightened up, adjusted his tunic and hat, and just as we passed spit vigorously in our direction, muttering, "Fucking Jewish rats" under his breath.

I felt the spittle strike the back of my neck, but only lowered my head and urged Samuel on faster. When we arrived home, I said nothing to my father of the incident.

That was not an unusual event for any Jew in Poland in those days. So why, I asked myself as I dug my bare feet into the still-warm sand, did it affect my path so dramatically? Others, my father among them, had been able to shrug off incidents like this as mere "undertow." For me, it had been a fault line that, once crossed that day, left my father and me on separate tectonic plates altogether. I had come to a clear, if not yet conscious, recognition that I had—and would always have—no place in the country of my birth. Indeed, I would never have a place in *any* country—except one of my own.

My path had diverged irreparably from my father's, fated never to realign itself.

I turned back to the moon path, which shimmered unperturbed by the adrenaline that still pounded in my temples. I dug my toes deeper into the sand and wondered if Sean's path and my own would yet cross again.

CHAPTER 13
Aron: Behind the Beauty

Kibbutz Beit Oren, Tuesday, June 23, 1942

"Goddammit Bert, don't you see?" Yochanan Ratner's voice rose dramatically over the background noise of the dining hall porch in Kibbutz Beit Oren. "There *is* no other choice! There is *nowhere* left to run! It will be *here*, and *soon*. There's no more room for your doubts. The leadership has approved it. You *have* to get me that funding! We need to move forward *now!*" The room fell silent as, his heavy brows furrowed, Ratner hurried out through the open wooden door.

I looked up from *Davar*. Yesterday we'd heard the news of Tobruk, and I'd not seen or heard from Sean since he left my flat. Now, I sat in Beit Oren, just southeast of Haifa, eating a bowl of cottage cheese and reading a report in *Davar* quoting "reliable sources" in the Mandatory government, who warned of a real danger of German advance troops being parachuted into Palestine. These troops would be only too welcome by the Arab population, most of whom secretly anticipated the arrival of *Abu Ali*, as they referred to Rommel surreptitiously. The British, *Davar* reported, urged "extreme vigilance" on the part of the populace, especially in remote areas.

We left Tel Aviv well before dawn in Hacohen's Mercury convertible, which he'd imported from the US—one of those luxuries the CEO of a major construction company like *Solel Boneh* could afford. Next to him sat Aharon Bert, my boss and the Chairman of *Kofer HaYishuv*, the fund set up to finance overt and covert Jewish defense activities in Mandatory Palestine.

"With those bald heads shining up there, this car would be an easy target for a German bomber, don't you agree?" My companion in the back seat, and partner in follicular prowess, was Yohanan Ratner—architect by trade, renowned expert in static defenses, and the creator of the *Hagana's* Northern Plan. He was the reason we were heading to Beit Oren at this ungodly hour—for it was still moonlight that reflected on the bald pates of Hacohen and Bert, not sunlight.

I tagged along as Bert's assistant on this official review of progress made on the defenses below Beit Oren, and the findings of the elite *Palmach* unit scouts, who'd been tasked with locating, fortifying, and stocking guerilla bases in the caves of the Carmel. The thinking was that a relatively small force of *Hagana* guerillas, if properly supplied and hidden, could seriously augment the physical defenses being put into place. This would perhaps buy the Jews of Palestine enough time for the Allies to regroup and counter-attack, ultimately pushing the Axis forces back south.

The *Yishuv* leadership knew the Northern Plan was a gamble, but I agreed with Ratner: with Jews being slaughtered throughout Axis-controlled Europe and North Africa, and given two thousand years of antisemitism that had only relented for short periods before being renewed each time with greater ferocity — there was nowhere left for Jews to run. I was not alone on this thinking. The Northern Plan was already being referred to on the street as *Masada on the Carmel* — named after the desert fortress in which Jewish rebels held out against the relentless Roman army, until its residents committed mass suicide in the face of defeat and enslavement. While Ratner and the *Hagana* had no overt plans for mass suicide in the face of a Nazi victory, I knew — as did every Jew in Palestine — what the Nazis had in store for us, and thus what the cost of failure would be. The name *Masada on the Carmel* was apt, I believed.

I followed Ratner out of the dining hall, and found him brooding on the porch outside. I turned to take in the spectacular view over the Oren Stream, which the Arabs called *Wadi Fallah*. Countless scrub Palestine Oaks clotted together into a bumpy wave of green felt, which flowed over and melded with the landscape, engulfing boulders and concealing paths. One could truly lose one's self in this landscape. It was the incarnation of surreptitious hope, and I knew the power of the shadows.

"I am *not* simultaneously contemplating the destruction of the Jewish people and watching this man's ass," I told myself repeatedly. But I was. On its dusty black fabric strap, our *Palmach* guide's STEN submachine gun bumped rhythmically and beguilingly against his tight posterior. *Step, bump. Step, bump.* It was hard to ignore, especially given the muscles of his sweat-streaked bare back, which glistened below the neck shade of his visor cap, only a meter ahead of me on the narrow path. I tore my eyes away, and tried to think of Sean.

By the time all were ready to set out from Beit Oren, the sun had already climbed high in the sky. The tension between Ratner and Bert remained as palpable and oppressive as the June heat. The path, completely hidden from our former lookout above, led across the dry streambed, in and out of deep Oak shade where crazy whirlpools of flies buzzed aimlessly. We were on our way to inspect the pillbox under construction on the south side of the winding, tamped dirt track that led up from the coast to Beit Oren, and thereafter to see one of several caves already being provisioned for the *Palmach* fighters.

Behind me, Bert and Hacohen puffed heavily, taking turns wiping their bald pates with white handkerchiefs, sweat stains spreading under the arms of their dress shirts. At their request, we'd scaled back the length of our hike and now planned on visiting only one cave. It was, they had both argued, only a *formal* inspection, after all.

Ratner walked far out in front of the *Palmach* guide, a man named Maxim, whose strongly Russian-accented Hebrew showed utter disdain for articles and prepositions. I'd started to breathe hard myself from the unaccustomed exertion of the march, and between breaths I asked him why he hadn't Hebraized his name, as many immigrants — and especially *Palmach* fighters — did.

"No need," was his curt answer. "I still me, here or Russia, name this or name that. Why need bother?"

I smiled and nodded in agreement. I too had kept my name, after considering it seriously, because so few ties remained to my father that I couldn't bring myself to destroy this last one.

We completed our cursory inspection of the pillbox, which commanded an impressive view of the approach to Beit Oren, in about ten minutes. Bert and Hacohen, still breathless and sipping from Maxim's canteen, seemed unimpressed with the view that stretched all the way to the Mediterranean.

"So, this is what will stop the entire *Wermacht*, Ratner?" growled Bert, making no attempt to hide his derision. "This pillbox is what will tip the scales in favor of the survival of the Jewish people?"

Ratner would not be baited. "Don't be ridiculous, Aharon. You've heard the details of the plan numerous times, and you of all people know our limitations, as well as our imperatives. The trick is using the latter to overcome the former. Let's move on to the cave, shall we?"

We set off uphill, following Maxim's bouncing gun. My tired mind had settled into the rhythm of that gun, which made a small metallic rattle at every bounce on Maxim's rear quarters. *Step, bounce, click.* The heat faded into the background, as did the thorny brush that grabbed at my legs with every uphill step. *Step, bounce, click.* For chunks of blessed minutes at a time, only that *step, bounce, click* resonated, and my mind slipped back to another hot hike, through very different vegetation, many years previously.

I grew up only a block from the Vistula, where the thin strip of undeveloped yet not quite wild forest along its banks served as playground, refuge, and treasure trove throughout my childhood. Together, my playmates and I scoured its ever-changing banks for items the river regurgitated, created forts among the piles of brush brought high by its swollen spring flow, raced our bicycles along smooth and occasionally muddy dirt paths. Thus, when I snuck out of the house that late summer day in 1920, I set my seven-year-old feet in motion directly towards the cool shade of the forest.

Samuel was napping, and with him our babysitter, Mrs. Chlebek. Her name meant "little loaf of bread" in Polish, and with her wrinkled face, round body and stubby neck, she did indeed resemble a loaf of the brown bread Mother now regularly purchased, when she could get it. The war had caused shortages.

Mother had rushed back out the door to the Praski Hospital, just down the street from our flat, to help soldiers that were hurt. She'd said we must be good and mind Mrs. Chlebek, and stay in the house, no matter what, because no one knew what would happen if the cursed Russians broke through. Only later would I understand that this was the peak of the Soviet-Polish war, and the Battle of Warsaw raged literally kilometers from our home.

Mrs. Chlebek snored in the armchair by the window, as I gazed out at the sunny day. I was bored, and the distant booms that had scared me at first had now settled in with the rest of the background noise, so I closed the door behind me and strolled down to the riverbank.

The hot sun reached down through the foliage, tickling the back of my neck with its golden hands and prompting me forward towards the cool water's edge. The water was low, and I had to pick my way carefully through the crusty mud to reach it. I fastidiously removed my shoes and socks, just as Mother had demanded the last time we'd walked on the bank, and walked barefoot upstream in the cool water, feeling the sand between my toes. Squinting into the sun, I watched the ducks riding the swirling eddies created by the giant brick pilings of the Poniatowski Bridge, still being rebuilt, and heard the gulls complaining overhead.

I found an off-green, peaked cap with a red star sewn on it bobbing gently in a small pile of foam, which the river mysteriously produced on hot days like this one. I fished it out with a stick and wrung it out. Only when I placed it on my head did I notice the two holes on either side of the cap, with edges so smooth they might have been cut with my mother's sharp sewing scissors—which I was never to touch. I took the hat off and inserted my fingers into the holes, wondering who would wear a cap so oddly perforated.

That's when the sun caught something shiny on the water, and I looked up to see the logs.

The river lapped at my toes more hungrily, it seemed, as the logs bobbed gently in the slow current, twisting and turning gracefully, bumping into one another and politely separating. This strange dance reminded me of the ballroom event Mother and Father had once taken me to see. I watched, mesmerized and smiling, as the logs put on a show just for me—a charming river ballet.

Then one log drifted closer to the shore, and lazily rolled as it passed me. This puzzled me because, even at age seven, I knew logs didn't have faces. I knew logs didn't have hands so bloated that they looked like the chubby cheeks of the little boy in *The Land of the Midgets*, which Father sometimes read to me. My stomach dropped, as did the cap from my hands. These logs wore uniforms, and left trails of red in the water as they floated by. The river mud grabbed at my toes as I began to run.

I arrived, scratched and barefoot—my socks and shoes utterly forgotten—at the door to our building, and threw one last glance over my shoulder at the hundreds of bodies of Russian soldiers making their deliberate way downstream. Beyond the profound horror which had yet to manifest itself in tears, I felt such a deep sense of *betrayal*. How could the beauty and charm I witnessed in the graceful river ballet have been something so tainted? How could such grace mask such horror?

Step, bounce, click. Step, bounce, click.

We rounded a corner in the path, yet my focus on this mantra remained so intense that Maxim's elbow nearly caught me under the chin when he abruptly stopped and swung the gun up, at the ready.

Snapping out of my reverie, I looked up and spotted a magnificent Griffon Vulture riding a thermal high above us to the west. Momentarily confused as to why this bird of prey should cause Maxim such alarm, I shifted my gaze earthward, and started violently.

I'd never had the opportunity to see a *Wermacht* uniform up close, but there was no mistaking the identity of the five khaki-clad soldiers who now stood, having appeared as if from nowhere, on both sides of the path.

Maxim slowly lowered his weapon and raised his hands. Bert, Hacohen and I followed suit.

The German soldiers, apparently unfazed at this encounter, looked curiously at Maxim, their rifles raised. The unmistakable sound of a safety catch sounded, and I felt my bowels loosen.

When I left Poland in late 1931, the name Adolf Hitler had been a sidebar, mostly the subject of ridicule in the Polish press. In fact, the last thing I recalled reading of him in Poland was sordid gossip about a lover's quarrel with a young half-niece, who had killed herself after he shunned her — or so the rumors claimed. No one had taken seriously the short and violent man that had led the then-forgotten Beer Hall Putsch, and spent less than a year in prison for his treason — perhaps a lesson for governments everywhere, in perpetuity.

Things have changed, I reflected through my fear. *Things have changed drastically.*

The German soldiers motioned for us to get to our knees, hands behind our heads, and we complied. I could see the sweat stains spreading farther down the sides of Hacohen's dress shirt, and could smell the fear dripping from Bert's sideburns next to me. Ratner had vanished.

The officer of the group, his field insignias clearly visible, approached Maxim with pistol in hand. He picked up the STEN gun, turned it over in curiosity, and surveyed the *Palmach* soldier. He used his own Mauser to tip Maxim's hat back and get a better view of his defiant face.

Then he bent close to Maxim, caressing the side of his face with the barrel of the pistol, and whispered something into his ear.

The effect was dramatic. Maxim jumped to his feet and shoved the German officer hard in the chest, first cursing in Russian and then yelling, "You son of a bitch!" in Hebrew.

The officer holstered his weapon. His soldiers looked on and lowered their rifles, but did not interfere. A tense moment of silence ensued, and the German soldiers looked to their officer for guidance.

Then, Maxim snatched his rifle back from the officer, yelled, "Not funny, asshole!" in Hebrew, and promptly broke into hysterical laughter.

The giggles spread to the German soldiers. As Bert, Hacohen and I watched incredulously, the officer and soldiers collapsed into utterly incapacitating laughter. One soldier literally rolled on the ground in hysteria, while another put his feet up on a boulder and lit a cigarette, watching the scene with a broad smile. The officer remained doubled over in paroxysms of laughter.

Finally, Maxim turned to us and motioned for us to lower our hands. "German unit. *Palmach* soldiers," he managed to choke out, wiping his streaming eyes. "They very good, no? This officer Shimon Koch. He chief *yeke putz*, in charge these bastards."

We all relaxed and got to our feet, and I brushed the gravel and dirt from my knees.

The German Unit was a minor *Hagana* legend, comprised of German immigrants, many with *Reichswehr* military service experience. Outfitted and trained with such attention to detail that its members spoke only German among themselves, the small German Unit would infiltrate *Wermacht* units in the event of a German invasion.

From his hiding place behind a boulder some meters beyond, Ratner emerged. "I see you've met reality, Bert. Sorry if it was a bit harsh, but perhaps you now appreciate what exactly we're facing. The fear you just felt was not abstract, and neither is the threat facing the Jews of Palestine. It will not be blown away by the electric fan in your Ramat Gan office. It is out there, waiting to pounce, hiding behind the façade of your theatres, your bank vaults, your red-tile roofs. We can either choose to face it, as our colleague Maxim has done, or stand petrified in its face, pissing down our legs, as you appear to have done. Which do you think grants us a better chance of survival?"

Bert could only glare, red-faced and shaking his damp trouser legs.

I thought again of the logs that were not logs, the power of shadows, the freedom that comes with accepting the ugliness that grace and beauty so often mask.

Realizing what lies behind the world's gilded façade is liberating. Only when we look squarely at the evil behind the beauty can we begin to hope to vanquish it.

CHAPTER 14
Samuel: Perfection

USSRS "Turkmenistan," Caspian Sea, June 1942

Our departure from Chelyabinsk was not harried. After all, they'd accounted for Jacek, but found nothing to tie us to his death or escape. We had time to plan and prepare, and we'd done so nightly in our doghouse, our breath fogging in the slowly warming spring air. The twins had immediately expressed their willingness to accompany me to Palestine, despite the danger.

I didn't completely understand their willingness to undertake such a dangerous journey—one from which they stood to gain little. They spoke vaguely of joining the British Army, but if they wanted to fight the Nazis, there was certainly no shortage of opportunities in Russia in 1942. I might have attributed it to friendship, but I feared it was more semi-blind loyalty, mixed with a bit of adventurism. Either way, I didn't discourage them—which I would soon add to the collection of regrets that weighed ever heavier on my shoulders. My spine seemed to bend under the pressure of Jacek, my parents, Aron, and Danuta, but I could not allow myself the luxury of mourning or the indulgence of self-doubt. Rather, I compartmentalized.

Jacek's death had happened to Past Samuel. Present Samuel needed to focus on getting to Palestine. It was inaccurate science, this experiment of emotional repression—but I was a child of Poland. When in pain, distress, or even awe, we were taught from a young age to internalize, not express. Thus, Viktor's and Igor's effusiveness still embarrassed me, even as it concurrently pleased me. This was how I pushed Jacek's frozen, contorted face to the back of my mind, and chose to focus instead on Danuta's warm and soft one.

With adequate time to prepare, our travel was comfortable, even luxurious in comparison to my own odyssey from Pechora to Chelyabinsk. As representatives of Salzman, on a part-sourcing mission crucial to the future of T-34 tank production, we traveled exclusively by train coach. From Chelyabinsk, through Orsk, to Makat, and finally arriving at Guryev—we sat on bench seats, behind dirty glass windows, amid the fragrant cigarette smoke of high-ranking Soviet officers and foreign businessmen. On the inevitable and often lengthy delays between trains, we stayed in hotels and ate gristly meat off actual plates. We grew to take this level of luxury for granted, and would soon miss it dearly.

"You're wallowing."

Viktor's matter-of-fact pronouncement, coming as it did from the dark of the deck to my left, jolted me from my engine thrum-induced reverie. I turned away from the lights of Guryev, now shrinking on the horizon of the Caspian Sea behind me, and away from the ship's blue-green wake, which chewed and regurgitated the freshly risen moon path.

"I'm not wallowing," I said. "I'm thinking."

"Yeah, dick breath, can't you see he's just thinking?" Igor's nasal voice piped up in my other ear, jolting me again.

"Shut up, butt crack. He's clearly *wallowing*." Viktor spoke firmly. "Perhaps weltering. Possibly foundering. But there's clearly little 'thinking' involved."

"Look...." My thought began, but trailed off. Far beyond the ship's wake, I stared at the moon path, now smooth as a crisply ironed sheet. It strove toward infinity, but was frustrated by the far-off shore's abrupt imposition. *Much like myself,* I pondered, annoyed at the simultaneous triteness and absolute veracity of my analogy. *No matter how far forward I try to see, my actions are inevitably frustrated by unforeseen obstacles.*

Every young man will face, at some point, a moment of absolute mortal clarity. This moment may be cloaked in the sudden and dramatic realization of human failing. Yet, at its core, it speaks a clear and dire prophesy. *You will not achieve the perfection of infinity. You too will disappear from this world,* it says. Following this singular moment, every following moment will be a futile attempt to overcome this truth: *the absolute joy and impenetrable anguish of existence is finite.*

I saw this as my moment, each thought both forever and insufferably instantaneous: the moon path, the thrum of the ship's engine, the corpses of my mother and father laying in the ruins of their building, the smell of the palms of Danuta's hands, Jacek's frozen body wedged unbearably in the ammunition crate for eternity.

Viktor's urgently sincere voice shattered my musing. "You couldn't have known that would happen. You know that, we know that, and if fucking Jacek were here, he'd tell you the same. He'd tell you to spend less time wallowing, and more time figuring out how to get back to that wife of yours."

"But he's *not* here, is he?" I turned violently away from the moon path. My words splashed to the deck like vomit and ran in chunky rivulets down the grooved floor into the sea.

"Yeah, shit cheeks. He's *not* here, is he?" Igor's parrot-like retort, born less of an actual desire to respond than a deep-seated sibling autopilot, bounced into the ship's wake and followed the moon path into the distance.

I put my hand in my jacket pocket and found the reassurance of Danuta's last letter. It had found me in Guryev, and informed me – as joyfully as its crumpled state would allow – of her arrival in Palestine several months earlier. The clerk at the grubby shack that served as post office had asked to see my ID and travel papers twice before relinquishing it to me. His single bushy eyebrow, which stretched nearly ear to ear, had risen with deep skepticism when he saw that the papers had been personally endorsed by Salzman, "Commander Tank" himself. I was used to this response, having put the papers, which I'd forged myself, to copious use since our departure from Chelyabinsk just two weeks previously. Finally, as in previous instances, my clean and well-fed appearance – thanks largely to the petty cash that I'd 'borrowed' from Salzman's office, along with the travel papers – together with my practiced air of authority and self-importance, had overcome Monobrow's hesitation. He passed over the precious letter, but not before making a circumspect note to himself – which, I suspected, he would in short order turn over to his NKVD contact in exchange for a few coins.

Now, hand in pocket, I caressed the letter and the others in the oilskin case, trying to conjure a memory – any memory at all – of her. Incongruously, an afternoon at the Warsaw Zoo jumped into my mind.

I never liked zoos until I went with Danuta. I still despised the idea of them, but with Danuta's hand tugging me forward through the Varsovian throngs, I momentarily ignored that the antics of the seals and the elephants were essentially the demeaning shadows of humanity's own self-importance. It was, after all, a gloriously sunny July day. Danuta wore a revealing summer dress with a matching scarf tied over her hair—*a la* Betty Grable in Campus Confessions, which we'd seen at the Era the evening before.

We squeezed out of the crowd surrounding the low fence of the concrete seal pool, and sat on a shaded park bench. Squirrels rushed frantically between trees. With the air hanging as heavy as breath, the occasional breeze offered a cool hand on a feverish forehead. And Danuta's presence next to me was like static electricity in the air.

"You've got that sardonic look on your face again, darling." Her voice penetrated my musing.

I shook my head sincerely. "I'm not sardonic. I'm pensive. It's a writer thing. We're supposed to contemplate deeply. It's in the handbook."

Danuta's laugh trickled from her lips like cool water from a mountain spring. "And what were you contemplating, my love? What inspiring thoughts can you share with a mere mortal?"

I fixed her with my best *I-know-something-you-don't-know* author gaze. "I would question your mortality, my love. Yet if you must know, I was pondering perfection, as various philosophers have historically viewed it. Would you mind standing for me, and turning around, just for a moment? Yes, there it is: the manifestation of perfection I was considering. Your ass. Don't laugh. I said *don't* laugh. This is serious."

I shook my head. "Look, have you considered how much more entertaining the shadows in the Allegory of the Cave could have been, had Plato but known your ass? Would Kant really have needed his whole 'future perfection of man' argument, had he simply been able to put forth your ass as proof of existing perfection on Earth? And don't even get me started on Rousseau's concept of natural perfection. Face it, my dear: half of Western philosophy... out the window, and all owing to one spectacular posterior."

I smiled, pleased with my cleverness.

She swatted me playfully, and turned mock-serious. "It may shock you to learn that Catholic girls are not just sexual objects, my Jewish Eros. I have no doubt that we have supplied wanking material for generations of little Yids like you, yet I contend that we have far more to offer. What would Aquinas have said about your obsession with my corporeal being? Not a particularly virtuous path, don't you.... My goodness, look at that squirrel. He really does look a bit like Jacek, does he not?"

We both burst out giggling at that. Our laughter escalated, until passers-by began to stare, and Danuta stood up suddenly, claiming that if she laughed any harder she was in dire danger of wetting herself.

I told her I'd like to see that, and that set us off again.

Back from my reverie, I thought it must have been precisely the glorious banality of that afternoon that had left it stuck in my memory. It was the summer before the war. We were in love. It was perfection because neither of us had yet met the limits of our humanity. Yet, as any theologian worth his salt would argue, any perfection — other than the divine — is by definition *transient*.

"So, what's the plan once we get to Bandar Shah, boss?"

A spray of fresh Caspian Sea water, thrown up from a wave that broadsided the *Turkmenistan's* rusty hull, stung my cheek. I had turned back to the stern, and the spray obscured my view of the choppy moon path that followed the nearly empty freighter on its southward crawl. I'd used the last of our funds to book passage to the Iranian port of Bandar Shah, with the vague intention of following the Trans-Iranian Railway south to the similarly named port of Bandar Shahpur on the Persian Gulf. This explained the cramped stateroom we shared, just slightly roomier than our Chelyabinsk doghouse. Getting to Bandar Shahpur with no money over some 1300 kilometers of tortuous rail, not to mention finding passage to the port of Aqaba in British Palestine, was not yet in the forefront of my mind.

Indeed, I could think of nothing at that moment except Danuta and, of course, Jacek. Perhaps I *was* wallowing.

"You can't *put* things behind you," my father once said, "because they're already back there. The moment you consider something that happened, it has by definition *already happened*. There is never any choice but to move forward." My father, who'd left an entire childhood and a loving family behind — like thousands of young Jews of his generation — to move from what he considered the darkness of *shtetl* life to the light of interregnum Warsaw, had known about not looking back. He'd known that each step forward left a footprint that could never be retraced. He, too, had left home, never to return.

And so I turned away from the churning moon path again — perhaps born of the same moon Danuta now contemplated in Tel Aviv — and towards Igor and Viktor.

I gave them a look of mock decisiveness, then softened and smiled. "Fine, I'm wallowing. You're right, and I have no fucking idea what's next. We have no money left, and the NKVD may well be waiting for us in Bandar Shah. I was kind of hoping that *you two* had a plan."

⸻ ❦ ⸻

That night in my pitching berth, the oneiric film projector in my brain worked overtime, as it usually did. During my waking hours, Danuta had faded to a collection of treasured stills. Yet nightly in my dreams, she lived and breathed in full and vivid Technicolor. She touched me with warm pink hands, kissed me with rose-red lips, and soothed me with golden-haloed whispers.

> *I sat in the flat in Vilnius. Streetcar noise and children's voices reverberated from the narrow alley, borne through the open window on a summer breeze redolent of car exhaust, sweat, and fear. Adriana's hushed voice crept from the kitchen, slipping under the bathroom door, wherein I soaked in a rapidly cooling bath.*
>
> *"Marry him? Marry him? But he's Jew! A charming, handsome, and talented Jew, of course. But a Jew, Danuta. What future could you have together? And who will even agree to marry you? Certainly no priest."*
>
> *Danuta's replied in less hushed tones, as if she knew I was listening and didn't care either way. "We don't need a priest, you goose. Don't you read the papers? The Soviets have abolished ecclesiastical marriage. Anyone with a passport can marry in a civil ceremony. All we have to do is go to the municipality and register. And it is below you, of all people, to reduce Samuel to an arbitrary ethnic definition. He is... he is... he is my soul, my dearest cousin. Can you not see that? Wake up! We are already joined. Wake up! This marriage will be just a formality. Wake up! Wake up!"*
>
> *My bath had grown cool in the extreme, yet I smiled at Danuta's proclamation of love, lolling dumbly in the chilly water. I opened my eyes slowly, and found Danuta and Adriana standing over the tub, urgency and concern marking their faces. My hands rushed of their own accord to cover my nakedness, but they paid me no mind.*
>
> *Danuta spoke now in a different, deeper voice. "Wake up! Wake up! WAKE UP!"*

Viktor's hand slapped Danuta's face away, and I opened my eyes to find him standing over me, urging me awake. Cold water lapped at my back, then at my torso as Viktor hauled me out of my top berth.

"Wake up, dream boy! We have to get out of here!"

Igor already waited at the bulkhead, two life preservers in his massive hand, his own preserver already strapped on. Water lapped at his belly, rising quickly.

Viktor hurried me through the bulkhead and up the stairs to the steeply inclined deck.

I had always pictured a sinking ship as a chaotic, Lusitania-like scene—women screaming, men stoic and grave, lifeboats overflowing with human detritus. Yet the *Turkmenistan*, which now listed so severely that I had to cling to a railing to avoid sliding backwards, remained nearly silent, as calmly expectant as a freshly dug grave. The air stunk of petrol and burning meat—a smell the origin of which I chose not to contemplate—yet a moribund peace prevailed. The absence of lifeboats indicated that whatever survivors there had been on the sparsely populated freighter had already left.

The torpedo had struck, Igor informed me, in the aft of the ship. He'd been forward, and by the time he'd made his way down to our stateroom, most had abandoned the ship.

Viktor's rebuke rang out in the silence. "If you had come a little faster, dong head, maybe we could have made the lifeboats. Why didn't you just tell them to wait?"

Igor grunted. "Maybe if you hadn't been sleeping like the baby-fuck you are, you would have been here already. And I *did* tell them to wait, pencil dick—they just didn't seem to care much."

The ship gave a sickening lurch, and a loud bubbling groan emanated ominously from its aft.

I struggled into my life vest, one hand precariously clinging to the rail, one hand working the straps of the complex device. I gave the straps a decisive final cinch, and turned to the twins. "Right. Who knows how to swim?"

Neither raised a hand.

The twins tried to make light of the situation, but they were scared. Despite having grown up in Leningrad, a port city, their faces were clearly etched with the awe of the land-locked when confronted with vastly large bodies of water. They betrayed none of the welcoming intrigue and sincere respect of those who live in harmony with the sea. Rather, they showed the soul-deep terror of those with keen awareness of their air-breathing nature. If being on a ship was an unnatural circumstance for Igor and Viktor, being in the water itself was utterly unthinkable.

"How is it you grew up next to a port and can't swim?" Exasperated and beginning to panic, I scrambled quickly across the nearly vertical deck, and found one dilapidated life ring attached to a railing. I chucked it to them, imploring them to share without fighting, for once.

The heavy rubber Soviet Navy surplus life vests we all wore were grubby orange, and had seen better days. Each had two inflatable sections, one on each side. However, we quickly discovered that between the three of us, only three sections — one on each vest, luckily — actually held air. One inflated section was sufficient for me, as the lightest of the three, to bob comfortably, if a bit lopsidedly.

I jumped as far clear of the rapidly sinking ship as I could, mentally thanking my parents for their insistence on swimming lessons. I smoothly kicked away in the oily summer waters of the Caspian Sea, which were warm and only slightly salty. I turned to watch Viktor and Igor as, gulping, they followed suit.

They landed heavily in the water, and came up spluttering and wide-eyed, their combined weight just barely supported by the sodden life ring and their half-inflated vests. They looked around confusedly, in panic, unsure what to do next.

In the eerie silence, my voice carried easily across the meters separating us. "Kick your legs, you Russian idiots! You need to get your fat asses away from the ship! Come on! You can do it! Hurry!"

I turned to swim farther away, and could hear Viktor and Igor laboring behind me, gasping and dog-paddling. I paused to look back just as the burning ship slid gracefully beneath the surface, then turned and swam back to the twins. For several minutes, we watched the burning petrol on the water's surface backlight the scene dramatically. Then all fell to blackness and silence — no lifeboats, no rescue ships, no stars, no moon. Just three men, two of whom couldn't swim, three half life vests, and one water-logged life ring. *Perfection.*

The *Turkmenistan*, in a final act of defiance, gave up not a single item of buoyancy — not a barrel, not even a damned plank. I scoured the inky waters for what seemed like hours, desperately seeking something—*anything*—which could conceivably support Igor and Viktor's bulk.

We tried over and over to patch and re-inflate the damaged life vests. With string I unraveled from my pants cuff, I tried to tie off the leaky corners where the glue and stitching had split with age and neglect. Then, I used the same string to create a life preserver from my tied-off and air-filled shirt, a trick I recalled from some novel. It held air for only minutes. Finally, I tried to teach the twins to float—first a dead man's float, face-down, with only occasional whale-like breaches of the head to breathe, and then a back float. Again and again, they forced themselves bravely, with my gentle urging, to release the life ring and relax into the float. Again and again, they ended up gasping, back on their stomachs and clutching the faltering life ring, too panicky to continue.

By the time the sky revealed the first hopeful traces of dawn, hope in our corner of the Caspian Sea had sunk below the level of the grey life ring, which now floated some ten centimeters below the surface. Igor and Viktor, exhausted and half-conscious with the long effort of keeping afloat, had only mortal anguish to keep them from slipping into a blessed faint. Still they struggled to keep their faces above the water. Still they kicked heavy legs futilely, in the feint hope of gaining a centimeter more of air. Still they hoped.

Finally, with my own life vest only half-inflated and showing signs of leakage itself, I came to a decision that I knew would haunt me for the rest of my days. Was it hubris to believe that I could survive? Was it selfish not to sacrifice myself in futile heroism? *Was it wrong to want to live?* I feared I might ask myself these questions every morning for the rest of my life.

Slowly and kindly, I explained to Igor and Viktor the little I knew of drowning: how it wasn't a slow death; how it was not supposed to be painful. I also explained about the drowning man's desperation, how he would unconsciously cling to, and possibly drown with him, any buoyant object nearby. And then, God help me, with tears streaming invisible down my wet face, I apologized profusely, and moved far enough away from them to remain safe.

And I watched.

"I'm going, and you're taking my life vest," Viktor gasped, struggling to extricate himself from the tight straps.

"You are not, worm-dick. I'm going, and you're taking mine," Igor immediately retorted.

"Shut up, shit for brains. You're taking mine. There's no argument here."

Their fraternal banter made me smile fleetingly. It continued — at a more halting and gasping pace than usual — for some minutes, yet they reached no agreement.

I felt it then, before I heard it — a faint vibration in the water, like the deep hum of a generator in a basement. With a glimmer of hope, I turned to see the distant lights approaching. It was a ship!

Gleefully, I called to Igor and Viktor, and began to swim in their direction even before I had fully turned towards them. There was no answer. When I reached the spot where they had been, all that remained were two partially filled life jackets and a submerged life ring.

In a vain attempt to escape the anguish that threatened to make me wrench off my own life jacket and pursue them, I tried to pick the issue apart objectively, philosophically.

What is the more moral choice, self-sacrifice or self-preservation? If the only moral imperative in our deity-free zeitgeist is to live well, to serve fellow humans, to make the world better — is not living, and taking personal responsibility for fulfilling these criteria, preferable? Yet if so, why does self-sacrifice still maintain such a strangling emotional grasp on our psyches? Why is that cursed internal voice reiterating, as it might well do even to my last day on Earth: It should have been you. It should have been you?

Why should it have been me?

Yet that dark night in the warm waters of the Caspian Sea was not the time for dialectics. I gathered Igor and Viktor's limp life vests around myself and waited for the ship to approach.

CHAPTER 15
Samuel: Three Letters

South of Sepid Dasht, Iran, July 1942

The air flowed as viscous and foul as my mood. It was so bad that stowaways and crew alike had to jump off and trot alongside the train, crouching low to gain what little fresh air cowered at ground level. Spurred by the spewing locomotive, temperatures in the unventilated switchback tunnel climbed to oven levels. Terror of suffocation from choking coal smoke quickly overcame fear of losing a hand or foot by stumbling into the unforgiving path of the train's hungry steel wheels.

I'd grown up in a city where trams were a way of life, and knew about the appetite of steel wheels for human flesh. From as early as I could remember, we 'rode the tit' everywhere we wanted to go. The 'tit', as every Praga boy knew, referred to the covered protrusion that housed a Warsaw tram's rear coupling mechanism. It was a comfortable perch, out of sight of the conductor, easily accessible as long as you timed your run to match the tram's pace, and—best of all—completely free.

Krystyn Broz had discovered the tram wheels' hunger on a crisp and sunny winter Saturday afternoon.

Aron and I were riding the tit of the Little Jew—we had names for every tram line. Only outsiders used the line numbers. The #1 was the Truncheon because it went by the police station; the #5 was the Piss because it passed by Praga's sewage outlet into the Vistula; the #4 was the Little Jew because it went to the Jewish section of town; and so on.

The cobblestones were slick that day with packed snow that had partially melted and refrozen. It had been a slippery chore, but Aron and I, and a number of other Jewish boys, had managed to mount the tit of the Little Jew, headed north towards the Zoo. We were halfway up Targowa Street when somebody spotted Krystyn Broz walking alone.

Krystyn was my age, but he didn't attend our *szabasowka* school, which was for Jews only despite being state-run. Still, we Jews knew *of* him, as did perhaps half of Praga. He was the small boy whose mother had no husband. Thus, most assumed her to be a member of the Oldest Profession, although nobody had ever proven this, or even knew of someone who knew someone who had. His nose was always runny, his jacket threadbare, his hat inevitably askew, and he had a leg brace — most likely the result of Polio, although the juvenile consensus was venereal disease caught from his mother.

Aron elbowed me, gave me a knowing 'watch this!' look, and cupped his hands to his mouth to better project his voice. "Krystyn! Yes you, *debil*! Got anything to do today? Want to come with us to the zoo? Come on up! Come on, you can do it! It will be fun!"

That winter morning of 1926, I saw in Krystyn Broz's eyes perhaps the most genuine hope I'd ever seen. It was the hope of the dying who knew they were dying and the hope of the dying who chose to remain willfully naïve. It was the hope of mothers scanning endless lists of battle dead, and the hope of fathers reading deportation orders.

We cheered him as he ran. The brace made his normally halting gait spasmodic and hysterical. Yet we reveled surreptitiously via sidelong glances and hand-hidden guffaws disguised as coughing fits. Anything, so as not to spoil the rare and legitimate opportunity afforded to us Jews to mock a Christian boy.

Krystyn smiled a beam of pride as one hand touched the tit. Then he must have slipped on a patch of ice, because we saw the grubby hand slip off. Then we heard a deep *thud* and the tram jumped a bit. Then we were confused because the brace, glinting meanly in the sunshine and still in possession of its leg, receded on one side of the tracks, while Krystyn Broz lay on the other side. Then the sound of his screams caught up to us, and the cheers from the tit of the Little Jew grew quickly silent.

I shook off the memory and its familiar companion, guilt, and shuffled in the pitch dark, scowling and stooped. Even if I'd been closer to the front of the train, the ancient engine had no lights. Doubled over, I felt my way with hands and feet already accustomed to the task. I was 100 kilometers north of Andimeshk, Iran, heading south in an empty military freight train, deep in the black of a railroad tunnel that ran under the Zagros Mountains, and even deeper in the black of my guilt and grief at the deaths of Igor and Viktor, and Jacek. Bandar Shahpur, the train's destination, remained hundreds of kilometers and countless tunnels away. The distance stretched in front of me dizzyingly. This journey, I knew, like the pain that bit into my sides deeper than time, would never truly end. The darkness in which I stumbled now would be the darkness in which I remained.

The rustle of a body falling heavily to the ground, and a curse in Russian, told of a fellow traveler tripping over one of the countless boulders that lined the tracks, and often blocked the tracks themselves. Rock fall was a constant problem in these hastily built tunnels, just as it was in the route's countless bleak mountain passes, which were held back by massive yet flimsy retaining walls. We'd spent hours at a standstill in the plantless lunar landscape of a switchback, watching the water flow by, shit-brown, in a nameless river far below while helping the train crew clear the tracks.

The train picked up speed, and my knee banged into a rock of its own. I cursed in Polish, just a short expletive. Burgeoned by the anonymity the darkness afforded, I took a breath and geared up to shout a satisfyingly juicy string of epithets. Just then, barely audible above the din of the wheels and the curses of the other tunnel-walkers, my darkness-enhanced hearing picked up another sound, this one markedly more pleasant.

A woman sang a song—in Polish—and a familiar song at that! As quickly as it started, however, it stopped—so suddenly, I thought perhaps I'd imagined it.

The train gave the familiar series of complaining clanks and squeals that indicated an impending halt, and the cars slowed and stopped. Expert at conserving my scarce energy, I immediately sat beside the tracks and leaned back against the rough rock wall. My eyes strained for a hint of light that never materialized.

I'd been on the Trans-Iranian Railway for nearly a week, and had grown used to this hop-on, hop-off, sit-down, get-moving routine. I'd found the train right after the fishing boat delivered me, broken and shivering in the night's chill, to the port of Bandar Shah. Despite my fears of imminent arrest by the NKVD—compounded by my lack of papers, money, or even a full set of clothing—it had been easy to bypass the Soviet checkpoints. The trains came from the south in a never-ending stream, bringing desperately needed war materiel provided by the Allies to the Soviets on a lend-lease basis. Once the boxcars and flatbeds had regurgitated their tons of armored personnel carriers, trucks, ammunition crates, and other wartime burdens, they were so urgently needed back in the Persian Gulf that no one paid much attention to what they carried. I ended up in a spacious boxcar at the end of a long train pulled by an ancient-looking coal-fired engine. My car had obviously recently carried machinery, given its pronounced oily taint, but it was shaded, and I was comfortable on a scrounged pile of dusty sackcloth for the three-day journey south to Tehran, where Allied and Soviet jurisdictions overlapped.

In the bustle of the rapidly growing rail hub in the Iranian capital, Soviet engineers handed over control of empty southbound trains to their English counterparts, and took control over northbound, materiel-crammed cars. Once, a railroad official looked into my car, nodded at me, and walked on—no papers checked, no questions asked. We were soon on our way for a week-long southward odyssey to Bandar Shahpur.

Once again, I had nothing but Danuta's letters, partially preserved from their Caspian Sea baptism by the oilskin in which I'd wrapped them. I dried them page-by-page over the course of the trip south, careful to weigh each down with its own rock. In fairness, "I had nothing" was not entirely accurate, as I did have new and dry clothes, along with a nearly intact pair of Soviet boots. The owner of both, a dead Soviet soldier lying by the tracks in Bandar Shah, had needed them no more.

I also had leftovers to eat and a regular supply of tepid water from compassionate British railroad workers. And thanks to the efficiency of the British consul in Bandar Shah, I had—miraculously—received papers enabling me to travel to Palestine and "rejoin" my compatriots in the Polish Army, which had begun to coalesce in a camp near Beer Sheva.

The Polish song started again, this time closer. I scanned the darkness with aching eyes for the source of the sad waltz, popular before I left Warsaw: *Trzy Listy*—Three Letters—a story of a woman writing her final farewell to her lover. It should have made me homesick. It should have brought tears to my eyes. It should have made me long for Danuta's comfort. It should have made me feel something—*anything*—except the black emptiness that coursed through my veins like crude petroleum. It did not.

The singing grew in intensity, as the singer gained confidence both in her own anonymity and in the emerging power of her contralto.

I sighed. Tel Aviv, Aron, and Danuta were only weeks—no longer worlds—away, yet I could take no comfort from this thought. *Three Letters. To whom would I write my Three Letters? To Jacek, who died owing to my hubris? To Igor, who died owing to my desperate fear of being alone? Or to Viktor, who had been to first to offer himself on the altar of self-sacrifice?*

It should have been you, the Voice reminded me.

I yawned and closed my eyes, loath to argue with the Voice, which I knew would prevail, in any case. I'd fought it in the beginning, but had quickly conceded defeat. It was there, like severe tinnitus, resounding in my head day and night: *It should have been you. It should have been you.* I tried to ignore the Voice for a moment, let the song slither warmly up my consciousness like a down comforter pulled over winter-chilled flesh, and opened my eyes once again to face the darkness. I had slept little these past days, to avoid the dreams. No longer the haven of Technicolor Danuta, they had become black-and-white vignettes of Jacek, Igor, and Viktor—my *Trzy Listy.* In my short nightly snatches of sleep, and the inevitable daytime naps into which I was lulled by the potently somniferous combination of heat and train rhythm, I saw each die in new and increasingly graphic ways.

The engine stirred to my right, and the train groaned to life. I stood and instinctively brushed dust from my clothes. The singing stopped, and I started walking, then trotting—doubled over to detect rocks, and alert to avoid losing my car, especially since it was at the end of the train. Inevitably, owing to the blackness and the confusion of keeping up with the train, people made mistakes—meager possessions lost, travelers left behind by the tracks until the next train came by.

Several minutes elapsed and a pinprick that rapidly deteriorated into a searing spotlight peeked from the darkness of the tunnel. I straightened on trembling legs and, after one last breath of untainted air, boarded the car next to me, happy to see the bed I'd scavenged. It was my own car.

When the train jauntily forayed into blinding sunlight prior to entering the next tunnel, I saw that I had a new car mate. He sat with his back to me, and I caught only a glimpse of him before the train plunged into the darkness of another tunnel. This tunnel was blessedly short—no need to get out to breathe. In the briefly renewed darkness, the haunting song began again, this time from within my car.

I called her Vera, after Vera Gran, the cabaret alto to whom Danuta and I had so loved to listen—on the radio, on my parents' gramophone, and once even live at Warsaw's legendary Adria club. Born Dwojra Grynberg, Vera had been the belle of Warsaw's dazzling 1930's cabaret scene, which was not surprisingly dominated by numerous other Jewish artists with Polonized names.

I had to call her Vera because she never spoke—but she listened, and she sang. Oh, how she sang.

Vera sang others' words, yet spoke none of her own. Occasionally, her songs degenerated into wordlessly lyrical, soul-scraping laments. In these times, she seemed to have foregone the power of words altogether, recognizing their futile impotence. *For which words will we ultimately treasure, and which will we forget?* She sang in a language beyond language. *Which will we heed, and which disdain? Which of these words—which pour so casually from our breathing souls that most are lost before they're ever heard—will we ourselves ever recall?*

As a writer, for whom words represented the sum of all being, I was bewitched by Vera's forays into the realm of musical muteness. As a man who had been alone for so long, I could not help but admire her high cheekbones, straight white teeth, small hands, and slim figure. Through the dust that streaked her smooth cheeks and frosted her short hair, I saw beauty. It was beauty I tried to ignore. It was beauty I truly did not want to notice. I had eyes for Danuta, I told myself, and only for Danuta.

She came silently across the car in the dawn of our third day together. Her hands were rougher than I'd imagined, her lips softer.

We offered no whispers, no romance, no love except the intrinsically fleeting variety shared by anguished humans. She never looked in my eyes. She was just there. Her small hands sandwiched my cheeks. Her tongue tasted of dust as it explored my mouth. Her warmth below enticed then engulfed me. She was there. I was there. We were together.

It was glorious.

Wordlessly, she moved on me to the rhythm of the train, slowing as the train slowed on a steep uphill climb. Her breath blasted a gentle fire onto my neck. As the train crested the rise, her hands grabbed double folds of the back of my shirt. I could feel her nipples on my chest through our layers of clothing, as she levered herself tighter against me. The train began to regain speed, and her urgency grew. The seam in my shirt complained and then split, and still she moved. The couplings between the railroad cars joined in the cacophony with their own complaints, as car followed car around a near 90-degree hairpin turn. The air of the car filled with the smell of scorched steel, sweat, and sex.

Now she ground harder, gasping. Now her dry tongue found and filled my ear. Now she gave a mute grunt. Now we both shuddered simultaneously. Now the couplings gave a final orgasmic scream of their own. Now a loud metallic *crack!* sounded from the front of the car.

Our breathing slowed as the ceaseless *clackity-clack* of the wheels abated.

Vera climbed off me. A sobering rush of cold air chilled both my wet nakedness and my mood. She wiped herself unceremoniously with a corner of my rag bed, the sight of which intensified the unbearable sordidness of the scene.

What have I done?

Vera caught and defiantly returned my somber, resentful stare. Her eyes answered wordlessly, kindly: *Only what's natural.* She moved towards her side of the car, and we didn't look at each other again. She began to sing, and our car began to move again. *Backwards.*

In the post-coital, guilt-ridden fog on our opposite sides of the train car, neither Vera nor I realized immediately what was happening. Only as the train rapidly gained speed did we realize, as simultaneously as our orgasms only minutes before, that the train was moving *in the wrong direction.* Or, at least, our car was.

"The couplings! We've separated from the train!" My voice came out in a morning rasp — she *had* woken me — and I had to clear my throat to make myself heard. I repeated myself, and shouted that she should grab her things.

I gathered my own meager possessions, rushed to the door on the valley side of the tracks, looked out, and gasped. Far below me, malevolently bare rock scraped the bottom of a brown river's chasm. The sheer drop, lit by pale morning sun, rushed by with rapidly increasing velocity. There could be no exit from this side.

I threw myself across the car, moving with difficulty against its now violent swaying. I yelled over my shoulder for Vera to follow me, and managed to get one hand on the handle next to the open door. I stuck my head out to get a better view, and almost had it removed by a jutting boulder. The car was traveling, now insanely fast, just centimeters from the mountain wall on one side, and just centimeters from a sheer drop off on the other.

The probability of exit without breaking a neck, skull, or back was low. The probability of decapitation under the razor-sharp bouncing steel wheels of our chariot was high. A sudden image of Krystyn Broz's severed leg shot through my mind, raising a dust trail of guilt. The car wheels rhythmically chanted: *It should have been you. It should have been you.*

The car wheels screamed, and through the open door on the gorge side, I saw around the tight curve through which we were barreling. The car leaned alarmingly in the turn, and the centrifugal force threatened to wrench my hands from the door handle. Desperately seeking a way off the car before it derailed, I followed the tracks with my eyes. Ahead, at the base of our current descent, a low curving bridge mockingly straddled a nearly dry riverbed. Thereafter, the tracks climbed slowly into a long tunnel—the very same tunnel which we'd passed through *in flagrante delicto.*

"I think we should jump into the riverbed," I yelled over my shoulder to Vera. "The water and sand will cushion our fall! Be ready!"

She didn't answer.

I turned towards where Vera should have been, seeking some hope, solace, or even empathy in what might easily have been our final minutes. Yet the car was completely empty. Vera—like Igor and Viktor, like Jacek, like Krystyn Broz's brace-clad leg, like my once-lovestruck soul drowning in Danuta's bottomless well—was gone.

CHAPTER 16
Danuta: Touch Me

Tel Aviv, Sunday, July 30, 1942

> *My Dearest Samuel,*
> *Touch me with your words. Touch me with words brighter than light, deeper than shadow, and softer than your sleep-heavy breath — which should be filling the void in this empty bed, but is not. Touch me with your words because, without their anchoring power, I fear I will simply float away. Caress me with your words, and I will reciprocate with my own whisper-soft caresses. Touch me, my love, because I cannot conceive of an alternate light in this terrible darkness.*
>
> *It's now late at night, and I shall mail this first thing in the morning. I woke early today, sweltering after a miserable night. It is ungodly hot this summer, Aron tells me. Just last month, the highest temperature yet recorded in Asia was measured in Tirat Zvi, 53.9 degrees Celsius. The July Tel Aviv air is so heavy that it sticks in one's lungs.*
>
> *I had a dreadful chicory coffee, which is all that even your brother can get hold of, and went to buy a Palestine Post on King George Street. The news from Warsaw was beyond horrific. The Nazis have converted part of the Warszawa Gdanska train station and now call it Umschlagplatz — collection point. Every day, according to Aron's friend Henryk Rosmarin, the Polish Consul General to Palestine, the Nazis "deport" 10,000 Jews. But they're not really deporting them, Henryk insisted. He also insisted I call him by his first name — everyone is so refreshingly informal here.*
>
> *We met him in Jerusalem. The Polish Military Theatre put on a benefit concert for Polish war orphans in the lovely courtyard garden of the Cafe Europe, right on Zion Square. Aron was of course invited. We arrived in Jerusalem after sunset, and the night air was beautifully clear and cool.*

I think you would like Henryk, my darling. He used to edit Moment Magazine in Warsaw, and was especially outspoken about the numerus clausus – from which you suffered so personally. He's also a lawyer and former member of the Sejm, the Parliament. He has deep-set eyes and delightfully fleshy jowls that shake when he laughs, very much like your father. But his eyes weren't laughing as he told Aron and I what was happening to the Jews of Warsaw, and indeed to the Jews everywhere in occupied Europe.

I'm an educated woman, but I have to confess I felt like a confused schoolgirl. Henryk simply used combinations of words that I'd never encountered – phrases with no meaning like "systematic extermination" and "industrial-scale murder." Aron shook his head gravely, as if he understood perfectly, but I finally had to interject because it simply made no sense. Henryk was kind and explained. They have corroborating testimonies from too many sources to ignore, you see. There's simply no further argument as to what is happening. And not just in Poland...

I've been in Palestine for several months now, my love, And my Hebrew has improved dramatically. I can now understand the rumors – whispered in intensely quiet conversations at the market or in small groups around public benches – but rumors are a far cry from personal confirmation by a government official. And now the Germans are coming here, the rumors (and Henryk) say. At the end of the El Alamein fiasco, just four days ago, the British captured documents from an Afrika Korps source, he told us. Hitler has authorized the SS to "deal with" the Jewish population in Palestine.

*Are we to be "dealt with?" Is our fate to be the same as those poor souls in Warsaw – our former classmates, your parents' friends? According to your brother, it will most definitively **not** be – not if he has anything to say about it. Yet his voice is only one of many. There's a huge rift in the Yishuv leadership, Aron told me. Some are supporting the British decision to send much of the Palmach, our best fighters, south to Kibbutz Gat and Kibbutz Dorot. Despite being ridiculously ill-equipped – some don't even have guns – the British expect them to hold off invading German tanks. This, instead of using them more effectively to stock caves and building defenses on the Carmel. The British, it seems, have their own priorities.*

Here in Tel Aviv, Food Control is calling on citizens with open land next to their homes not to grow flowers, but rather food. The Haifa-Beirut railway line was dedicated, and the British are already moving unneeded staff and materiel directly from Cairo to Beirut. In Cairo, Henryk says, they're burning sensitive documents, and the Egyptian newspapers carry pictures of a new German locomotive with armor plating as thick as a tank.

If only I had such armor, my love. If only these words, this terrible news, would bounce off me, leaving no marks. But I am scarred by the evil that so mercilessly chips at my soul, nibbling at my façade like the shrapnel from the Italian bombs that ate at the buildings on Bugrashov, just one street over from where I now sit. I am scratched. I am torn. I have no loving balm to soothe me. Hurry to me, Samuel. I long to be touched not only by your words, but by your soothing and beautiful hands.

I love you with all my heart,
Danuta

CHAPTER 17
Aron: Powerlessness

Tel Aviv, July 30, 1942

What are words in the face of the pain and rage, the cries of agony of the martyrs of Polish Jewry? Words will not express these agonies. Our deeds will!

Berl Katznelson wrote this in the morning's Davar. The words stuck with me throughout the day, ineffectually circumnavigating my sweltering office like the hot air pushed by my feeble desk fan.

They continued to resonate when the sun finally took its daily cooling dip in the Mediterranean, lifting the cloak of summer heat. As Tel Aviv drew a collectively deep breath and exhaled with cool relief, I walked down Bugrashov, then along the sea breeze-swept promenade until I reached London Square.

The humble Armon Hotel on HaYarkon Street stood starkly dark in the blacked-out twilight, but crowds had filled the bar within. The smell of sweat, dust, and alcohol easily overcame the fickle breeze that trickled in around the blackout curtains. I scanned the mass of suits and uniforms—all male, of course—for Sean's blond curls, in vain. He was late, at best, or more likely a no-show.

My face must have reflected the lump in my stomach, for Theo, the Armon's iconic bartender, winked at me and deftly slid a chubby bottle of Eagle Beer across the bar. He'd seen me coming in here alone, and occasionally leaving in company, for many years. If the Armon Hotel bar existed as the solar system for homosexuals in Tel Aviv, Theo was its sun. Lives lived in darkness were quietly and cautiously illuminated in the Armon. No matter what face you presented to the rest of the world, no matter who you had to pretend to be, Theo knew you not only as you really were, but as you truly wanted to be known.

I nodded in thanks to him, but returned the bottle and asked for a seltzer. On the third and hopefully last day of a severe stomach flu, I feared alcohol would loosen floodgates that had only recently closed. I mopped my damp brow with my handkerchief, running a tender finger over the monogram. Sean had ordered them from London for me as a six-month anniversary present. I felt weak and must have looked peaked, yet I persisted and scanned the crowd again.

Words will not express these agonies. Our deeds will! Katznelson's words resonated in my head, turning into an unconscious mantra in which I found *some* validation, but mostly anguish.

I strolled gently through the crowd, bumping an elbow here, a dangling slouch hat or rifle barrel there. I nodded, smiled thinly, exchanged a passing word in English or Hebrew with men I knew, and some whom I had *known*. Sean wasn't here; there was no question. Would he come? He was either busy with the British retreat from Palestine, I told myself, or conducting his own personal retreat from a relationship that had become complex at best, potentially deadly at worst.

I stepped through the blackout curtains onto the balcony, which faced the street. Here the air was fresh, yet no matter how deeply I sucked the briny sea air, I couldn't dispel the poison that seethed in my lungs, or the gurgling of my guts, which still protested at having been dragged out of bed.

Words will not express these agonies. Our deeds will!

Only last week, the Palestine Post reported mass deportations of Jews from Warsaw. Now, even the most recalcitrant doubts in the most optimistic minds had been dispelled. Now, in July 1942, the entire *Yishuv* viscerally understood the fate of European Jewry — and remained collectively powerless to substantially change it.

I felt nauseous, and spit over the balcony rail into the garden below. I tried to distract myself by surveying London Square — tasteful and newly completed. The black asphalt of HaYarkon Street gracefully arched its back around a switchback and glided down to the sea, leaving behind a deeply shaded garden on one side, and a beach-facing kiosk on the other. At night, the garden's shade turned to shadow, and the venue had quickly become popular for nighttime trysts. The lack of streetlights under Tel Aviv's wartime blackout contributed markedly to the garden's seclusion and mystique. I spit again over the railing.

"*The perception of powerlessness breeds desperation.*" I recalled my father's words at the train station on Chmielna Street in Warsaw, the morning I left for Palestine. His hands felt comfortingly heavy on my shoulders. He looked deep into my eyes with a fatherly knowledge and love that made me look away in shame. "*You are in what Nietzsche called the 'hour of the great contempt,' but you are not desperate, my son. And though I understand why you feel powerless, I also know to the depths of my soul that you are not.*"

The sea breeze flowed past me, leaving my face cooled, my back sweat-soaked, and my insides still gurgling. Voices surged in waves from the bar. My father had expected me to overcome myself like Nietzsche's *ubermensch*, yet I'd devolved from would-be redeemer of Zion to conniving embezzler. Now, in a pathetic attempt to redeem myself, I'd become a low-level office cog in the Zionist machine. To complete the picture, I was in love with an Australian officer. If anyone ever discovered our relationship, I would face not only immediate dismissal from my job at *Kofer HaYishuv*, but likely covert execution by *Hagana* or *Irgun* operatives as a collaborator.

Truly, my deeds spoke louder than my words. I was powerless, I realized with a sudden visceral pang of longing for my father's embrace. Why had I been unable to meet his gaze that day, that last time I saw him? What had I been — or what had he *made me* — ashamed of?

My stomach flip-flopped again, this time with more determination. My return trip through the packed bar was less convivial as I pushed past the obstacles that the revelers had become. Unshed tears clawed at the backs of my eyes, seeking release.

The voices from the bar pursued me closely across the fresh asphalt of HaYarkon Street, yet abated in the sudden quiet of the hidden garden that lay in the embrace of the elevated road's curve. The noise from the bar faded, as did the thrum of the Mediterranean's gentle summer waves. As my nausea subsided, I found a bench in the shadows, sat, and was immediately overcome by sadness so deep that it could not but burst forth.

I doubled over and wept into my hands as I had not wept in years. I wept for the countless unavenged corpses of Polish Jewry — people I had lived with, grown up with, nodded to on the streets of Praga. I wept for the years lost following my abandonment of home and family. I wept for the look of disgust in my father's eyes when he confronted my true face, yet simultaneously for the comfort of his cool hand on the back of my neck, along with my mother's warm palm on my cheek. I wept for Samuel, who — if he was even alive — doubtless yet carried the soul-scratching disappointment of a spurned younger brother. I wept for the ideals that had brought me to Palestine — then questionable in their loftiness, now quashed and unrealized. I wept for Sean, whom I'd seen only once in the past weeks. Most of all, I wept for my utter powerlessness in the face of love and death. I was no one's *ubermensch*. I had overcome nothing. I was as alone as I'd ever been in a lifetime of loneliness. I wept, and my stomach churned afresh.

"Oi! This one's just 'ad a fight wif his boyfriend, that's wha' I say!"

The slurred voice, and the loud guffaws that followed it, split the fabric of the silent park. Above on the roadway, the *phut-phut* of a British Austin staff car meandered by indifferently. Still higher above, the half moon slipped demurely behind a thin summer cloud.

"Awww, the poor lad! Maybe what 'e needs is some cheerin' up, mates! Eh?"

I wasn't scared as the group of four clearly drunken British soldiers surrounded my bench. Certainly, the area was deserted. High walls muffled the street noises from above, as they would any noise from within the garden to outside ears. The streetlights sat dark, and the moon fell behind its veil of clouds. Yet I knew that picking on homosexuals in the area of London Square was a regular pastime for Mandatory Cro-Magnons. It was demeaning, but generally physically harmless.

Generally.

Only when I rose to slink away, and was pushed rudely back down by a calloused hand, did I begin to feel fear.

"Oi! Where do you think you're going, Sally? We was just going to cheer you up. So boys, what do we think would make Daisy here most happy? What do queers like to do most? Let me think here...."

"*Powerlessness is a conscious decision,*" my father had reiterated as we parted.

Had I consciously chosen to be bent over the back of a park bench, my trousers around my knees? One beer-soaked soldier pinioned my arms, another my legs. A third's shorts-clad leg rested on the bench, using one tobacco-smelling hand to immobilize my head against his knee, and the other to cover my mouth tightly. The fourth took his time undoing his belt. Was this my choice? Had I somehow influenced this fate, through action or inaction, thought or deed? Or had my metaphorical powerlessness simply corporealized, its noxious fumes escaping into the outside world like exhaust from a poorly-tuned engine?

"Now then, Fanny, be a good girl and hold still, wot?" The fourth soldier hocked and spit luridly into his hand, and reached down to put the lubricant to good use on himself. "There we are. Now, don't you get the idea that I prefer this, right? But a bloke's gotta grab opportunity when it presents itself, right boys?"

The other soldiers gruffly concurred.

The pressure on my abdomen from the bench's hard back set off a wave of fresh cramps. The soldier's hand slipped from its tight grip over my mouth to cover my nose as well, and I writhed, struggling to breathe.

You were wrong, Father. Powerlessness is not a decision. It is imposed.

The coolness of the soldier's saliva touched me, and I cringed. I clenched my buttocks with all my might, and bucked against the hands holding me, driving the wedge of the bench back further into my midsection. Desperate, I wrenched my head from the soldier's grasp, turned it to draw a blessed and ragged breath, and found myself face-to-face with the trench knife sheath strapped to his calf, its restraining strap hanging loose from the struggle.

From the corner of my eye, I saw the fourth soldier approach me. I felt the pressure and heat of his body against me, pushing me further into the bench, turning the pain in my gut into red-hot agony. The three soldiers were engaged in the action now, and less attentive to their restraining duties. I clenched tighter, fighting the fourth soldier with all the resistant force I could muster. He began to pant in anticipation, using his hands to spread my buttocks and bending drunkenly low to line himself up.

That's when I realized that powerlessness, even if imposed, need not be *accepted*. The constraints of any situation, however ugly, can always be manipulated, however slightly. Microscopic advantages, some even as small as intestinal bacteria, can always be leveraged.

As the soldier's face came in line with me, I suddenly relaxed and released what I'd been holding back. The immense pressure on my abdomen from the bench, together with my doubled-over posture, amplified the explosive effect. The noise was deafening by bodily standards, the smell overpowering, and the blast radius of hand grenade scale. The soldier who had been about to rape me staggered back, gagging. He tripped over his lowered shorts and fell gracelessly to the ground, cursing and wiping his face ineffectually.

The other soldiers each raised an arm against the smell, and I used the opportunity to wrench my own arms free. I snatched the trench knife from its holster next to my face. Without hesitation, I slashed wildly at the soldier still holding my head. A gurgling sound followed, not unlike that which emanated from my bowels, and something warm and sticky flowed over me. I pushed myself up off the bench, reeling from the pain in my abdomen, half-blinded by what I quickly realized was the soldier's blood, and tangled in my own trousers, which were still around my ankles.

The moon slithered guiltily from behind its cloud and illuminated the scene. The air was a miasma of feces and blood. Another car drove by above, backfiring on the climb from the beach. The soldier that had been holding my head lay slumped over the bench, motionless. The would-be rapist struggled with his shorts, the brown stain covering his chest and head visible even in the dim light. The other two soldiers had run out of the garden, leaving their comrades to fend for themselves.

The rapist overcame the fight with his shorts, rose, and briefly met my eyes.

With my face likely unrecognizable with clotted blood, I advanced threateningly.

Sensing the desperation of this blood- and shit-covered figure brandishing a bloody trench knife, he retreated silently like his comrades.

I expected to hear the trill of his whistle echoing off the white buildings, followed by a hoarse cry of, "Murder! Murder!" Instead, I heard only the echo of the waves and distant voices from the balcony of the Armon, where I had stood eons previously.

I dropped the knife and bent to pull up my pants, ignoring the filth caking my legs. I wiped the remaining blood from my eyes with my still-damp handkerchief, and assessed the situation quickly, my mind surprisingly clear. Obviously, my attackers—especially the one covered head-to-waist in my shit—would be hesitant to throw themselves under the wheels of British military justice. They would more likely prefer to leave the mysterious death of their colleague a mystery.

Suddenly, to my amazement—even through my shock, pain, and fear, and even as the soldier's blood dried on my face and congealed in my hair—I smiled.

Who's powerless now?

I had advantages that could be leveraged. I would no longer be imposed upon. Tonight, I had done the imposing, and would continue to do so.

Words will not express these agonies. Our deeds will!

Still smiling, I took off at a run into the welcoming darkness, whose power, like my own at that very moment, seemed limitless.

CHAPTER 18
Aron: Trust

Tel Aviv, July 31, 1942

I imagined him waiting for me at home. I pictured him sitting at my kitchen table, his slouch hat hanging from the back of the chair, a cigarette clutched deep between first and second fingers, his hair falling into one eye as he leaned over the Palestine Post. I pictured him thus as I groped through pipe-lined, trash-reeking alleys, stumbled through well-kept flowerbeds in gardens surrounding low apartment buildings, and clambered clumsily over cinder block walls.

I stayed off the streets, realizing even in my elation that it would not be prudent to be seen covered in blood. I imagined him meeting me at the door, gasping, then taking my face in his rough hands: he sits me down, strokes my hair, gently undresses me, bathes me, lies me on cool sheets, and kisses me, long and slow.

All this I imagined as I struggled home, desperate to wash it all away: one soldier's blood from my face, another soldier's spit from my ass, my own excrement from my legs, and the feeling of power that so consumed me as to render me giddy.

He'll be there, I thought as I skittered around the corner onto Bugrashov. Ducking into yet another yard, I pushed thoughts of comfort briefly out of my head to assess my situation.

Assuming I made it home without incident, which now seemed reasonably likely, I had a chance—a good chance, even—of not getting caught. The police would have staggeringly little to go on. They wouldn't even find the weapon, since I'd discovered it still clutched tightly in my hand just minutes earlier. It now rested at the bottom of a storm sewer on a side street whose name I couldn't recall.

Although numerous patrons of the Armon Hotel bar had certainly recognized me, most—likely all—would be reticent to come forward. Everyone knew why men frequented the place, and no one would freely admit to patronizing the establishment. The whole crowd probably had instinctively melted away when the first sirens approached, in any case.

Theo would have remained, of course, and he knew me, but he was busy at the bar all evening, and would have no idea what I did or where I went after I left the bar, if it even crossed his mind to mention me.

I turned onto Buki Ben Yagli Street, and paused in the shadow of a tall myrtle hedge across the street from my building. I tried to catch my breath, and reconnoitered the entrance carefully. The hour was very late, and there were only a few apartments in my building, yet running into a neighbor when I was in this state could be a literal death sentence.

Two steps from home, I waited with a patience the origin of which was unfathomable, and continued to review the facts in my head. I felt certain no one had seen me entering the London Square gardens, which were nearly pitch black in any case. My attackers would have only barely been able to see my face when they'd first approached, and seen only a blood-clotted Golem thereafter.

My mind slipped back into Sean-longing mode. *He'll be there*, it said with what I knew to be false reassurance. He wouldn't be there, another more rational part of me asserted. *In any case, what I really need*, I thought with urgency—my patience dissipating as suddenly as air from burst balloon—*is to wash this dried mask of blood off my face and these clumps of dried blood from my hair... now!*

I truly couldn't stand another second, and lurched out into the street just as a truck rumbled down Bugrashov. I jerked back into the hedge's shadows. My stomach twisted again with tension, and the memories of the flu. The truck continued past, and breath came to me again. I skipped quickly across the twenty meters separating me from home, then slunk up the two flights of stairs and into my apartment without encountering anyone or—as far as I knew—being seen.

He wasn't there.

I jerked awake to the sound of trucks, horns, and shouting, certain that the entire British police force had pulled up to my door. Yet a tinny voice in Hebrew, coming from the direction of King George Street, urged all citizens of conscience to lend their able hands to the war effort, and join up this very day.

"Come meet us in London Square," the voice called, "to see how you, yes *you*, good citizens, can make sure that good, not evil, will be triumphant. The power is in your hands. Your fellow citizens trust you to do the right thing." Faint cheering followed these words, and the engines faded southward.

I lowered my head back onto my pillow, which still smelled faintly of Sean's cologne, hoping that someone had found and removed the dead would-be rapist prior to the arrival of thousands of patriotic revelers.

I brushed my teeth, threw on some clothes, and hurried to the corner kiosk to buy the thick Friday newspaper, fully expecting to find "Murder in London Square!" on the front page of *Davar*. Instead, I learned that the Germans had suffered over 400,000 casualties in the past weeks, and that Stalin was calling for resistance to the last man. Still standing at the kiosk, I flipped rapidly through the pages, and found no mention of the incident, not even in the police reports in the back pages. Perhaps it had happened too late at night to make the morning paper, I reasoned. *Or perhaps,* a small voice whispered in my head, *they're withholding publication until they arrest a suspect.*

I shook my head to silence the voice, and bought a fresh pack of Simon Artz's, smiling in passing at the gaudily decorated pack. Artz's wise-looking, fez-wearing head stared blithely back at me. I opened the pack and managed to light one after two attempts, owing to my shaking hands. Having succeeded, I turned abruptly toward home, and ran smack into the soldier who had been standing close behind me in the small kiosk. Not looking up, I excused myself hastily and sidestepped him.

"Bloody rude yid," came a familiar voice.

I looked up into the soft eyes and smiling face of my lover, and something in me melted. My eyes filled with tears. I blinked them away, but not before he saw them.

Worry crossed his face, but he could clearly say nothing there on the street.

"Excuse me, I didn't see you there," I managed to choke out in English. "I was... uh... just on my way home, and I... uh... I didn't... I need to.... So, g'day then." I walked away quickly, not looking back.

Ten minutes later, he knocked faintly at my door, knowing it would be unlocked, and let himself in, bringing with him the smell of *Shemen* shaving cream, Woodbine cigarettes, comfort, and compassion—all of which I was determined to resist. He locked the door behind him.

I sat rigidly at the kitchen table, my tea rapidly cooling, and let him embrace from behind.

"I missed you," he whispered to the back of my neck. "I just got back from Beirut. They sent me on some errand, very hush-hush, very urgent, very last minute. I'm sorry I couldn't tell you."

The previous day's *Davar*, still open in front me on the table, displayed the article about the British Eighth Army's valiant stand at El Alamein. They'd repelled Rommel's relentless attacks, but just barely. There was no doubt that when the Axis forces regrouped, the Italian dictator Mussolini and Nazi Foreign Minister von Ribbentrop—who were rumored to have personally traveled to North Africa in anticipation of Rommel's triumph at El Alamein and subsequent drive into Egypt—would be back.

My own resistance was slightly less effective. My defensive lines held until Sean's lips reached my shoulder blade, then they utterly crumbled.

Afterwards, we lay in my rumpled bed. The smoke of our cigarettes intermingled and dissipated languidly in the late morning heat. Knowing it was unwise, I nonetheless spoke the words that had been on the tip of my tongue since he stepped in my door.

"Why the bloody hell didn't you send me a note, at least? If you want out, you can just say so." I propped myself up on one elbow, to better look him in the eyes. "Is that what you want?"

He seemed genuinely surprised, and my heart leapt. He propped himself up to meet my gaze, thought for a moment, then his eyes narrowed and his brow furrowed.

My stomach churned faintly.

"Look," he said. "This may come as a shock, and I'm sorry to be the bearer of bad tidings, but you see, there's a war on. I know, I know. It was quite unexpected, and it turns out that we're on the losing side. The British army is preparing to retreat from Palestine, when—not if— Rommel breaks through into Egypt. I'm attached to the office that's organizing it. I *had* to go to Beirut. I didn't even have time to pack underwear or a bloody toothbrush, if you must know. And go find a bloody toothbrush, not to mention bloody decent underwear, in bloody Lebanon, by the by. You'd think the buggers didn't have *teeth* or... you know, things that underwear... ah, crikey! I *don't* want out, okay?"

I smiled vaguely, trying to hide my elation, then put my hand under the light sheet that covered us and stroked the fur of his thigh. "Sorry, were you saying something? You lost me at the mysterious reference to Lebanese underwear. My mind does wander so."

He smiled and lay back in the bed. He reached for yesterday's Palestine Post, which I'd left on the nightstand, and opened it.

I nestled into the space between his shoulder and the base of his neck, and continued to absently stroke his bare thigh under the cover.

"Bloody hell, quite a way to go. There was some butcher in Haifa that stabbed himself in the heart, by accident. Put his knife in his pocket, point-up, and when he bent over, bang-o. Which reminds me, did you hear about the to-do last night at the Armon?"

I froze, and quickly withdrew my hand. "No. I mean, I was there early last night, looking for you, but you weren't there, and I wasn't feeling well. I came home, and I... didn't hear anything. So... what happened?"

He told me. "...seems like the police are downplaying the killing. They're saying that it may have been related to 'deviant activity', which—as we both know—does not officially exist. There were no witnesses, and nobody has real interest in pursuing an investigation. They'll probably just let it blow over."

I had scoured myself, my clothes, and my shoes the previous night before collapsing onto my bed. There was literally not a shred of evidence connecting me to the killing. However, there was also not— and I had checked and rechecked until I had begun to feel ridiculous— any sign of the monogrammed handkerchief I'd been carrying, with which I distinctly recalled mopping the blood from my face. Of course, it could have fallen from my pocket on the way home, a safe distance from the murder scene. Then again, it may have fallen *in London Square itself.* Either way, according to Sean, the police had all but dropped the case. Aside from the burning ember of my conscience, and the seed of worry planted by the missing handkerchief—both of which I knew could be controlled—there was absolutely no reason in the world that I need ever recall, let alone *mention,* the incident again.

Yet I was empowered, and what is trust if not the ultimate empowerment? Trust is always granted, not accepted. I had granted Josef Warszawski, my first love, my trust. I never regretted that decision, despite the misery it prefaced. I had not granted trust to my father, had never truly harnessed the power of his love—a choice I regretted deeply to this day. I realized suddenly that my internal barriers to trust—those concrete obstructions that had held me back from so many opportunities—were born of *weakness*, not caution or self-preservation. Confidence in the righteousness of one's actions, a willingness to look one's self in the eye with fortitude and true empathy—truth was the key to empowerment, and trust was its natural extension.

I sat up in bed, removed the paper from Sean's hands, cupped his cheek in my palm, and turned his face towards me. I kissed him and looked him in the eye. "There's something I need to tell you...."

CHAPTER 19
Samuel: Desert Wind

Zagros Mountains, Iran, July 1942

If I had been in front of a typewriter, I would have been composing an ode to the freedom of the desert wind that whistled like a death-scream in my ears. *Stopping for neither manmade nor natural barrier, I would have written, it rampages, moving mountains grain-by-grain with persistence known only to gods, mothers, and tax collectors.*

Yet, regrettably, there on the roof of a rogue train car rocketing downward towards a dead-man's curve over a nearly dry riverbed in the Zagros mountains of Iran, there was not a damn typewriter in sight.

I had caught a flashing glimpse of Vera's skirt as she stepped off the ladder and up through the hole in the boxcar's roof. I fought my way across the car, which gained even more speed on the long downhill approach to the curving bridge. Upon reaching the top of the ladder, I stuck my head through the hole, and met the desert wind. I blinked back wind-drawn tears and watched as Vera displayed superhuman balance.

She stood atop the car, her arms outstretched as if offering an embrace to the infinite, and rode what she must have assumed to be her last ride with glory and aplomb.

The desert wind scratched at my cheeks, and its hands pushed me back down the ladder, but I fought the fight of the righteous. I too would have my ride of glory. I too would look Fate in the eyes. I forced my body up into the wind, watching the curving bridge approach in slow motion, and centimeter by centimeter, fought to stand. In the end, I was a man triumphant. I looked unafraid into the eyes of nature's power, and would have spit in them had the desert wind not threatened to return my gift of moisture with geometrically stronger force. I felt as if I'd left behind my regrets over Igor, Viktor, Jacek and — yes — even my betrayal of Danuta.

The train plunged downwards, its wheels screeching metal. I squinted against wind-borne sand, watching rocks and track slide by in a blur below me. The wind's wild scream sounded like the Stuka dive bombers I'd fled from in terror on that terrible night in Warsaw. The bridge, and imminent derailment, seemed only seconds away. I reveled in the immortality of the moment.

Then, as if received via cosmic message, a sudden awareness of our mortality overcame both Vera and myself simultaneously. As the car's formerly rear-facing wheels crossed the threshold between earth and sky onto the brown stone arches of the bridge, we threw ourselves forward, landing face-down and hugging the roof of the boxcar. Our hands clamped, vice-like, on the safety of the roof's handholds. In stark contrast to the epic bravery of the seconds before, we surrendered to our humanity at the exact moment of our demise—not with literary bravado, but with clinging whimpers brusquely swept away by the desert wind's cynical guffaws.

The car lifted hesitantly skyward, then slammed back onto the tracks. It writhed, shimmied, and squirmed, eager to break free of its earthly encumbrances but held back by the curse of gravity. It gave a final unearthly screech, metal searing metal, lifting one last time in hopeful triumph, and... slowed as it ascended the hill beyond the bridge.

We remained facedown for some seconds, unsure if this was life or death. The car was still moving fast, but it soon became clear that it was gradually slowing. The wind's shriek softened. I looked up and found Vera's incredulous face. Then I sat up, pushed myself to my knees, and glimpsed the bridge receding behind us over the edge of the car's roof.

Vera did the same.

The car moved farther from the bridge, and slowed to a safer speed. Vera and I struggled to our feet and stared dumbstruck at the trickle flowing through the riverbed far below, which we had tacitly assumed would be our final resting place. The sun scoured the valley and glinted off the brown water, creating sparkles that looked like joyful aquatic fireflies. Above, a blue sky flowed by, cloudless and warm. This majestic landscape, in a divine world, momentarily dazzled us with the beauty of life itself.

Yet Fate is an intimate bedfellow. She knows more than we admit to ourselves, and ultimately extracts payment for every favor. She was intimately aware that I had caused the deaths of three innocent friends. She was intimately aware that I had betrayed Danuta. She was intimately aware that I would likely take any of these actions again, given another chance to choose self-preservation over nobility.

Thus, as the desert wind's whistle faded from my ears, I turned to stand proudly with Vera, facing away from our direction of travel and ready to take her in my arms for a triumphant kiss. That was when we both—nearly as simultaneously as our orgasms just an hour before—gained acquaintance as intimate as Fate's with the side of the mountain, when our boxcar rolled swiftly into a low tunnel.

I awoke to the sounds of groaning. Grains of sand danced in the desert wind against my forehead, and the sun, now high in the sky, seared through my eyelids. I raised one hand to brush the dirt from my eyes, relieved to find I could still move. My hand came away gritty and sticky from what I guessed was my own blood. I tried to raise myself to locate the origin of the sound, which I could only assume came from Vera, but the movement sent a wave of white-hot pain through my leg, past my groin, up my spine, and directly into my brain. I cried out and jerked my head around. Over my shoulder, I could see my left knee bent at an unnatural angle. I felt the sickening beginnings of shock settle into my stomach.

Yet the groans persisted, and I forced myself to raise my upper body and look around.

I lay ten meters below the level of the train tracks, and perhaps fifty meters away from the tunnel entrance chiseled into the mountain's face, into which we'd both smashed so unceremoniously. Behind me, the bridge we'd crossed reclined lazily in the sun, as if content with a job well done. To my right, the boulder that had apparently kept me from rolling down the embankment and over the drop-off into the river below smiled in recognition of my gratitude.

I reckoned I'd been unconscious for several hours, as we'd ridden our last ride of glory in the late morning. Now, the sun had moved past its welcoming morning caress into the daily tantrum of afternoon abuse, and already burned the skin of my neck. I lay my head down and closed my eyes, seeking comfort and escape in the still-cool sand under my face. I longed for the relative cool of my boxcar, for Danuta's hand on my cheek, for my father's heavy arm around my shoulder, for anything external to me that could strengthen my precarious, faltering resolve.

The groans grew in volume and intensity, shaking me from self-pity, but not yet spurring me to action. Should I cross the chasm of doubt and self-interest, and go to her? I could survive, even if I didn't move a muscle. The next train would hear my cries, and stop to help. I would live, even if I looked away from conscience's accusing eyes — as so many others did regularly, and as I myself had done so recently.

Will I ultimately benefit? I asked myself, *and if so, how?*

Benefit notwithstanding, I made the decision. Gritting my teeth against the expected pain, I reached to pull my body forward through the sand, gravel, and rocks in the direction of the groans.

Sweat tickled my temples, and the desert wind obligingly kissed it cool. Elbow over elbow, I worked my way laterally up the embankment, every movement pre-calculated to tenderly avoid shifting my bad leg. After awkward initial efforts, I fell into a tediously slow, back-wrenching yet effective serpentine slither. The minutes passed, the sun shone, the flies buzzed, the desert wind sang, and I climbed. Vera's groans — alternately intensifying and waning — spurred me on.

My face was dust-caked and my arms throbbed by the time I reached the tracks. I placed one hand on the reassuringly manmade steel, already viciously hot from the sun, and looked up and down the rail line. The immotile lump that must have been Vera lay perfectly still fifty meters away from me, towards the tunnel entrance, her body fully in between the two rails. Only her head and shoulders lay draped across one of the tracks, on the side closest to me. Suddenly, she twitched her legs in an apparent attempt to move, but then groaned piteously.

Between us lay a field of rough-cut rock fall, strewn viciously along the sides of the tracks as if to thwart any crawling thing's hope of progress. How could I possibly reach her?

The desert wind kissed my ears, then momentarily faded. Free of its incessant singing, I heard another sound over Vera's groans — the faint yet distinctive *chug-chugging* of a steam engine laboring up a steep grade. Its sound echoed from the mouth of the tunnel. It was the next southbound train! In the rush to supply the Soviet Union with war materials, the British ran trains at minimal intervals, several a day in each direction, closely timed and coordinated to avoid collisions on the single track.

I looked again at Vera. She lay, I realized, just outside the line of shade demarcating the tunnel entrance. This would make her nearly invisible to an engineer's light-starved eyes as his train exited the tunnel. Moreover, this train, like ours, would likely have no light on the engine. That meant the engineer would never see our boxcar — which had probably stopped somewhere inside the level tunnel. The train's slow speed meant that the boxcar would not derail, but it would be pushed uncontrollably out of the tunnel ahead of the train, eliminating whatever small chance there was that Vera would be seen before the train was upon her.

The chugging grew louder. I wiped ineffectually at the sweat and dried blood on my face with a dirt-caked hand, and took a deep breath. Time slowed. I was never a competitive man, preferring an *ex post facto* backstab over a punch in the nose, but I would, I vowed, beat this train. I would save Vera. I would do so now, for I had not done so before. I had not saved Jacek, Igor, or Viktor. I had not saved my parents. I left Danuta to her own fate in Vilnius, and then betrayed her the first chance I had.

Not this time!

I slithered urgently in Vera's direction. I even tried to use my bad leg, despite the burning swords of pain that the slightest pressure drove into my side. My progress was achingly slow across the rocks that, like burning shards of glass, sliced my hands, belly, and legs. The desert wind had begun to blow in earnest now, as it did every afternoon. Sand whipped my ears, but could no longer drown out the growing noise of the train.

Vera's legs twitched in agitation. She heard it too, perhaps feeling its thrum in her track-bound head, yet she seemed powerless to move.

The desert wind whistled now, and a voice—previously muted—emerged from its low howl. *It should have been you*, it hissed, keeping time with the beating heart of the approaching engine. *It should have been you. It should have been you.*

I crawled to the rhythm of this mantra. I crawled as the desert wind spat sand into my eyes. I crawled as the rocks ripped at the flesh of my torso and chewed my fingernails. I crawled as a metal-on-metal crash echoed from the tunnel—the boxcar, I guessed—followed by an alarmed shout and the ineffectual screech of brakes. I crawled as Vera gave another twitch, this one like the climax of a grand mal seizure—she was facing the tunnel, and could see the train coming.

I could see it now too, the vague sliver of sparks from its locked wheels glowing ever brighter in the tunnel's ground-level darkness. She was trying, I guessed, to get her head and shoulders in between the tracks, where they would be safe from the tons of metal rushing at them. She was on my side of the tracks, so I could push her to safety in just seconds if I could only reach her.

The desert wind blew at my back now, whistling and urging me forward like a sergeant pushing troops out of the safety of a muddy trench. I heeded its call, now pulling myself up to hobble crookedly on two arms and one leg. The sparks from the brake-locked engine grew brighter, illuminating our boxcar from behind as it rushed out of the tunnel. I was only meters away from Vera.

It should not *have been me. It should* not *have been me.*

I changed my mantra now, breathing hard. As I reached Vera, I collapsed back to my stomach. Balancing on my left elbow, I leaned forward with my right hand. Just as the rumbling of the engine broke free from the tunnel and the ferrous beast burst forth, I pushed her head and torso gently off the tracks to relative safety between the rails.

It should not *have been me.*

Yet Fate had not yet extracted her full payment that day, and she did so with an irony that could have graced an ancient Greek comedy. For how better, truly, to compensate a writer for his narcissism? How more graceful a *coup de grace* than one that separates a man who lives to put words to paper from his literal means of doing so?

For I paused, you see. I paused to caress Vera's head reflexively, for a split second. I paused to impart a microscopic measure of comfort to a terrified and grievously wounded girl, who sang like a goddess, and to whom I'd made illicit love just hours previously. I paused and caressed Vera's head in its train-bound nest, even as the desert wind ruffled my own hair comfortingly, as if it knew what was to come only seconds later. I caressed her head, but I never withdrew my hand. It stayed, gently resting on her head. It stayed, an eternal beacon of comfort that I saw clearly even as the train passed. It stayed, as fate drove the razor-sharp wheels of the boxcar over my wrist, separating it from me as surely as I had separated myself from Danuta.

CHAPTER 20
Samuel: Absence

HMHS Somersetshire, Port of Bandar Shahpur, Iran, August 1942

"A gigolo without a penis. A parfumier without a nose. A runner without a leg. A sharpshooter without an eye. An opera singer without vocal chords."

I droned my list as slowly as possible, to consume the maximum possible tedium.

"A pilot who's afraid of heights. A sea captain who gets seasick?"

Jacek—who was not *my* Jacek, but another Pole bearing the same name, and whom they'd placed in the bed next to mine—picked up where I trailed off.

"Now you're just being stupid. We're talking about *physical attributes* that are lacking. Physical attributes. Get it? Like—uh, hmm, let me think—*a right-handed writer without a fucking right hand?*"

I held up my thickly bandaged stump demonstratively, wrinkled my face in a cruel gesture of disgust, and turned away. We'd been trying to alleviate boredom by coming up with the most outlandish games Fate could possibly play with human ambition. This Jacek, however, was not *my* Jacek. My Jacek was more glib as a frozen corpse folded into an ammunition crate—where he conceivably still *was*—than this Jacek. I preferred conversation with *my* Jacek... in my head.

During the first week on the sweltering hospital ship, prior to the arrival of Jacek II, I'd conducted numerous conversations with Jacek, Igor, and Viktor in my head. I tried to conduct conversations with Danuta, too, but I couldn't summon her voice, even when I read her letters, which they brought to me from the post office in Bandar Shahpur. Her voice had been absent since the tryst with Vera, as if the Danuta in my head was furious at my betrayal.

Throughout the endless train ride south to Bandar Shahpur, with Vera next to me—first twitching, then still—Danuta stubbornly refused to make a comforting appearance. She wasn't with me as the first doctor unwrapped the makeshift bandages, pronounced the amputation the cleanest he'd seen since the Great War, and nodded in professional respect to the kindly British rail worker who had wrapped the tourniquet around my wrist by the side of the tracks—as if he, and not the boxcar, had done the job. With a nod in return, and a wink in my direction, the man—who had cared for both Vera and myself for three days and nights—took his leave. I never learned his name.

I imagined Danuta smiling in feminine *schadenfreude* as the doctor gravely examined Vera, then sent her with some urgency to another ward, and ultimately to another ship. Indeed, Danuta stayed away, deaf even to my screams during the reduction of my knee, which had only been dislocated.

As anyone who's ever lost a loved one can tell you, absence is a powerfully palpable presence. The indentation that remains on the other side of the bed, the clothes that still hang in the closet—these things take up so much more space than their owners ever did.

Now that her voice had left me, I felt Danuta's overwhelming absence. Not only had she fallen silent, I worried that she was fading. Her touch, her kiss, her warm breath—I used to be able to feel these things, much as I still felt the fingers of my right hand. Now, they were absent.

Jacek, I reasoned, had had nearly two decades to imprint himself on my psyche. This made his memories deeper and his wisdom—or his silliness, or just his banter—easier to summon. Danuta had been with me less than three years. Could I have expected better? What would it be like when we were finally reunited?

The *HMHS Somersetshire*, a converted troop transport ship, had 514 beds, a skeleton staff, and a partially closed hole in her forward starboard hull from a U-Boat torpedo. She was being provisionally repaired at Bandar Shahpur, to make her safe to sail to the nearest port with dry dock facilities for a full refurbishing. In the meantime, she held few patients and even fewer distractions.

I'd seen nothing of Bandar Shahpur on my arrival, but now had a unique shipboard perspective on what had become a strategic asset in Allied support of Stalin's war effort. The area itself was the dictionary definition of "wasteland." Treeless, isolated, and laughably desolate, Bandar Shahpur was a like a child's seaside model of a port: a haphazard collection of mud-brick buildings, telegraph poles that leaned like twigs at various angles, countless lines of toy-like narrow-gauge train track that extended out into the water on a Y-shaped pier. It seemed that one wave would wash the whole thing away. Indeed, only high embankments saved the entire operation from daily inundation by the five-meter tides.

The summer heat blazed so intensely that most dock work took place at night. They initially confined me to bed, with just a round slice of porthole-framed sky, a cracked-paint ceiling, and a poor Jacek-substitute for company. After I was allowed to put weight on my knee, I slept during the day and spent every night at the deck rail, basking in the still-warm night air, and watching the beehive of port activity as the night hours slipped by.

One after the other, ships approached one of the two brightly lit berths at either side of the pier, where workers unloaded them from both the pier and sea sides. On the pier side, an endless collection of trucks, troop carriers, artillery pieces, and crates of all shapes and sizes were craned directly onto railroad cars, destined to travel north on the same railway that had borne me south. On the sea side, lighters — unpowered barges — were piled high with goods and slowly pushed by tugboats to the single lighterage wharf.

I lived this odd nocturnal existence for my two motile weeks aboard the *Somersetshire*, prior to my departure for the port of Aqaba in Transjordan, from where I could travel overland to Tel Aviv. I saw the staff only occasionally, when I retired for the morning to the relative cool of the stifling ward. They seemed to barely notice my absence. Perhaps, as Viktor had accused me just weeks before, aboard a different ship in the Caspian Sea, I was "wallowing." I preferred to think of it as adjusting to my new manual reality.

I wanted one day to write an Ode to the Hand. I would sing the praises of what I now knew to be the most sadly underappreciated and abused of our appendages. What evils we made our hands perpetuate, and how ungrateful we were for their unquestioning obedience! Like loyal lovers, family pets, and flush toilets, the hand was ever taken for granted. I would yet write this Ode, if my limping, one-handed, typewriter key pecking would ever again be deserving of the title "writing."

My lack of a dominant hand manifested itself in those early days — and still does — at every turn. The phantom pains that plagued my stump were inconsequential compared to the pain in my face and, primarily, my ego when I punched myself for the umpteenth time while trying to scratch my nose or push hair out of my eyes. Eating, bathing myself in our daily seawater baths, dressing, using the latrine — *especially* using the latrine — even masturbating silently in the ward's darkness — all were, it turned out, highly hand-centric operations.

Absence was a strict master. Unlike presence, it refused to be ignored, growing only bolder in the face of such attempts. It expanded to fill more than the space allotted it. During those first weeks without my hand and without Danuta's voice, the absence of each fought the other for primacy in my consciousness. I'd left my hand cradling Vera's head—much as I'd left Danuta, Jacek, Viktor, and Igor. Now, I feared that they would leave me, too.

It was a particularly soft evening, the night Danuta returned to me. The fingers of a light desert wind caressed my head, as my own former fingers had once so briefly caressed Vera's. I reached up to gently grasp the hand that seemed to brush my hair, longing to bring its cool palm to my cheek. Instead, I punched myself in the ear, and simultaneous jolts of pain emanated from both my face and the stump of my right hand.

The spell broken, I cursed and turned back to my nightly port vigil. For the previous week, I'd been tracking the comings and goings of each man, and creating maudlin stories for each piece of equipment unloaded. How many ultimately inconsequential human tragedies—all of them still more consequential than my own growing collection— would play out in the back of that ambulance? Would the man ultimately driving that half-track return to his farm at the end of the war, only to find his wife and children gone? Which of the soldiers wearing boots from that crate would freeze to death the very first night they wore their newly acquired leather trophies?

My reverie and field of vision were punctuated by the bow of another ship, which slid silently by on its way out of the harbor. The noise of its engine far astern, only distantly audible, could not yet mask the sweet strains that skipped lightly across the water between the ships. It came from an open port, or perhaps from a hidden corner of the deck—I couldn't tell, but it was unmistakable.

Vera sang *Bo to sie zwykle tak zaczyna*—Because thus it Begins. The song told the story of a woman ashamed to have fallen in love with the wrong man, and wrestling with her decision to end the liaison. Vera's voice rose sweetly and clearly in the summer calm, unwavering and, I gathered, healthy. She sang as she had sung to me, though she could not have known I was there. With a quick flash of jealously, I wondered if she was singing for another man, but then I realized that Vera sang then, as she always had, for no one and everyone simultaneously.

I was flooded with an impossible mixture of joy at Vera's apparent recovery, and with my visceral longing for Danuta, with whom I had danced to this very song on an equally mild yet imminently more memorable late summer Warsaw evening in 1938.

Then, as anyone who loves a woman might have already imagined, Danuta returned to me. As the passing ship's stern drew parallel with me, and Vera's voice was determinedly crushed by the engine's heavy *thrum*, Danuta whispered in my right ear, as if remembering herself that evening at the Adria Club.

"That's right, my love," she said. *"I chose you because you were the right man, and I've never been ashamed. Not Felix Kaspar, darling, you."*

Everyone has 'If Only's.' *If Only I hadn't left at the end of that summer. If Only she hadn't been seeing him when we met.*

I had mine, and Felix Kaspar was Danuta's. The big difference was that, unlike most 'If Only's,' Felix not only reentered Danuta's life in 1938, just six months or so after I'd met her—he actually *moved into her house*.

Danuta's father, Lech Kumiega, was a financier. This is why he knew my father—the Warsaw financial community was small enough that everyone knew or had worked with everyone else at some point. In 1933, he moved his family—his wife Marianna and their children Stanislaw and Danuta—to Vienna to pursue a new business venture. Mr. Kumiega explained the nature of this venture to me once over a sweet *digestif*. As suitors have done for millennia, I nodded with feigned interest as he gestured with his cigar throughout the lengthy explanation—understanding not a word and stealing surreptitious glances at Danuta the whole time.

She sat by his side, demure and just out of his field of vision. For the entire conversation, she mocked each of his gestures and mannerisms so accurately that I was forced to mask my outbursts of laughter with quasi-sneezes and coughs, which ultimately blew dessert wine all over my lap.

Danuta was sixteen, her brother just ten, when they moved to the large flat in Vienna's Landstrasse district. Although she found the lyrical Austrian German puzzlingly different from the German she'd learned in Warsaw, she quickly grew to love Vienna's stern beauty and endless diversions. She first saw Felix Kaspar ice skating in what was then the largest indoor ice rink in the world, near the Heumarket. His broad smile, broad shoulders, and high-jumping figure skating prowess had entranced her. He was already then a national champion, and they expected great things of him in the 1934 European Figure Skating Championships.

The next time she saw Felix was in her family's own flat in Vienna. Felix's father, it turned out, had business dealings with her father. Thus, the Kaspar family showed up for dinner at the Kumiega family's residence one evening, with eighteen-year-old Felix in reluctant tow. Perhaps, on seeing Danuta, his reluctance faded rapidly.

It was to be an intensive, yet limited, year-long 'If Only' romance. In 1934, just before the European Championships in Seefeld, in which Felix would place 7th, the Kumiega family moved back to their flat in Praga, Warsaw. Though the fathers continued their close business cooperation, the love letters that traversed the 700-kilometer expanse between Vienna and Warsaw quickly faded in both frequency and ardor.

This should have been the end of Danuta's 'If Only' story. However, Felix Kaspar had the unfortunate luck to have been born Jewish. In 1938, after Germany annexed Austria, and the wave of antisemitism that had already been sweeping the country for years intensified brutally, Felix fled, along with tens of thousands of other Jews of foresight. He showed up on Danuta's doorstep in July 1938, his father having arranged for him to be safely hosted in Warsaw by his old Catholic business partner, Danuta's father.

To her credit, Danuta had been forthright with me about Felix. She told me he had arrived, what he had meant to her, and why he had come. She also told me that I had nothing to worry about, that her 'If Only' — even if he was now a *proximate* 'If Only' — remained just that.

If I were to be diplomatic, I'd describe my initial behavior as sub-optimally reasonable. If I were to be straightforward, I'd just say I was an ass. To my credit, I was a disenfranchised young man in an increasingly antagonistic society, who'd recently been expelled from university. I also loved a Catholic girl who was — I felt — far, far above my station. To my discredit, I was still an ass. I ranted, raved, and broke it off with her, but not before making a few disparaging remarks about her perhaps unhealthy penchant for Jewish men.

What began with me storming out of her parents' flat continued as a week-long self-pity binge, in which I was inconsolable and utterly unapproachable. Even Jacek had had enough of me after several days, requesting that I inform him upon my return to human society.

I was unrelieved when he brought me the news that Felix Kaspar was leaving the following week for America. Jacek told me conspiratorially that Danuta was waiting for me. Still, I kept up my infantile act. I didn't see her for nearly two weeks, and had actually begun to accept the sad inevitability of life without her. In a vain attempt at self-commiseration and reentry into society, I took myself out for an evening at the Adria Club to see Vera Gran perform.

Danuta didn't know I would be there, and I certainly hadn't known about her. I actually didn't recognize her when I scanned the room, looking for an acquaintance on whom to foist myself. Then I realized that the source of light by the bar, around whom men flitted like moths, was actually Danuta. I watched her with the incredulity of an ornithologist observing a rare species of hummingbird, ashamed of myself for being unable to look away, yet desperate for her to glance my way.

She did glance at me, of course, and as Vera Gran stepped to the microphone to begin what became our song, I mouthed its opening words across the room to Danuta: *Tak mi wstyd, strasznie wstyd*—I'm so ashamed, terribly ashamed.

"I never gave you a reason to mistrust me," Danuta's voice whispered in my ear, jerking me from the memory back to the deck of the Somersetshire.

And I don't mistrust you, whatever you may have done. Come back to me.

In the distance, Vera sailed away down a moon path that first engulfed, then purified in white light the rusting freighter that carried her. With her sailed Danuta's absence. Throughout my uneventful days of travel to Palestine, my trip from Aqaba to Tel Aviv, all that followed, and until this very day—her voice never left me again.

CHAPTER 21
Danuta: Panic

Tel Aviv, Sunday, August 16, 1942

My Dearest Samuel,

Panic is here. It throbs in wispy tendrils just below the surface, like blood dripped into water, like a riptide waiting to carry away an unsuspecting swimmer. What was once spoken in whispers is now heard in full-throated terror: the Germans are coming, the British are leaving, and even before the Nazis get to us, the Arabs will have their own day.

In Jerusalem, well-meaning Arab families are offering to adopt Jewish children, to protect them when the rioting and slaughter begin. The Irgun, it is said, is making covert plans to take over the Old City of Jerusalem, evict its Arab residents, and make a last Jewish stand within its walls against the Nazis. Jews are scrambling for visas to India, to America, to anywhere that will accept them. There is discussion of mass evacuation – some say just women and children, some say just the leadership – yet no one seems to know how and to where, exactly.

There is even talk – by the more deluded among us – of cooperation with the invading German forces. These poor souls think they can persuade the murderers to spare our lives in exchange for leveraging Palestine's industrial capacity. But Aron knows from his sources that the SS have already created a Einsatzkommando – the same murder squads that now operate throughout Europe – tasked with 'dealing with' the Jews of Palestine once Rommel breaks through British lines.

And the Einsatzkommando, it is clear, will enjoy the whole-hearted assistance of our neighbors, Palestine's Arab population. I see them, my love. I see the eyes of the Arab day laborers in Tel Aviv. The way some of them look at us makes my knees turn to jelly. No one has forgotten the slaughter in Hebron, only 13 years ago. What will become of us without British soldiers to intervene?

The Arabs listen to their leader, Haj Amin Al-Husseini, who is the guest of the Reich in Berlin, and moves in the highest Nazi echelons. I've seen the transcripts of his broadcasts, which are monitored by the Hagana. They are bloodthirsty rants, and his rabble understand — and seem to look forward to — what is expected of them. What did we do to them to inspire such hatred? We are a community of 500,000 Jews. We built all our settlements on land bought and paid for. What kind of culture produces people that gleefully plan how to divide up Jewish property, post-slaughter?

Panic sits mutely like a clenched fist in every stomach. In every household, it tingles the limbs and trembles the hands, waiting for the right moment to spring. Families are buying up cyanide capsule kits as fast pharmacies can stock them. Parents are instructed to dose their children first, then themselves. It is said to be quick and painless. I understand and frankly admire these people, who insist on living the lives they've built, then dying on their own terms. Perhaps, if we had children, my love, I would follow their path.

But I have work now. For there is talk, there are endless rumors, there is never-ending debate on the street and in the corridors and backrooms of the Jewish Agency, there is unremitting angst, and there are nightmares. Yet there is also action.

I see less of your brother these days. He arranged a one-room flat for me on Bugrashov Street, just a block away from his own. He craves his privacy, as you will learn when you finally arrive. I wonder if you know why. I found out quite quickly, and care not a whit. He claims you must know. I have learned so much about Aron, and I wonder if you truly understand your brother, my love. When he left, you were still a child — the little brother abandoned. This is why I have always understood the anger you carry at Aron's 'desertion.' Yet I fear you have grown, while your judgment of him may have remained adolescent.

In any event, we will sort out your relationship with your brother when you arrive. "There's little a drink and a warm fire can't solve," as my father used to say — although even thinking of a warm fire makes my sweat trickle faster down the sides of my cheek, dropping to my shoulder and sliding sweetly down my chest. Yes, I am thinking of you, my sweet, as I write this...

There will be time enough for that when you arrive. I mentioned that there is action alongside the panic. Well, I am now part of it. I have joined the Hagana! Together with Aron, I am part of the Northern Plan now.

Aron speaks constantly of empowerment: national empowerment, personal empowerment. He's quite loquacious, your brother. He paces when he talks, the palm of one hand grasping the back of the other behind his back, save the occasional beard stroke, when he is unshaven. The Northern Plan, he says, is the ultimate Jewish empowerment — much as I see the cyanide capsules as the ultimate family empowerment in this twisted world in which I find myself. How sad to say this! Yet what is power if not absolutism and adamant faith in self?

The street talk, of course, is of 'Masada on the Carmel' — a fortress holdout until death. This could, of course, come to pass, but the Hagana leadership is made up of chess players, apparently, who think many moves ahead. There are only half a million of us here in Palestine, and it is not infeasible that we could all be concentrated in one place. The Axis will ultimately lose the war, this has become clear to all. The question is, when? The Yishuv leadership is banking on the fact that even if the British retreat to India, they will ultimately regroup. They believe we could conceivably hold out at the Carmel until the Allies return. They believe there's a chance of survival. Certainly, no one has proposed a better solution — nor one that will so definitively safeguard our national aspirations once the war is over. For, having held out against the Germans and so markedly contributed to the British war effort, how could His Majesty's Government refuse in good conscience our demands for autonomy?

Indeed, Aron claims the British are cooperating in full. In British military installations across Palestine, orders have been given that when the retreat begins, they will leave behind sufficient weaponry for the Jews. The Hagana, myself now among them, is working tirelessly to stockpile and transport enough food and medical supplies to Haifa. The physical defenses on the southern side of the Carmel are being strengthened. The guerilla bases in caves throughout the mountain range continue to grow in equipment and sophistication.

Today's Davar reports that Adam Czerniakow, the Jewish head of the Warsaw Ghetto, committed suicide following the Nazi's demand that he prepare a list of 100,000 — a fifth of the

Ghetto population — for deportation and likely murder. The Nazis, it is said, simply appointed someone else, and the population of the ghetto hand themselves over to their oppressors like sheep.

The Germans are used to a certain type of Jew, my love, but they will be surprised when they approach the outskirts of the Haifa Ghetto, as we've taken to calling it. For at every step they take toward this Ghetto, Aron believes, they will be struck by a new kind of Jew. A Jew unafraid to defend himself. A Jew unwilling to submit. A Jew for whom boldness is not anathema, nor self-sacrifice foreign. We have created this new Jew over the past generation in Palestine, Aron says. Now, it is time to show the world who he is and what he can achieve.

We will do this together, my love, for I am certain you must be close. Your letter from Tehran was a cool breeze in this unbearable August heat. Where are you now? On the train to Bandar Shahpur still? On a ship to Aqaba? I dream of you. I wake nightly, expecting your rough hand to slide across my cheek in comfort. It is the thought of you that stems my own panic, for I am distracted by my work on the Northern Plan, but not fully immune to the nightmare of the Einsatzkommando. Come back to me quickly, my love.

I love you with all my heart,
Danuta

CHAPTER 22
Aron: Close to Hell

Jerusalem, September 11, 1942

What could I possibly have wished for the eve of the new Hebrew year? Prosperity? Abundance? Health? *Rosh HaShana* greetings for the year 5703 were more visceral. That year, Jews around the world — in Europe, of course, but also in Palestine — prayed for *life*. Full stop. For one cannot live a good life, a bad life, an unexamined life, or even a squandered life... without the prerequisite of *life itself*. They prayed for life, though there was no one to hear their prayers. They prayed for life, though millions of identical prayers were mockingly ignored.

I secretly longed to pray, yet could not. The purity of belief in beauty and trust in humanity's potential for good — prerequisites to prayer — always eluded me. I could at least enjoy, however, the caressing call of *others'* prayers. These whiffs of the divine drifted lightly like the sweet smell of home baking from the synagogue across the courtyard of the Russian Compound. They flitted through the bars of the small window near the ceiling, and alighted gracefully next to me on the cold stone floor of my cell. They sang into my ears with voices of butterfly delicacy. They called to me, these strangers' prayers. They sought a way in, yet could not pierce my armor of cynicism, which I'd worn with pride for too many years to readily shed.

I imagined the prayers squeezing through the crack under the rough-welded iron door — my sole portal to the outside world for the previous week. Then I pictured them turning on their heels and leaving the same way, in search of more fertile ground to sow their seeds of hope.

I had no need of hope, as I was in hell. Almost literally. Prisoners referred to the solitary confinement cells in the Central Palestine Prison in Jerusalem's Russian Compound as *gehenome*. What many did not know is that *actual* hell, according to Jewish tradition, was less than a kilometer away from their cells. The word for hell in Hebrew evolved from *"Gai Ben-Hinnom,"* the Ben-Hinnom Valley, whose curved palm cradled and caressed Jerusalem's Old City from the south. In that place of beauty, one could gaze at the majesty of the golden stone walls from below. Yet its rough stones were, according to legend, stained with the blood of countless children sacrificed to the Canaanite god Molech by the good citizens of Jerusalem, many hundreds of years before Jesus.

A fitting setting for hell on Earth, if ever there was one.

So, in fairness, I wasn't *actually* in hell—but I was close—close to hell, and close to despair. I was close to embracing the finality of the searing aloneness that had pursued me since childhood. I was close to accepting that my estrangement from whatever family remained living had become irrevocable. I was close to finally rending the veil of naïve optimism from my face, the veil that had for so long enabled me to see light—however elusive and faint—around the next corner.

The loss of Sean and my imprisonment had brought me this close to hell, but I'd been closer. Alone in that cell, the devils of memory exploited my loneliness, tormenting me in an endless mental matinee. For depravity leaves a scar, and fourteen years previously, what happened in the mud of a verdant summer forest on the banks of the Vistula had scarred both Samuel and myself.

"What are you *doing* to him?"

Samuel's annoying little brother voice ripped me back to the here and now, the summer of 1928. It ripped me, damn him, back from a heaven more than just physical pleasure. It ripped me from the bliss of sharing myself, in a visceral sense I'd not previously conceived, with another human being. It ripped me so cruelly away, and thrust me so quickly into the murky waters of shame, that I immediately began to question whether the bliss had ever actually existed.

"He... I... he... he was hurt. I was... helping him." I drew the back of my hand roughly across my lips, wiping Antoni Wawrzaszek's saliva away and smearing dark river mud across my cheek. At the first sound of Samuel's voice, I'd pushed myself away from the tree against which I had pressed Antoni.

A slight boy, Antoni stood a head shorter than me, and now looked up at me with surprise and longing as I pulled away. His long smooth hands still clutched my shirt. His swollen lips called me back to their moist warmth.

"It looked like you were *kissing* him," Samuel said.

"Shut up, you little shit. I *wasn't*. He was hurt and I was helping him. That's all. What the fuck are you doing here, anyway? I told you to wait by the sandbar! Are you too retarded to follow a simple instruction? Are you fucking *stupid*?" My breath was still ragged, and my voice hoarse.

Antoni's fingers had uncurled from my shirt, and he was already busy straightening his own rumpled clothing.

"You *were* kissing Antoni. *Ew!* Why were you kissing Antoni?"

My hands, which had just seconds before been caressing the impossible softness of Antoni's lower belly, curled into fists. My voice steadied, and my breathing slowed. Samuel was supposed to have stayed by the river — I'd told him very clearly, and he'd nodded in agreement. As ever, the job of watching him had fallen to me at the worst possible time. Mrs. Chlebek, who spent the vast majority of her time sleeping while babysitting Samuel in any case, was ill the very day that Antoni had agreed to meet me in the thick woods by the river's edge.

I turned to see Antoni running off towards the roadway high above us, still fidgeting with his pants as he ran.

At that moment, my younger brother Samuel turned into something different. He was not the pesky yet lovable burden that others seemed to see in their own younger siblings. He was far beyond this. At that moment, and for many moments thereafter, Samuel became the embodiment of the anguish that had been growing in me for the past years. He became the corporeal angst of knowing I was somehow different, yet unable to understand how or accept why. He became the knot in my stomach when I passed groups of kids chatting amicably in the school halls. He became the flush at the base of my neck when someone called someone else "faggot" or "Jew-boy." He became the essence of my shame, and was — I say with no pride — sadly proximate whenever I needed a scapegoat.

Now he stood there, my scapegoat, with a mocking grin on his face, making kissing sounds, hugging himself and laughing — and my fists clenched so tight my knuckles grew white. He laughed, and pointed at my reddening face, aiming for my most tender wounds as only a sibling can. His laughter stripped me bare.

The silent forest swirled above me as if I were on a merry-go-round. I could hear my pulse throbbing in my ears.

The next moments I experienced only in jerky snapshots, like a kinetoscopic movie — me moving toward Samuel, the pain of a throat-burning yell, my hands on his neck, the terror entering his eyes, the river wetting my sleeves, the bubbles rising from his mouth, his feet twitching.

His stillness.

As he came to, I sat near him, still breathing hard, my shoulders aching with the violence.

He whimpered, coughed, and spat water. Then he sat up, and his eyes focused enough to find my own. The look that crossed his face at that moment was a cross between abject, pants-wetting terror and deep betrayal.

I looked away, still too deep in my own pain to accept the existence of his. I could offer no solace or even apology. My voice came flat and numb, but steady. "I was *not* kissing him. And if you ever say anything about this, I'll fucking kill you. Do you understand?"

He nodded, wide-eyed, and he never said anything, as far as I knew.

Later that year, I joined the youth movement with the clear intent of moving to Palestine. Samuel and I saw less and less of each other, despite living under the same roof. The interactions we did have, at least until my return from the Vienna debacle, remained cursory and politely correct. I was broken and jagged, and during my fall to the hell that was the muddy Vistula bank where I nearly killed my brother, I had sliced too deep for the fraternal flesh ever to heal.

I betrayed Samuel that day, I thought, gazing again upward toward the source of the prayers that still filtered into my cell. Yet my violence had been the culmination of the years of carelessness that preceded it. I'd been careless with Samuel's fraternal admiration and love. I'd been careless with my parents' trust in me as his protector. I'd been careless, in a very real sense, with the unwritten yet pervasive law of family cohesiveness and loyalty.

Now, my carelessness had again cost me, for carelessness had brought me here, and put Sean on that ship to Ceylon. The question was, would my carelessness again beget betrayal, as it had on the banks of the Vistula in 1928?

I'd been careless over the weeks preceding my arrest. I'd been euphoric, filled with renewed purpose, and immersed in the daydreams of love, ridiculous fantasies of a future that did not involve the drudgery of daily subterfuge—a future in which I could stroll down the shady boulevards of Tel Aviv on a cool late summer evening, openly holding hands with my love. In this future, I would wake up next to him every morning, smile at his tousled hair, and kiss the sleep-warm nape of his neck before getting up to make coffee the way he liked it. In this future, I would greet him at the end of each day. I knew, of course, this future would never come to pass.

It was, I believe, these daydreams—fueled by elation over surviving the London Square attack, killing the British soldier with apparent impunity, and sharing this information with Sean—that had blinded me to my own vulnerability.

Thus, when I threw myself into Sean's arms, surprising him daringly in his quarters that evening, I was blind. When I drew him irresistibly—as I knew I could—into my passion, I was blind to the chance that a fellow officer might enter the shared room at any time.

They arrested me the following night, quietly at my apartment. The officers shackled me hand and foot, and roughly threw me into the back seat of their unmarked car. The loquacious officer that interrogated me in the Abu Kabir police station had explained, with no attempt to disguise his disgust, that I was under arrest pursuant to Chapter XVII of the General Penal Code for Palestine, for Offences Against Morality. He showed me a copy of the code, as if trying to convince me of the clear moral basis for my arrest. He did this despite me being utterly submissive to the Code in my shackled state—right or wrong, moral or immoral.

"You are accused," he said in a clipped voice sharper than the ends of his waxed mustache, "of attempting to have carnal knowledge against the order of nature, a felony that carries a maximum sentence of seven years." He paused for apparent effect. "Now, I'll let you mull on that, pervert. I'm sure your fellow Fannies will be pleased to—how shall I put it?—make your acquaintance in prison. I hear they have a lovely initiation rite involving petroleum jelly and a cucumber."

The officer sneered, turned on his heel primly, and left the interrogation room, slamming the door behind him with a deep thud.

Several hours later, they transported me in the back of a lurching lorry to the Russian Compound, where I would remain while awaiting trial, 'for my own protection' in the solitary confinement cell into which only prayers passed unimpeded.

During that first week alone, my demons relinquished their hold only infrequently, yet I did not dread the future. I still hadn't yet reached dread. Instead, I struggled simply to regain the *terra firma* of reason after having my rug of reality yanked so swiftly from underfoot. I could not dread my future because, alone in that cell, *I literally saw none.*

Then one was presented.

Early one morning, they shackled me, herded to an interrogation room, and abandoned me. As hours passed, my arms ached from being trussed behind my back, and my bladder felt as if about to burst. Finally, as the sun reached its peak through the grimy barred window, the door banged open and an unfamiliar figure stepped halfway into the room. Before I could get a good look at him, he turned on his heel and left. I heard him summon the guard and bark a string of commands.

The guard entered immediately, efficiently released my arms and legs from their shackles, and asked me if I required the toilet. I replied in the affirmative, and he escorted me courteously.

When he brought me back into the room, a steaming cup of tea awaited me on the table. The unfamiliar figure, grey-haired and wearing a suit instead of a uniform, sat in the interrogator's chair. He gestured politely for me to sit and drink, and I was at last able to study him.

He was at least ten years older than myself. Quicksilver strands of grey streaked a full head of wavy hair parted fastidiously directly above his left eye. His square Hollywood-star jaw line and flawless aquiline nose could not offset a pair of disturbingly thin lips, which he held in what seemed to be permanent disapproval. After I sat, he glanced up, and starkly grey eyes pierced, held, then relinquished my own.

When he spoke, he did so in the elegant baritone of no-nonsense gentry. "Mr. Katz, I am Thadeus Heathcliff. I work for the Joint Technical Board, which is attached to the War Office. I'd like to offer you a fairly simple way out of the mess you seem to have gotten yourself into. Are you interested in hearing what I have to say?"

Without a moment's hesitation, I shook my head 'no.' I knew of the "Joint Technical Board," a bureaucratic pseudonym for the Special Operations Executive — British Intelligence, and I immediately understood what he would ask me.

Heathcliff blinked at my audacity, sighed, and looked momentarily skyward as if in silent reprimand to the gods of pliability. Then he shifted his lanky frame in the uncomfortable wooden chair and continued anyway.

"Mr. Katz, I think you would agree that the British and Zionist interests in Palestine—leaving aside the notably volatile issue of Jewish immigration—are fully aligned at the moment. We all face one overriding peril, Rommel's army, together. This is the basis, indeed, for the deep nature of the cooperation between the leadership of your *Yishuv* and the portion of His Majesty's government that I represent. We share a common enemy, Mr. Katz, and are thus allies in the truest sense."

He leaned forward, rested his right elbow on the table, and met my eyes again. "And allies, Mr. Katz, help each other *unreservedly*."

"No," I said simply.

"'No' to what, Mr. Katz? I haven't asked you anything."

"But you are about to, and the answer is no. No, I will not spy on the senior Zionist leadership, to whom you know I have access. No, I will not betray their trust, and no, I will not commit treason. Does this clarify my position for you, Mr. Heathcliff?"

He sat back and deftly fished a pack of Simon Artz's from his shirt pocket. He offered me one, and I accepted. He lit his own cigarette with an expensive-looking metal lighter, and passed the flame across to me. He drew deeply on the cigarette, exhaled smoke to the side, and continued.

"I admire your adamant loyalty, Mr. Katz. I too, consider myself a man of principle. Yet it seems to me you've already betrayed the very leadership you now seek to protect. Carrying on a personal relationship with a British officer carries a very stiff penalty in *Hagana* circles, does it not? In fact, I can think of a number of recent instances where gentlemen such as yourself ended up dead owing to mere *suspicion* of just such a liaison."

"It's not the same thing—"

"Let's just save our time, Mr. Katz." He cut me off with a dismissive wave of his cigarette, which sent flakes of ash drifting down over the tabletop. "Here's what I can offer you: charges for your indiscrete behavior will be immediately dropped. You will return home today and can be back at your desk in *Kofer HaYishuv* tomorrow morning. There will be no repercussions whatsoever from this incident, save the reassignment of Major—now *Captain*, I believe—Sean Deakins to an outpost in Ceylon. He's already left, by the way."

He paused to let this sink in. Then he lit another cigarette from the stub of his first, leaned back in the creaking chair, crossed powerful arms across his chest, and continued.

"All you have to do for me, in exchange, is answer a few questions now, and make yourself available to answer any future questions I may have, or provide any documents I may request. There won't be many, I assure you. I'm quite careful not to over-extend my assets. And I'm sure you'll agree that my offer, unpalatable though it may seem now, is your best option. It's better than jail, and certainly better than what will happen if the *Hagana* discovers your relationship."

Again, I shook my head.

He nodded as if in understanding, gathered himself to leave, then swung around so quickly that I never even saw the open-handed slap coming. Even before my brain registered 'pain' from the slap, Heathcliff had viciously pushed my chair backwards. I lost balance and crashed backwards to the floor. My cranium met the floor with a dull *thunk*, and then his shoe was on my windpipe. With a practiced movement, he fitted the depression between sole and heel just on my larynx, and leaned forward with just the right amount of pressure. It was a choking lead weight, immune to my ineffectual attempts to loosen it. He leaned further toward my face, increasing the crushing pressure on my throat, and pointed his lit cigarette directly at my left eye. With each pause in the monologue that followed, he jabbed the fag a bit closer.

"Let me put it bluntly, Mr. Katz. I don't give a shit (*jab*) who or what you fuck, but any way you look at it, you are fucked (*jab*). If you don't agree to work with me, you will be fucked (*jab*) the moment you step out of this jail by the very heroes in the *Hagana* that you're protecting. If I send you to prison, I will ensure that you are fucked (*jab*) by a long line of lonely, large men. With my deal you can fuck (*jab, jab*) whomever, whatever, and wherever you please—as long as it's not *me*. I'd strongly suggest that you choose to be the fuck*er*, Mr. Katz, rather than the fuck*ee*."

With that, Heathcliff relented.

I gasped for air and blinked wildly to clear the cigarette ash that was burning my eye. I back-scrabbled away from him and ended up with my back pressed against the cold wall, trembling, coughing, and trying to regain a semblance of composure.

Heathcliff ground out his cigarette on the floor at my feet. Then he turned and half-sat, half-leaned on the table's edge. His grey eyes said, "*Well?*"

In the war of principle against self-preservation, self-preservation almost always triumphs. What does a martyr gain from his own death if not relief from the very ills that led him down the convoluted path to the Reaper in the first place? In this sense, self-sacrifice and self-preservation are one and the same, and I could choose either in good conscience.

Yet I'd had my fill of betrayal. I'd betrayed my family, betrayed my integrity, betrayed Sean with my recklessness, and—according to the British—betrayed the very foundations of morality itself. I was not ripe for more betrayal.

At the same time, every betrayer seeks—consciously or unconsciously, overtly or subliminally—to return stasis to the chaos of his soul. He seeks the pressure valve of conscience that the churches and poets call redemption. I'd started down a path that could lead me back to my younger brother, and could not bear to abandon it, no matter what the cost.

Thus, when I nodded and then voiced my hoarse assent to Heathcliff's offer, it was, in the truest sense, both self-serving and self-sacrificing. There, in such close proximity to the bloodstained golden stones of hell, I'd discovered a path that led to both betrayal and redemption.

CHAPTER 23
Danuta: The Raw

Tel Aviv, Sunday, September 20, 1942

> My Dearest Samuel,
>
> Surely, this scratch is on another's hand. I stare at it, knowing that it's mine – just a scratch from some household chore – yet what it reveals is utterly foreign. It's a window to the raw just below my surface – the raw that now percolates inexorably from within me – and this raw no longer carries the ravishing essence of life, but the putrescence of despair. It simply won't stop emerging from depths I never knew, nor – now that I've made their acquaintance – ever desired to plumb.
>
> Your brother is in crisis, as am I. I send this letter to your care in Aqaba and Bandar Shahpur, in hope that you will receive it on one end of what must be the final leg in your journey to Palestine, and make haste. Although you may not realize it, my darling, you are our lifeline, and we are slowly sinking below the surface without you.
>
> Your brother has suffered some terrible loss, although he adamantly refuses to share its details with me. He disappeared for a week, and returned transformed. His sallow face and thin frame certainly support his alarming story of sudden hospitalization during a business trip to Jerusalem, as do the medical documents chronicling an emergency appendectomy, and his matching bandages. Yet I fear something deeper, a flow that no surgeon's needle could possibly staunch. For I know – as I know you do too, my love – at what depth the reservoir of raw pain lies. And I know that once this well is tapped, it is far less easily capped.
>
> My own raw, and that of your brother, mixes with the collective raw that has risen to everyone's surface. Gerhard Riegner's report to the US State Department, which reached the Yishuv leadership via Chaim Berles, scratched so deep as to leave no possibility of scabbing. There is not yet, I believe, a word for

what he describes. Nor could, perhaps, a single word ever aspire to encompass the enormity and horror of systematic mass murder on an industrial scale.

Now, more than ever, the fate of European Jewry is clear. Now, more than ever, the threat from the SS units attached to Rommel's army is indisputable. And now, more than ever, your brother should be redoubling his efforts with Kofer HaYishuv and the Hagana. The Northern Plan grows more desperately relevant with every passing day, with every British tank destroyed, with every piece of news I read in Davar. His efforts are needed, yet daily he sits, writes, and does nothing.

He does nothing, he says, because he cannot cap his own well. The vitriol simply forces its way to the surface too rapidly – as it does now through this little scratch on my hand. He greets each morning with the tired eyes of dread. Each morning, he thinks, 'what additional twist of the hot blade, already stuck so deeply in my ribs, will I suffer today? What new betrayal against me, or that I have perpetrated, will I relive? What love that was given to me will be ripped away?'

Yet the answers elude him, as does a bandage that can hope to cover his emotional wounds. Thus, he spends his days reaching out to the one person, he believes, that can help him. He writes – yet never sends – countless letters to the one to whom he is so deeply tied, yet with such a convoluted thread, that he fears he will never succeed in untangling it.

He writes, my love, to you.

And this is what you must know, on this day before Yom Kippur: your brother needs not just your presence, but your true forgiveness. Although neither you nor Aron have shared with me all that passed between you, I am sure that there is much to forgive. Yet forgive you must, my darling. It is the human gesture you must make in this terrible time of inhumanity. It is also, I truly believe, what your mother and father, of blessed memory, would have most fondly desired.

Forgive him, and hurry to us both. I love you with all my heart,

Danuta

CHAPTER 24
Samuel: Cost

Port of Aqaba, Transjordan, September 1942

I awoke with a deep feeling of foreboding. My neck ached as if it had borne some terrible burden throughout my fitful dream. The morning sun angled through the porous reed roof and walls of my rented hut, turning flesh into striped zebra hide, and creating myriad spotlights wherein dust mites floated with abandon.

The flies had begun their daily pestering dance on lip and limb, which would last until the midday heat became too intense even for them. I roused myself from the thin mattress that lay on the straw floor mat, and threw the hut's door open, almost blinding myself as the sun leapt in at me. The brown strip of bare sand at my feet dragged my teary, blinking eyes across its featureless expanse, then plunged them abruptly into the coolest, deepest blue water I had ever seen. I started, for when I debarked last night and arrived at the "hotel," I had seen only blackness.

The Red Sea, it seemed, was not really red.

I stepped out of the hut, which had cost me the last coins in my pocket, to better survey the majestic scene: red-brown mountain crags locked in distant struggle with lighter brown sand and rockslides, which tugged their foes inexorably towards the sea's azure maw.

I frowned, recalling snippets of the night's dream. I cradled the aching stump of my hand and thought about loss, but then heard Viktor's voice accusing me of wallowing, and shook off the dread with which I'd woken. I forced myself to grin.

What if there really is a light at the end of this tunnel? What if I've paid my fare in full? What if I've been crawling so long that I've forgotten how to stand?

I straightened up and smiled, this time for real. *I'm almost there, my love,* I told Danuta silently. *I'm waiting for you,* she answered in my head.

I washed myself clumsily in brackish water from the pitcher by the chipped ceramic basin, for which I'd paid extra, struggling to accomplish yet another two-handed task with only a single appendage. Then I gathered my few things and walked across the already-hot sand to the restaurant, with the aim of finding a creative yet quick way to get to Tel Aviv with no money.

The "restaurant" was a squat structure supported by stout palm trunks and roofed with dry palm fronds. British stevedores crowded its low-slung wooden tables, sitting on dusty cushions scattered across the woven rag carpet floor. I gathered that, owing to the heat, they worked at night like their compatriots in Bandar Shahpur. They'd just finished their shift, and were tiredly raucous. The hotel owner nodded that I could join them, as lodging included breakfast at no additional cost. I hesitated, chose a less crowded table, and plopped down on a cushion.

Over breakfast that consisted of sandy, flat, blackened *pita* dipped in tangy *tehina*, chopped salad, and some kind of salty cheese, I gathered from the stevedores at my table that bus fare to Tel Aviv was high, and service was spotty. One could also, for a hefty bribe, hitch a ride with a British army convoy for the two-day trip. Yet the prices the stevedores mentioned would take me weeks to earn, if I could even find work suitable to one hand.

A stevedore from the next table, who'd been listening to our pidgin-English parley, leaned over and spoke up. "Oi, you should talk to Bashir. He's the ticket. Runs the camel caravans to Jaffa. You'll find the little pisser down the beach a bit. Just follow the trail of camel shit." He winked and turned back to his meal.

The others at the table nodded in agreement.

I thanked them, rose from the table and headed down the beach, bidding the owner farewell.

There really was a trail of camel shit. At its end, I found a group of ten or so of the beasts, sitting with legs folded underneath them at incongruous angles, near the water's edge. Each chewed a cud thoughtfully and turned to catch the last memory of cool morning breeze that rose from the water.

A boy of perhaps fifteen leaned against the largest of the camels. Short and skinny, he had dark curly hair that framed a round dust-streaked face. Dark, dull eyes sat behind a flat nose whose nostrils flared into cheeks still graced by baby fat. Two dark-skinned, stick-like legs, capped by white-dusted bare feet, protruded from his ragged grey cotton *thawb*.

I'd read and heard much about the Bedouins, but never encountered one. Savvy herdsman and adept desert survivors, they were considered rather slow-witted — especially the younger ones, since none were formally educated. Thus, as I approached this boy, I donned the large smile I'd learned to use when facing particularly ignorant Russian peasants. I greeted him in the few words of his own language that I'd learned from the stevedores — hoping fervently that I wasn't actually cursing his mother. Then, I spent the following minutes pantomiming my urgent need to get to Tel Aviv, and my willingness to work at any job to do so.

He stared at me blankly, one eyebrow raised in vague interest — as if, despite the novelty of my appearance in his line of sight, I yielded little other entertainment value. A fly crawled across his lips, and he did not wave it away.

His dim eyes remained directed at me, though, so I tried again. This time, I accompanied my grandiose arm gestures with an elaborate pidgin English soliloquy. "You Bashir? Me Samuel! Me need go Tel Aviv. Bashir take me. Yes? We go Tel Aviv? Bashir and Samuel. Yes?"

Still Bashir stared.

Obviously, the stevedores were pulling my leg. This boy is clearly stupid, mentally deficient, or a bit of both.

Moreover, everything I'd read and heard about Bedouins was apparently true. Resignedly, I turned to go back to the hotel, intending to ask the owner for his travel recommendation. As I left, I muttered to myself in Polish about ignorant natives and wasted time.

A clear voice stopped me in my tracks.

"Kto nie ma w glowie, musi miec w nogach," it said in perfect and nearly unaccented Polish — *he who falls short in the head, had better be long in the heels.* My father had loved to throw out that phrase at Aron and me whenever we did something particularly stupid.

I spun around. *"Mowisz po polsku?"* — *you speak Polish?*

"Nie chwal dnia przed zachodem slonca," Bashir answered — *don't praise the day before sunset.* He continued in clearly fluent Polish, "I'll take you to Tel Aviv, but it will cost you."

Cost was something my father had understood. A man of science, of finance, and of education, he was a student of enlightenment, a universalist who truly believed in humanity's power to deliver itself from ignorance and superstition into a state of reason. When he returned from the Great War — Aron was just five years old and I was yet to be conceived—his break with the inborn spirituality of his *shetl* past was complete. He never spoke specifically of his wartime experiences, yet he imbued us with their lessons constantly. The battlefield, he liked to repeat often, stripped existence to its barest elements. In the trenches, you could rely on two things: your own hands, and the man next to you. God, he'd learned and shared repeatedly, had nothing to do with either. We must therefore take responsibility, he would tell us, for each of our actions, no matter how seemingly insignificant. And we must always accept that each has a cost.

After the war, Father returned to Warsaw to resume his financial career and his family life. He examined, researched, and cautiously executed every step. Life, he told us, was a minefield. If you didn't feel like losing a foot to it, you had to judge each step. When he purchased the new apartment on Wybrzeze Szczecinskie Street, he'd visited the land registry himself to ensure the soundness of the property ownership. When he brought Mother a dog for her birthday, he spent hours in the library, researching the relative merits of each breed before selecting the little Kundel we called Max, yet who lived with us for only a week until we discovered that Mother was allergic. He measured, checked, considered, and rechecked every step through the minefield of his life. The successful life, he claimed, was simply a science.

Thus, Father's decision to take Aron for "treatment" in the fall of 1928, just months after he nearly drowned me by the Vistula, did not surprise in and of itself. Following extensive research and consultation with Warsaw's leading Freudian scholars and endocrinological experts, Father had found a way to help Aron overcome his "delicate issue." He would take Aron, he announced one evening somewhat officiously to Mother, to Vienna to see the eminent Dr. Eugen Steinach himself.

I stood behind, stiff against the wall, hidden between the end of the kitchen counter and the frame of the door leading into the dining room—my frequent parental listening post. Father's excited voice carried quite clearly through the thin swinging door. The Steinach Procedure, he explained to Mother in what Aron and I called his "Eureka!" tone of voice, was widely accepted and exceedingly in-demand in Europe and America.

"Even Karl Kraus came out in favor of the procedure, my dear. You fancy his work, do you not? He joked—with no small measure of truth, mind you—that Steinach could make suffragettes into Madonnas and journalists into real men, just by doing this simple testicular transplant.

The key is the testosterone in the donor testes, you see. Aron needs more, and this transplant can provide it. He can overcome his unnatural proclivities, using nature itself. There's really no danger, and Steinach's results have been quite positive."

My mother remained unconvinced.

Father's voice grew lower and more urgent, and I strained to hear. "This can make our son *whole*, dear. This can make him a whole man. Why would we not take this opportunity to offer him a life of true fulfillment, instead of one of depravity? How could we look ourselves in the eyes, knowing that we did not do everything in our power to change him into what he should be?"

He persisted, and Mother acceded to a compromise in the end. Father would take Aron to Vienna for an *examination* only, then consult her via telegram before agreeing to any *procedure*.

I momentarily considered sharing this information with Aron. My parents were, I understood even at the age of ten, essentially planning to mutilate my brother—even if it was for his own good. Yet the incident by the Vistula remained too fresh in my mind, and I contented myself with a smug look at Aron as he and Father left the flat late Monday afternoon.

He caught this look, and returned a cursory, puzzled look of his own—raising eyebrows as if to say "What?" Then they were gone.

On Wednesday morning, two days later, as I prepared for school, the door slammed open. Aron burst through, my father close behind. He rushed over to me and tried to grab my shoulders. I instinctively shrunk from him, still leery from the attack just months previously, and moved across the room.

Across the dining table now sitting safely between us, he said in a voice dripping with accusation and vehemence sadly familiar to me, "You knew. You knew, and you didn't tell me. Did you think I wouldn't find out? Did you think I'd *let them* do that to me?"

My father looked pleadingly at my mother, who turned away.

Aron's stare burned into me, and I looked down at my toes at first, unable to meet it. Then I straightened my back and neck, and looked directly into my brother's eyes defiantly, silently. Without saying a word, I asked him with my eyes: *who crossed the line between mischief and hostility first? Who raised their hand against whom? And given this, why should I have been obligated to inform you of anything?*

Over a lifetime, we both acquire and inflict deep wounds. Most of these wounds never fully heal. They scab over, only to be reopened constantly by one emotional concussion or another. In some rare instances, we acquire or inflict wounds so deep that they *won't even scab.*

I acquired one such wound with Aron's hands around my throat on the muddy banks of the Vistula. I inflicted one such wound when I neglected to tell him that my father was taking him to Vienna for a doctor to cut his scrotum open.

There is a cost to everything, brother, my eyes silently told him across the dining table.

My parents looked on, utterly unaware of the silent Clash of the Titans underway right in front of them.

I have paid, and now so have you.

"What will it cost me?" I asked Bashir in Polish.

One of the camels lowed loudly, and Bashir swatted at it, eager to make himself heard.

Flies buzzed at my eyes, and I waved them away.

"You are educated, are you not?" he responded.

I nodded, and shaded my eyes against the sun now reflecting off the water's glass.

His husky voice resonated in the range between boy and man, yet remained purposeful and unwavering. "Outstanding. So, I'll take you to Tel Aviv, and you teach me along the way."

CHAPTER 25
Aron: Hope

Tel Aviv, September 30, 1942

> *My Dearest Brother,*
> *Hope came to visit me. It flitted, skittish and moth-like, around the candleflame of my soul. It danced just out of reach, and I knew that if I reached out to grasp it, it would dissipate. So, I simply watched and took comfort in its illusive presence.*
>
> *Then it flew into the flame. The stench of its death-smoke still taints my nose.*
>
> *This fleeting glimpse of hope was born, I realize now, not of presence but of absence. Of love's memory, not of love itself. It came from my too-transient taste of love's delicacy. It came from his melting smile, which I still see every time I look over my shoulder, and the tingle of his breath, which I still feel on my neck when I wake.*
>
> *My hope stemmed also from the African front. Maybe, I thought for the briefest of moments, there is hope for all of us. Maybe there is hope for you and me, as well.*
>
> *And now I know there is none.*

I ripped up this letter, too, of course.

What emptiness do I seek to fill with these fragments?

They were shards of glass, the sharp corners of myself that needed to be expunged so they wouldn't cut me from inside. And it didn't matter, I had long lied to myself, whether they were ever actually shared. I knew for whom they were intended, and had thus communicated what I needed. The response, I rationalized, was immaterial.

But I had loved.

Now, I understood that the response one receives from a shared feeling defines, in a very real way, the feeling that follows it. It is the symbiosis of love — thought feeding off thought, touch feeding off touch — that makes it so powerful. It cannot be, and is never, a one-way street.

I knew this because I'd been on a one-way street for more than a decade. I'd emotionally divorced my parents, and by association, Samuel, when I left for Palestine. I'd loved them in a vague, reminiscent sense, yet I'd had no need to share with them. After all, they only knew Old Aron — the child of icy cobblestones, lumbering streetcars that took unsuspecting limbs, and unforgivable violence in the summer Vistula mud. They didn't know New Aron. There was no connection between the two, I thought. I had become the new Jew, taking part in the ideological adventure called Zionism. This had, by definition, transformed into me into New Aron — freed of the shackles and repercussions of my past.

Yet New Aron never quite expunged Old Aron. He would return, frequently and accusingly. *I reside inside you*, he would say in the darkest hours of a lonely night. *I will never leave.*

I mentally shoved Old Aron away yet again, and New Aron wrote another letter.

I signed my name, sealed the envelope, addressed it *post restante* to Aqaba, and set it aside to mail in the morning. With any luck, it would await my brother's arrival in Aqaba. The last letter I'd received from him was from Bandar Shahpur. The letter had been written in a strange hand, with no explanation, yet it was signed Samuel, and the words were clearly his. Surely, he must have been close by now.

In my letter, I provided instructions to him for accessing my flat in my absence. I left a key and instructions with a neighbor, and another letter to Samuel on my desk. I would be in Helwan, near Cairo, indefinitely.

Look at this as an opportunity, Bert had said in the meeting in Jaffa. It would be an opportunity to bring my skills to bear on a truly pressing challenge. It would be an opportunity to learn a skill that could be of great use to the *Hagana*. It would be an opportunity to prove myself worthy of the renewed trust the *Yishuv's* leadership had placed in me, following what was — after all — a grave violation of trust.

An opportunity.

I had my own thoughts as to whether being sent to within kilometers of the North African front was opportunity or punishment. However, I had no choice in the matter, and it *did* give me an opportunity of sorts: the opportunity to be absent when Samuel arrived in Tel Aviv.

My journey to Helwan began, in essence, with my walk to the bus station in Jerusalem following my release from the Central Palestine Prison. I felt as if Heathcliff's palm print lingered fresh on my cheek, yet the sky above Jerusalem was clear and tepid. Slowly, my newfound freedom sunk in, and I began to bask in the sunshine of my own false confidence. Idioms of salvation bounced through my mind: I'd dodged the bullet; the hangman's rope had broken; my ship had missed the reef. I had come out ahead.

Hours later—disheveled, starving, yet markedly heartened—I disembarked the green snout-nosed Egged Ford with a new spring in my step, and hopped down into the noise of Tel Aviv's new central bus station, opened just months previously. I smiled at the white rounded concrete roofs that covered each platform of this admirably modern transportation hub—the largest in the region, it was said. I flipped a two mil coin to the boy selling elliptical *bagela* rolls, sprinkled *zaatar* on the still-steaming white insides from a package made of a twist of newsprint, and ate ravenously.

The fall sun shone hotter now, and Tel Aviv's humidity pressed in. Cars honked, people jostled, hawkers trailed and called. The burgeoning city, frantically trying to live its life despite the yoke of doom dragging at its head, threatened to engulf, devour, and assimilate me—as it had so many times before—yet I paid it no mind. For the first time in weeks, I was pleased with myself, not only for being saved from prison, but also for formulating a viable plan of action during the bumpy ride down from Jerusalem. For the moment, I had—if not actual hope itself—at least a clear view of hope, which waited for me just beyond the horizon.

I walked to the nearest taxi stand and took an extravagantly expensive cab straight to *Kofer HaYishuv*. When the heavy wooden lobby door swung shut behind me, it cut off both my uncertainty and the noise of the street. I climbed the smooth stairs and marched into Aharon Bert's outer office. I smiled sweetly at Dvora, Bert's buxom and overprotective secretary, also rumored to be his lover. Her lipstick-gilded lips began to open in protest, but quickly formed an open-mouthed silent snarl as I marched past her.

I entered Bert's office, closed the door behind me, and stood in front of my boss' desk with my hat in my hand until he looked up.

He'd rolled up his shirt sleeves, and beads of sweat bobbed between the wisps of hair crisscrossing his broad forehead, despite the mighty chugging of his electric desk fan and the late summer breeze drifting through the large street-facing windows. He took me in with his soft, shrewd eyes, raised one eyebrow in interest, mopped his brow with a once-white handkerchief, and leaned back to hear what I had to say.

I took a deep breath, and proceeded to succinctly and calmly tell the Chairman of *Kofer HaYishuv*, whom I knew had the ear of the highest levels of the *Hagana* leadership, everything. With the glaring exception of the would-be rapist's killing, I left out no detail about my arrest, Heathcliff, and the exact nature of my relationship with Sean.

Bert listened with the impassive interest of one whose wisdom and experience frequently vanquished his dismay. When I finished, he nodded coolly and called out loudly for Dvora to order his car. To me, he said simply, "Wait here."

So I waited, sipping a glass of tepid water grudgingly provided by Dvora, watching cars meander by on the street below Bert's office. It had gone well, I reflected. Bert seemed to understand that this was no rash confession on my part. I was not throwing myself at his mercy, for what I'd realized on the bus ride from Jerusalem to Tel Aviv was that my position, far from being disadvantageous, had in fact never been more valuable.

In turning to Bert, in baring my soul in the most dangerous way possible, I'd banked on the fact that I had value as a British agent. I could serve as a natural conduit through which the *Hagana* could pass on whatever information they desired. This, I was sure, would trump any outrage over my conduct or perceived moral indelicacies. Despite the *Hagana's* close wartime cooperation with the British, the long-term interests of each side clearly remained at odds. Owing to this ongoing yet quiet rivalry, they would regard me—I believed—with understanding.

Two hours later, Bert returned. An hour after that, I was back in my flat. The following morning, I was back at my desk. The gamble seemed to have paid off. Far from being a traitor whose life was destined to be short, I would be—if not celebrated—at least tolerated and put to good use.

The term "good use," it turned out, could be interpreted in many ways.

The note came a week later.

I started that day with a grim smile. *Davar* carried news of a bomb that killed two and wounded twenty at the Paris screening of a notoriously vile antisemitic propaganda film, *The Jew Suss.*

My schadenfreude was short-lived, however. The bus from Tel Aviv to Ramat Gan arrived late, its wooden benches already packed. I finally walked up the stairs to the second floor of the *Kofer HaYishuv* building ten minutes late. I tried to slink past Bert's office, but a smirking Dvora hailed me, informing me that Bert had assigned me yet another old account ledger. He'd been doing this all week, ostensibly using me to prepare for an audit that we both knew was unlikely to materialize. He'd likely designed this boring work to keep me busy while the *Hagana* leadership masticated my story, trying to decide whether to swallow me or spit me out.

After a day of inhaling old ledger dust and meaningless columns of figures, I finally stood at one minute before 4 p.m. with my timecard in hand. As the minute hand of the time clock clicked forward, I shoved my card into the slot and received a satisfying click in reward. I walked down the stairs, thinking of Samuel, missing Sean, and wondering whether I could stand another evening of silence.

The note was tucked next to the handle of the door to my flat. At first, I recoiled at its sight, but eventually gathered courage and plucked it with two fingers, much as one picks up a particularly loathsome insect. On it was printed the name and address of a coffee shop in Jaffa, and a time two hours hence. It contained no signature, but it was clear who the sender was.

I would meet Heathcliff for my first debriefing.

I washed and groomed slowly, trying to pass the time, yet I still arrived at the coffee shop twenty minutes early. I sat on the sea wall and smoked, willing the butterflies in my stomach to calm themselves before the meeting. I had no idea what I would say to Heathcliff, or what I was even *allowed* to say. *Hagana* intelligence hadn't yet briefed me, so I would have to think on my feet.

I ground out my cigarette, walked briskly to the coffee shop, and quickly picked out Heathcliff, facing me from his seat at an interior table. Two men sat with him, their backs to the entrance and their faces hidden from me by the shadows.

Fellow agents? Contacts?

My questions were rapidly resolved as I approached the table. To my shock, Aharon Bert turned to face me, as did the man next to him, whom I recognized as Yisrael Amir, the head of the Soldier's Welfare Committee, the cover for *Hagana* intelligence. My stomach dropped, and I stopped in my tracks, unsure whether to run.

Heathcliff turned, smiled at my shock, and narrowed his eyes. "Mr. Katz, how good to see you! Surely, you know my colleagues. Well, don't just stand there like a figurative deer in the headlights, Nancy. Sit. Just try to keep your poofster hands to yourself, if you don't mind." He chuckled at this.

Bert and Amir looked dire.

I sat, wary, but still sufficiently dumbstruck by the presence of these three together that I obeyed the order automatically.

Bert turned and addressed me in Hebrew. "Sorry for the delay, son. The three of us only find time to meet like this once a week. And ignore my rude British colleague here. We just wanted to let you know we're already sharing all the information we need. But we do appreciate your offer and your willingness to sacrifice."

I blinked, dreading what I knew would come next.

Bert cleared his throat uncomfortably. "Look, son, here's the thing. About those... uh... personal details we discussed. We think you might be a bit more useful to us all in a different capacity, for the time being. We need some truly urgent assistance down south. So, pack your things for an indefinite stay, and Dvora will fill you in on the details tomorrow morning."

Heathcliff turned to Bert and interjected in fluent Hebrew. "Oh, just tell him, Bert. Don't leave the poor girl hanging. Oh, never mind, I'll tell her myself." He turned to me and sneered. "Listen, darling, since you've proven yourself so inept at deception, your colleagues and I have decided to send you for, shall we say, *training and practice* in this art. So, pack your tutu, dearie, because it may be a bit hot there — in more ways than one."

Puzzled, and more than a little revolted by Heathcliff's crass self-satisfaction, I turned to Bert, who explained.

"Look, son, you've dug your own grave here. There's no easy way around this. The *Hagana* leadership would be pleased to see you dead for consorting with the enemy and agreeing to spy for the British, even if you did try — somewhat clumsily — to double-cross them. Heathcliff and British Intelligence would love to see you dead for making them look like the assholes that they are. The *Yishuv* leadership needs you out of the way. The only reason you're not lying in the dunes north of Tel Aviv with a bullet hole in the back of your neck is that I intervened, and suggested we send you to learn a skill that might be of use to us down the road. They reluctantly agree, and we're attaching you to Geoffrey Barkas's unit in Cairo—well, perhaps somewhat *west* of Cairo. But you'll start off at Helwan Air Base, which is completely safe. You need to look at this as an opportunity of some relative value. The skills you can learn from these people will help you reestablish yourself when you return—"

"—*if* he returns," Heathcliff snorted. "Look, Bertie, just tell it straight. We're sending you to the *front*, Nancy, and without a gun. These Deception boys work right up close and personal with the Germans. But you can either stay here and die or go there and die. Personally, I don't really care either way." He turned to Bert and Amir, gestured impatiently, and raised his eyes to the heavens in mock supplication. "Now, can we please move on to some more *savory* points of discussion, like bestiality, pederasty, cannibalism, or even *Zionism*, for that matter?"

I stood silently, and turned to leave as Heathcliff and the others huddled their heads together and began discussing something with intensity. I walked stiffly and slowly, intent on recovering some dignity, at least, in my exit, but Heathcliff was having none of it.

Catching my retreating figure from the corner of his eye, he stood and called out loudly enough for the whole restaurant to hear. "Why so glum, Nancy?"

All eyes turned to him, then in my direction as he continued.

"Lots of nice farm animals down south, I hear. Should keep you romantically occupied for *months*. Best of luck to you, my girl!"

His loud bark of laughter, together with the other patrons' puzzled amusement and Bert and Amir's indifferent silence, stabbed me between the shoulder blades on my way out.

Thus, I wrote my brother one final letter and arranged my flat for his arrival.

Hope had come to visit, then abandoned me. Samuel would come, too, and learn what I could not tell him without the necessity of my presence. Then he, like hope, could decide either to stay or to leave.

For hope, I now understood, was powerful even when fleeting. Yet even more powerful was the vacuum left by hope's demise, and I did not want to be witness to what filled that vacuum.

CHAPTER 26
Danuta: Demons

Tel Aviv, Thursday, October 1, 1942

> *My Dearest Samuel,*
> *Where are you, my love? I'm desperately worried. I've had no letter from you for weeks. I'm not even sure where to send this, so I'm again copying it to both Bandar Shahpur and Aqaba, in the hope that one copy will reach you.*
>
> *It's your brother. He's gone again. He left behind only this rather alarming note. I'm copying it out for you:*
>
> *"Danuta, I've visited my demons, and I know them well. I used to descend nightly to their cages. I used to nurture them through their bars in the vain illusion that – when they inevitably escaped – I could still control them. Now I realize I cannot, for I am my demons, and they are me."*
>
> *Surely you can understand my concern, darling. The note continues in this vein, and in the end, he offers me the use of his flat in his indefinite absence. I'm here now, in fact – and was secretly pleased to have had a reason to leave my small, dreary rental flat. Yet here I now sit, watching the door and knowing that none but Aron, one of his demons, or you will next enter. I pray it will be you.*
>
> *I haven't seen much of Aron these past weeks. I believe I can say with some finality that I've begun a life here, you see – one that I hope we'll soon share. I have my job at Kofer HaYishuv, which is tedious but pays the bills, and is – I truly believe – making a difference to our collective hope of a future in this place. I also have some new friends that still laugh at my Hebrew, and will forever mock my accent, yet accept me. Or rather, they accept my Jewish alter ego, and I'm not sure there's a difference anymore. They love me, and I am beginning to feel the same. Of course, having you next to me is the only thing that will ever complete this life.*

So, I watch the door handle, looking for the beginnings of movement that might suggest your arrival. I imagine you – gaunt and dusty, perhaps injured or sick – taking me into your arms. I imagine your lips, the taste of which is just a memory, again on mine, and two hands, rough from the road, on my waist.

Unlike your brother, I choose to ignore my own demons. These demons whisper nightly that you're never coming, that you're dead, or that you've forgotten our love and found another. I do not nurture them, unlike Aron, nor do I go anywhere near them. My demons remain where your brother's should have, tightly stowed and locked away. I don't need to release them, my darling, because you will soon be here. I need you, and I fear your brother – wherever he is – needs you nearly as direly.

I love you with all my heart,
Danuta

CHAPTER 27
Samuel: The Trail

Outskirts of Beer Sheba, Palestine, October 1942

"Fine. Name your favorite Polish composer." I waved my hand in front of my mouth as I spoke, having quickly learned that thirsty flies wasted no time in finding moisture, and would fly into an open mouth faster than even the briefest words could exit.

I looked at Bashir expectantly, raising my eyebrows. I'd finally decided to challenge him, following three days of listening to his boasting that he was — by culture, if not by birth — more Polish than me.

"Please. Paderewski, of course. Surprised? You weren't expecting me to just spit out 'Chopin,' were you? Give me a little credit." His scoffing smile bounced up and down with the rhythm of his camel, which loped along out of synch with the stride of my own. High above one of the crumbling canyon walls towering above us, a lone hawk appeared. It silently sliced the sky in two and disappeared over the opposite wall.

"All right. Favorite Polish food?" I turned away and lowered my eyes to avoid a wave of sand swept past us by the omnipresent wind. The canyon in which we'd been traveling for the past hours offered relief from the sun, which scratched mercilessly at any piece of exposed skin, but not from the afternoon wind.

"That's an easy one. *Bigos*. Although I'm partial also to *Pierogi*, when we can get it." Bashir clucked his tongue, urging his camel into a trot as the uniform tan in front of us turned suddenly, magically green.

My own camel, who I'd mentally dubbed Smelly for obvious reasons, perked up at the scent of water. It—I was as yet unclear as to the beast's actual gender — picked up its pace voluntarily. We'd arrived at our camp for the evening: the spring of Ein Abda.

"We?" I said, knowing that he was likely referring to the true source of his Polish *savoir faire*. I guessed that his "we" included a Polish soldier — likely an officer, given the clear level of education and sophistication—stationed near Beer Sheva. The Polish garrison there was awaiting the arrival of Anders' Army, which was working its way south from the Soviet Union and would be arriving within months, according to reports.

I had, of course, been asked to join the Polish Armed Forces in the East, also known as Anders' Army after its commander, General Wladyslaw Anders. They'd asked, cajoled, pressured, guilted, and once nearly physically coerced me. Of course, this was before I parted company with a certain appendage that soldiers find handy—pardon the pun—for trivial tasks like pulling a trigger. In any case, Anders' Army was months away from Palestine, and I'd not been willing to wait to see Danuta.

Danuta. I looked around the oasis, tasting her name through the dust on my lips, as I did every time it crossed them. Yet even with her constant letters—which I cherished, and which drove me forward throughout the impossible journey I'd undertaken—and even in the expectation of our impending reunion, I felt uneasy. I still heard her voice, could still feel her touch, yet she had become, in a sense, an ideal. The closer I came to her, the more she retreated from the world of the tangible into the realm of the possible. I tried to shake off the feeling, explaining it as an expression of my intense longing, coupled with my fears of her repulsion at my injury. But it persisted.

"We?" I asked Bashir again.

He gave a small smile that gently honored my right to interrogate him, while firmly asserting his own right to ignore my questions. He hopped deftly off his now-kneeling camel, threw off his *thawb* with abandon, and plunged his brown naked body into the green water of the oasis pool with a whoop that echoed again and again from the stratified rock of the cliffs above us.

I sat in the deep cliff shade, my back against a cool rock, reveling in the sudden absence of motion. Being on Smelly all day was like a never-ending ride on a merry-go-round that smelled like decomposing cow farts and snapped at you viciously if you dared to fidget. The shadow in which I sat lengthened with the coming dusk, and the oven-like temperature moderated, as if an unseen hand had lowered the dial from 'broil' to 'bake.'

Bashir stopped splashing and whooping, and floated placidly on his back. Smelly and his colleagues sat regally, tails flicking flies, satiated after their long drink. And the silence of the desert, which I had come to love, settled over the oasis.

If I'd had a typewriter, I would have pecked out an essay about how desert silence was unlike any other. In the forest, I would have written, silence hides behind the trees' wind-driven singing, graspable only in the brief breaks between songs. On the riverbank, silence is masked by the myriad burbles and gurgles of moving water. In the desert, silence is raw. Within it, you can feel the gentle thrum of Earth's deepest inner machinations. Desert silence is silence unbound from time. Desert silence is silence from which you cannot hide. It rips the bandages from your deepest wounds, strips the emotional pretension from your darkest thoughts, and lays bare all for rational examination. Yet even as it exposes them, it soothes and dresses these wounds with its balm of reflection.

I had no typewriter, of course, nor two hands to operate one. And, as the sun's last rays slipped down from the crevice of sky framed by the canyon's walls and illuminated the trail of blood leading from the pool's far side, neither could I revel in the luxury of desert silence for long.

I jumped up when I recognized the trail, engorged with jubilant flies yet still reflecting in the rapidly failing twilight, as congealed blood. This blood spatter had come not from a mere wound. It looked more like the remnants of a vibrant stream that would emanate, for example, from a slit throat. I checked my instinct to call out to Bashir, who now dozed under the spreading boughs of an Acacia tree. Instead, I stepped silently to his side, bent over, shook him, and held a finger to my lips when he opened his eyes.

He recognized the urgency in my face, and rose quickly. When I showed him the trail, his eyes widened and he reached for the dagger that hung loosely from his belt.

The last rays of sunlight dissipated. Our sandals crunched gently on the rocks of the streambed as I followed Bashir. The only other noise violating the desert silence was the buzzing of the flies, who ignored the fall of dusk in their feeding frenzy. We traced the gory path step-by-step toward its apparent origin on the opposite side of the canyon.

I'd followed such a trail once before, in the apartment in Vilnius, in February of 1940. That trail had meandered from our bed to the washroom, yet drew no flies in the midst of the coldest winter ever recorded in the city. With temperatures below -30 degrees Celsius, and with heating rationed owing to the city's burgeoning population and dwindling energy and water supplies, this blood trail had been nearly frozen by the time I woke and discovered it.

I'd rolled over, deep under the immense pile of blankets, sheets, towels, and even a children's-sized down duvet, under which Danuta and I had slept in a vain attempt to keep warm. I reached for her as I did a dozen times a night, and found her side of the bed cool. I'd poked my head from the pile of bedclothes and called her name, my breath fogging thickly in the crisp air. When she didn't answer, I rose, puzzled when the liquid soaked through my socks. A burst pipe, I'd assumed at first, but then I looked down and saw that the bottoms of my socks were black.

My stomach had dropped, and Danuta's name flew from my lips in a vapor cloud of increasing urgency. Ariana had poked her head out of her room, woken by my calls, and together we followed that trail.

Just as Bashir and I now followed the trail in Ein Abda.

The woman, who'd not been dead long, lay at the base of the cliff with her knees curled up to her stomach. A bag of small green melons lay near her, and the back of her filthy *thawb* was clotted with dark blood from the waist down. Bashir shook her shoulder, and her head lolled back, revealing a pretty, young, and unblemished face. Barely visible in the twilight's last rays, her expression seemed one of peace, as if she'd realized her goal and, in doing so, could rest soundly.

Bashir knelt and surveyed the scene, shifting his gaze to the bag of melons, then back to the woman's bloody posterior. "Baby," he pronounced. "She didn't want a baby. That's what the *handhal* was for. Come, we need to bury her."

By the time the moon had fully risen, we'd dug the shallow grave. As we worked, digging with hands and a stick liberated from the Acacia tree, Bashir explained to me about the desert melon they called *handhal*. Among its other medicinal uses, some women used them to end pregnancy when taken in large doses. Unfortunately, it could also cause massive bleeding, which is what had happened to this poor woman. She came by herself from a nearby tribe or village, either to avoid the shame of a child born out of wedlock, or to rid herself of an unwanted, yet legitimate, pregnancy. Either way, it had not ended well. Or... perhaps... from her perspective, it had.

Together, we piled rocks on top of the grave to keep out scavenging animals.

Bashir sat to rest, but I turned to methodically cover the trail of blood. The flies had left it alone for the night, but I could not bear the thought of their inevitable return in the morning. The trail caught the moonlight and shimmered—a ghoulish crimson moon path leading away from life, not toward it. I scraped sand over the trail, erasing the sanguine moon and seeing in my mind's eye the trail down the hallway in Vilnius. It too had reflected the pale moonlight, yet it had led me to a very different place.

"The *babka* said there might be some bleeding." Danuta gasped as Ariana and I reached her. "But I'm feeling a bit better now." She lay sprawled on the floor in the washroom, her back against the tub, looking anything but better. Her usually ruddy face was pale and sunken, like a balloon with a pinprick hole. Blood had pooled beneath her. She lifted one hand, which had been resting in the puddle, and pushed the hair back from her eyes in a weak attempt at making herself more presentable. The gesture left her with a thick dark red streak across her forehead, which ran in sinister rivulets like tears down either cheek.

Ariana sent me to bring the doctor who lived, thankfully, just two floors below.

The doctor came quickly following my urgent banging on his door. He shooed me unceremoniously from the washroom as he and Ariana stripped Danuta. Her moans followed me through the door while I changed our bloody bed linens, and persisted when I began on the floor, chipping and then scrubbing the remnants of the trail of frozen blood. They subsided as I washed away the last traces of what had been, I realized then, my son or daughter. The doctor and Ariana had Danuta cleaned up and back in bed by the time I'd finished.

The doctor took several minutes to berate me for risking a back alley abortion with the *dabki*—the Russian word for midwife abortionists.

I remained silent in the face of his onslaught, eyes downcast, as if ashamed of my actions. In fact, any shame I felt arose from my utter ignorance of the pregnancy and its termination.

Danuta slept for three days, and I slept in snatches sitting next to her, ever expecting her to awaken and call for me. She never did. Finally, her eyes opened, cleared, and met mine. She gave a faint smile that belied no guilt or apology, and before drifting off again, she said simply and weakly, "This is no world for children, my love."

With the memory of my child's blood still lingering under my fingernails, I could only hold her hand and nod in agreement.

After covering the desert trail, I walked to the side of the canyon and curled up on the straw mat to sleep.

Is the world ready for children now, my love?

I dreamt relentlessly of Danuta and babies — those who had never come to be, and those yet unborn.

CHAPTER 28
Aron: The Production of Nothing

South of El Alamein, Egypt, October 15, 1942

"All warfare is based on deception," read the plaque on Geoffrey Barkas' desk.

He caught me looking at it, and smiled vaguely. "Sun Tzu, from *The Art of War*. Familiar? MacArthur's a big fan, or so I hear."

I shook my head, though Barkas didn't notice. It seemed a bit unusual for the head of the British Middle East Command Camouflage Directorate to meet with a prospective ditch digger assigned to his unit, even one with an impressive-sounding title like mine. Thus, I didn't bother him during his lengthy perusal of the manila folder that presumably contained all the British Army knew — or cared to present — of me. Waiting patiently, I studied his downturned face.

It was a hard, ironic face, with a sardonic twist etched on lips that sheltered, umbrella-like, a round, full chin. Narrow cheeks drew attention from a broad forehead accentuated by slicked-back hair. Most striking about Geoffrey Barkas, I discovered quickly, was his gaze. It pierced whatever it fell on — stripping away pretense and laying bare motive.

Finally, he looked up from the folder. His eyes flayed me thoroughly before he spoke. "Jesus Christ, Private Katz," he said in clipped English, then read aloud from the typed orders in his hand. "'To maximize the learning experience, the Zionist Liaison shall be intimately exposed to all facets of camouflage activity — from the ground up. To this end, he should be assigned field work of a type requiring no specific skill set. There is no need for any formal classroom instruction, nor necessity to supply him with in-camp accommodation.'" He set the paper down. "So, who in the hell did you piss off?"

I smiled wryly. "Just about all of them, sir."

He snorted. "All of them, indeed. I'd say so, young man. Well, what the hell am I supposed to do with you, then?" His eyes once again interrogated me at length, and I imagined I could see the wheels of his

- 176 -

mind turning rapidly. After a long pause, he finally broke the silence with another, more decisive, snort. He jotted a note in my file and handed it across the desk to me. "Very well, Mr. Katz, you shall learn from the ground up. You will be attached to an engineering group building important infrastructure for Operation Bertram. That will be all."

I took the proffered file, but did not yet turn to leave. "Operation Bertram, sir? No one in Palestine mentioned that...." I let my voice trail off, hoping for a semblance of explanation as to what I was doing here.

'Here' was in British Army Camp E just outside of Helwan, Egypt, a sparse, nearly colorless Cairo suburb most notable for the large military airstrip on its southern edge. The bus from the throbbing iron-girded monstrosity that was Cairo's Ramses Station had first meandered at length along the refreshingly reed-skirted Nile. Then, regrettably, it had turned away into a bland, flat, and tan uniformity broken only by the occasional green-topped date palm. The monotonous landscape persisted as we pulled into a dusty enclave of wooden huts and squat concrete houses. The driver had stopped, allowing the trailing dust cloud to catch up and settle over us, and called out "Helwan!"

I'd alighted into a throng of khaki-clad British soldiers and *thawb*-wearing Egyptian *fellahin*—none of whom seemed to know anything about the Camouflage Directorate or its head. After an hour of aimless wandering, during which time everyone either ignored me or misdirected me, I found Barkas' office.

His eyes now spoke of fatigue, yet his face momentarily lit up. "Operation Bertram, my boy, will be written and spoken about for generations. We're creating the single largest campaign of deception in the history of military conflict. Sun Tzu would shit himself if he could see what we're up to here. Now, off to work with you. See the Major out front about the details of your posting."

I shuffled from his office and stood expectantly in front of the desk of the Major, whom I'd registered only in passing when I came in. He looked up from his typewriter with a bored expression, and I handed him the note I'd received from Barkas.

With a sullen sigh, he grudgingly shuffled papers and filled out the forms required for my transfer. After several minutes, without looking up, he explained in a monotone that I was to assist in the laying of a water pipeline that would carry no water. At this, he looked up slyly, clearly regarding this paradox as inescapably intriguing. He waited in expectant silence for my inevitable query, clearly eager to launch into an explanation.

I offered none.

I was no longer curious about what I was to do, bone-weary from the two-day trip from Palestine, and desperate for a bath, which I guessed would be long in coming. Mostly, I simply cared little where I would end up and what they would force me to do. Thus, I looked back at the Major with the same dumbly bored expression he'd given me just minutes before.

He stared back at me.

Finally, to break the standoff, I raised a querulous eyebrow, which was all he needed. I'd granted him a victorious spark of interest in a subject that clearly delighted him.

"It's all part of the grand and brilliant farce that is Operation Bertram," he sang out merrily, boredom dispelled. "The pipeline you're to help lay is codenamed Diamond. It runs from an actual water pipeline—" He showed me on the large map behind his desk. "—to a fake supply depot to the south. The idea is to convince the Germans that the upcoming offensive will begin far to the south of General Montgomery's actual plan. The fake pipeline's construction schedule is also timed precisely to make it appear that the job will be finished by a date far after the offensive is scheduled to begin."

He droned on, explaining far more than seemed appropriate. "During the day, your group will work with heavy earth-moving equipment to dig an eight-kilometer stretch of two-meter deep trench. When the trench is dug, you'll lay out *pipe*—" he made little air quotes around 'pipe.' "—made of wood and covered with tin from spent petrol cans—next to the trench, as if ready for welding into place. When night falls, you'll fill in the trench and move the same fake sections of pipes ahead to a staging area for the next section.

"Thus, to the ubiquitous high-altitude Nazi surveillance aircraft, it will appear that we've completed a section of the pipeline overnight, and are preparing to lay the next section. We'll even be building fake watchtowers and supply stations—placing scarecrow men and decommissioned vehicles next to these installations to make them look real from the air."

I listened to the Major's explanation in skeptical silence.

Catching my expression, he smiled in condescension. "There it is. That's the look they all give me. It's too bad I never get to see their faces when they actually get to the field." He slammed my file onto a pile of files that started on the floor and ended just above desk level. He ripped the final form from his typewriter, handed me two pieces of flimsy carbon-copy paper, and directed me to the transport hut.

My Darling Sean,

I said ten thousand goodbyes to you. I began right after we first said hello. I said goodbye every time I woke with your hand on my arm. I said goodbye every time I caught you looking at me across the Armon Hotel bar. I said goodbye over breakfast, when the morning sun slid through your curls like melted butter. I said goodbye every time you unlocked the door to my flat, undressed, and crept silently into bed with me – army dust and your own sweat still clinging to your skin.

I said ten thousand goodbyes to you because there are too many hellos in the world. They're so common as to dissipate without a trace. We say hello to strangers on the street, to bus drivers, to nameless neighbors – but we're stingy with our goodbyes. These, we reserve for those whose absence excavates an open pit in our stomachs, which cannot be filled. This is why goodbyes leave a residue. Microscopic pieces of each goodbye stick to the soul like burrs in a field-worn pants leg. Thus, I carry with me ten thousand pieces of you, tangled irretrievably in the fabric of my soul. I can't get rid of them, nor do I want to.

I didn't send this letter to Sean, just like the countless letters I'd never sent to Samuel.

I'd always been my own harshest judge. Yet in objective fairness, I couldn't have sent the letter even if I'd wanted to. I was kilometers from any post box, lying face down in a shallow, hastily scrabbled foxhole in the sand, next to the foundations of a water pipeline that would never carry water, in the vast desert emptiness south of El Alamein, Egypt. Even if there had been an incongruously located post box in this wasteland of tan, getting out of my foxhole during a Luftwaffe bombing run seemed rather imprudent.

Through my cheek, pressed tight to the sand, I felt the ground groan, as if the planet itself were grumbling about the punishment being inflicted upon it. The Luftwaffe directed the bombing not at us, but at the artillery set up some distance to our rear. Yet my superiors had ordered me into the foxhole, and I was frankly glad for the rest.

Flashes from the bombs illuminated the desert emptiness with stroboscopic persistence. Over and over, the flashes of light revealed the slice of our deception that was visible over the rim of my foxhole.

Deception and goodbyes, I thought. *Why are these always so intertwined for me?*

The guns answered, and I closed my eyes against their insistent mocking.

When the raid ended and the guns fell silent, darkness reasserted mute dominance over the landscape. My eyes readjusted to the starlight, and I grabbed my shovel—the only weapon they'd issued me on arrival in the camp—and moved to get back to creating nothing.

For what was our fake water pipe if not nothing? What was the goal of my daily and nightly labors with the rough-handled shovel—which in just five days had turned my hands into calloused mitts—if not nothing?

I had said ten thousand goodbyes—to Sean, to my parents, to Samuel, to my life in Tel Aviv. I had no more letters to send, no more goodbyes to say, no further secrets to reveal. Now, I had only deception, which was, after all, the production of nothing.

CHAPTER 29
Aron & Samuel: Secrets

Samuel: Outskirts of Tel Aviv, October 23, 1942

Smelly complained with a bitter grunt, but finally came to a halt. Like a long-married couple whose intimacy fostered an equal mixture of tolerance and revulsion, we'd come to a tacit understanding. I knew that if I tugged long enough on the reins, he — Bashir had clarified that Smelly was indeed male — would eventually respond. He knew that I would not stop interrupting his profound camel contemplation with my tugging until he did so.

I started tugging Smelly to a stop just as the minarets of Abu Kabir loped into view. By the time he *actually* stopped, the square tower of St. Peter's church in Old Jaffa — just a few kilometers south of Tel Aviv — had popped onto the horizon, too.

I gazed so long and so intensely that my eyes began to burn. At first, they burned with hope and longing. Thereafter, as Smelly moved forward again, they burned with the glare of the blue Mediterranean, which threw hot daggers of late afternoon sun into them. The sea, it seemed, was attempting to wrench me from the desert, yet the desert was reluctant to yield.

"Kropla do kropli i bedzie morze," Bashir murmured, as he gazed at the deep blue. *Drop after drop, there will be a sea.*

I rolled my eyes in exasperation as if to an agreeable, yet invisible, companion. I considered explaining to Bashir the actual meaning of the adage, but decided against it. As we'd drawn closer to Tel Aviv, I'd grown increasingly less patient with the boy. His vast repository of proverbs and overenthusiastic affinity for all things Polish had morphed from novelty to tedium. He'd been a pleasant and fair companion, however, and I'd kept my end of our bargain. As Smelly swayed over countless kilometers of sand, scrub trees, and rocky canyons, we discussed what I recalled from my university philosophy studies. I'd spoken to him, as he'd requested, exclusively in Polish. I'd corrected his grammar and vocabulary gently but consistently.

One night, as the stars smiled down on our smoky cook fire and a pita charred slowly on the domed *saj*, I told him about Danuta.

He reciprocated by confirming my suspicions about his clandestine love of a Polish officer named Amadei, who was to be attached to Anders Army and encamped outside Beer Sheva. Once he realized my indifference to what most still considered unspeakable perversion, he spoke openly.

I explained that I'd once been close to someone like him, and he nodded gravely. As with Smelly, Bashir and I had reached a level of mutual understanding and appreciation, but could simply go no further owing to our own inherent limitations.

Smelly cleared a rise, and I gained a clear view northwest. I looked over the sandstone walls of Abu Kabir, past the red roofs of the Neve Zedek neighborhood, and into the heart of Tel Aviv, wherein she waited.

She. Tel Aviv.

Surely, *now* I could say it out loud. Surely, now I could finally say the word I'd barely allowed myself to speak since Chelyabinsk. Now I could say aloud this word that carried such power, promise, and passion—without being afraid that it would curse the shrinking distance. For this word had propelled me from the frozen wasteland of the Pechora River, over 5,000 kilometers of rail, road, track, ice, blood and sea. This word had pursued me down every moon path, tickled my mind, and blown gently into my ears every time I closed my eyes. This word possessed a wizardry that made my right hand seem present, my empty tummy seem full, and my heart seem whole. Indeed, now it came—unbidden and drawn from deep within, dripping like sweet saliva from my slightly parted lips.

"Danuta."

Aron: Helwan, Egypt, October 23, 1942

I learned the depth of Sadness. It didn't hide deep, lurking just two meters below the crust of the Egyptian desert, awaiting the blade of my shovel. Nightly, I reached it, and nightly it kissed my burning, blistered hands. It soothed the dusty furrows from my brow and explained patiently that desperation was not, as I'd always believed, shameful.

"It is simply dark to hope's light," Sadness said. *"It too can be embraced. It too can be treasured. It too can be loved."*

I listened to Sadness, and—on its recommendation—embraced Desperation.

We had a rare afternoon off, and I sat in the corner of what passed for a pub just outside of Helwan, nursing my third or fourth pint. It was comfortingly warm in the rough-walled mud brick structure, a welcome respite from the late fall chill, in which we worked and slept nightly. The thick fog of alcohol clouding my mind, combined with the clouds of pungent cigarette smoke, caused the room to thrum pleasantly.

I watched the voices and motions of life—which seemed to have continued despite my own absence from it—remotely, with reminiscence but without remorse. On the piano in the corner, someone banged out an off-key rendition of *Somewhere Over the Rainbow*. From near the bar, a good-natured cheer arose when someone's glass shattered, having been nudged to the floor by an itinerant elbow. I raised my hand to the waitress and ordered another pint.

Is this number five or six? I paused to reflect on that. *Does it matter?*

"Here's to deception," I slurred to the waitress, who'd brought my beer. Pleased with myself, I repeated the phrase with greater volume and lesser diction. "Here's to deshepsun... uh, despeshun... ah fuck, *deception!*" My hoarse yell momentarily rose above the din in the room. Heads turned in my direction. Embarrassed, I lowered my own head back to my new beer.

Nature called, and though reluctant to relinquish my cozy corner perch, I rose and stumbled through the crowd, out into the gathering dusk of evening. The cool air flowed over me, but couldn't penetrate my beer-fueled inner warmth. By the last light of the sun, I found a handy palm tree. Halfway through a piss of epic proportions, I heard a familiar voice call my name.

I turned so quickly that I almost urinated on his shoes. I looked into his face, and then turned back to my tree. In my drunkenness, I reasoned that six pints had been enough to make me see Rommel himself singing a duet with Judy Garland. I chuckled. Clearly, the beer had caused me to imagine that Sean was standing behind me. He couldn't possibly actually be there, so I finished my business, buttoned my fly, and turned back.

He was still there.

Samuel: Tel Aviv, October 23, 1942

"Danuta."

Now it seemed that her name could not leave my lips frequently enough. It had become a wellspring newly tapped in my soul, gushing uncontrolled. "Danuta," I said as I dismounted Smelly for the final time. "Danuta," I said while gathering my meager possessions into a corner-knotted, dusty cloth. "Danuta," I said prior to my farewell to Bashir, who promised to come find me later, having heard me repeat the street address—*8 Buki Ben Yagli Street, Tel Aviv*—like a Rosary, over and over to myself during our days and nights together.

Her name, it seemed, was an entire dialect that everyone could understand. It was the dream of Esperanto realized, the universal language of love corporealized. I said her name to the driver of the first bus I boarded, which took me—to my horror—in the opposite direction, *away* from Tel Aviv. I said it to the second bus driver, who returned me northward. I told it to the man in the newspaper stand, who pointed with curiously vague hand motions towards what I hoped was Buki Ben Yagli Street. I spoke it again to the woman in the kiosk on King George Street, who smiled kindly in understanding and motioned me to go up one more block, turn left, then turn left again.

Now, I inhaled and exhaled her name like oxygen, as I ran around the corner onto Bugrashov Street. "Da-nu-ta," I breathed with each footfall. "Da-nu-ta," I said, metering my steps with her perfume in my nostrils until I stood below the street sign that proclaimed joyously in Hebrew and English: *Buki Ben Yagli Street.*

"Danuta," I said reverently as I ticked off the house numbers on the left side of the street—number 2, number 4, number 6. Then I stopped and looked up at the rounded façade of number 8, dumbstruck, like a pilgrim to Mecca when he first glimpses the *Kaabah*. I had a sudden urge to prostrate myself. Yet from somewhere, my mother's voice found me, and I drew on a hidden reserve of Polish filial dignity. I stopped, caught my breath, smoothed my hair, and tucked in my shirttail.

Then—as Danuta had instructed me so long ago on our wooden bench in Vilnius, where the Neris and Vilnia rivers joined to become stronger together than they could ever dream of being apart—I found my words. I found and spoke the words I'd so long withheld from the world.

"I'm here, my love."

Aron: Helwan, Egypt, October 23, 1942

I'd experienced much in my twenty-nine years on Earth—some good, much very bad, and more even worse. I'd responded emotionally, as anyone would—sometimes with powerful emotions difficult to surmount. Yet in my adult life, I'd always controlled these feelings, just as my father had taught me so many years before. I responded with the socially acceptable responses of a rational man facing daunting challenges. Even when Josef Warszawski brutally rejected my advances in Mishmar HaSharon; even when I learned of my parents' death; even on the cold rock of the Jerusalem solitary confinement cell; even with the blood of the British soldier still wet on my hands—I'd retained the veneer of control that I understood to be essential. I'd done it not only because society expected it of me, I reasoned, but because I expected it of myself.

Yet seeing Sean here, with my belly full of beer and months of desperation seeping from my very pores, stripped away any remaining obligations my psyche felt to the social contract. I was, at first, mute. Then, incapable of enunciating discernible words, I simply opened the floodgates. I let the rage flow out of me like an unchecked orgasm. I released the incoherent, full-throated scream that had been building in me for the past months. I lashed out in murderous flailing that—owing to my inebriation—caused harm neither to Sean nor to myself.

My tantrum drew patrons out of the bar, excited at the prospect of a fight, but they quickly drifted away when my voice and strength gave out. After all, a drunk soldier sobbing face-down, saliva mixing with sand to create a paste that coated cheek and lips, was not worthy of rubber-necking.

After what seemed like hours, I looked up.

Sean was still there.

"You left," I slurred hoarsely. "You never wrote. You *left*."

His voice wavered, lacking the determination I'd once so admired. "I had to. I had no choice. They *made* me."

My strength, along with my anger, rallied, yet my voice remained scratchy and soft. "They *made* you? This is what you have to say to me? How old *are* you? No one 'made' you. You made a choice, and it wasn't me. And what the hell are you *doing* here, anyhow?"

"Half the British army is here, you idiot. I was transferred here from Malta to help prepare for what's going to start." He checked his watch self-importantly. "In about an hour, in fact."

I was unimpressed. I didn't care what Montgomery and Rommel did any longer. I didn't care what would start or end in an hour. I didn't care about Operation Bertram, or the war, or Masada on the Carmel. I didn't care if the Zionists would win their state, or if the Nazis would break through, overrun Palestine, and ship its Jews off to God-knows-where. I didn't care that Sean was here. I didn't even care whether Samuel made it to Tel Aviv, or ever realized what I'd done for him, or perhaps *to* him. Most of all, I sincerely, truly, and genuinely no longer cared what happened to *me*.

I looked up at the eyes I'd gazed into when they first opened on so many mornings, and found that they were no longer familiar. My fury, I found, had shifted. It no longer had use for Sean. Instead, it chose a more proximate, familiar, and infinitely more vulnerable target: myself.

Still on my knees, with snot running from my nose and sand caked on one cheek, I shifted my jaw, and grit crunched between my teeth. It was not Sean at fault, my fury reasoned. Who would want to stay with me?

Forget him, a familiar internal voice said. *You're not worthy of him, anyhow. No one has ever wanted you. Not Josef Warszawski, not any of the countless men you met in London Square, not your brother, not even your parents. They didn't want you because there's nothing to want. You've always been translucent, and now you're fading ever faster towards invisibility. Who will notice when your clothes, unsupported by a body that's been reabsorbed into the Nothing from which it came, drop empty to the sand? Who will care?*

"You had a choice," I spat in Sean's direction as the tears came hard and thick. "You *had* a choice." Then, I rose to my feet, wiped at my face, spat sand from my mouth, and ran.

Samuel: Tel Aviv, October 23, 1942

I bounded up the stairs, found the door labeled 'Katz,' and forced myself to knock reservedly on the door, as if simply visiting a friend. I waited, listened, then knocked again and called out her name softly. I repeated this cycle several more times, ignoring the logical conclusion that she wasn't in. Each time, my level of urgency grew, until the intensity of my pounding and shouting drew the neighbor, an elderly man, from his own flat.

He pushed his glasses onto his grey-topped head, and looked at me suspiciously. Then, he nodded with understanding and said something in Hebrew. When I shrugged to show I didn't understand, he switched to pidgin English. "You Aron brother," he said. "You look him... uh, you look *like* him. He not here, left key. I bring." He shuffled back into his flat, and the rustling noises of his search continued for what seemed like hours.

I mentally urged him to hurry, despite the fact that my logical brain had reactivated itself. Clearly, Danuta was not at home, so I had no cause to hurry. It was Friday, late morning, and she would be at work at *Kofer HaYishuv* in Ramat Gan, in her small office, at the wooden desk with the squeaky chair and the electric fan, all of which she'd described in a previous letter. She'd be back after work, and I would surprise her. In the meantime, I would revel in her absence. I would smell her smell. I would touch her things. I would lay my head on the pillow where she'd laid hers just hours previously. I would breathe in her very essence.

Finally, the neighbor brought the key.

I thanked him, and with trembling hands let myself into the flat, filled with the anticipation of reunion.

Aron: Helwan, Egypt, October 23, 1942

I ran for no reason, as if I could outrun myself.

"Wherever you go, there you are."

I ran, blinded by tears and pursued by—I thought—only my father's words. I ran to escape this body, this sorely limited mind, the ethos I'd finally stretched to a breaking point. I ran to escape a life that had trapped me in a cage not of my own making, a cage that had contained me, yet never fit me. I ran until I felt my lungs had burst into flame, and I ignored the increasing urgency of the voices faintly audible behind me.

Nothing. No one. No reason. Nothing. No one. No reason.

The voice inside my head chanted to the rhythm of my pumping legs until I fell, exhausted. The voices behind me grew ever more urgent, but came no closer.

What do they want? Why can't they leave me alone?

I raised my head to look around me in the gathering darkness. It had been dusk when I'd first seen Sean. Now, the moon hung low on the horizon, and the stars shone fully visible. I sat up and took in the expanse of flat sand surrounding me, bordered on all sides by embankments.

Voices floated from just beyond these berms. "Don't move, mate!" they said, but I didn't understand what they meant.

Then, one voice rose above the others with a confidence and command that I recognized instantly. Sean yelled, "You're in the middle of a minefield, you dolt. Don't move, and I'll get the sap—"

Samuel: *Tel Aviv, October 23, 1942*

The lock clicked open, and I swung the door inwards. I took it all in: the hook on which she hung her coat, and the kitchen in which she cooked her—and possibly Aron's—meals. To my right sat the table at which she'd drunk her ersatz coffee this very morning. To my left lay the bedroom in which she slept. And here... here stood the desk where she'd written her letters to me—the letters I'd kept even to this day, in the waterproof pouch tied around my waist.

I smiled as I passed through the darkened doorway into her bedroom. I thought I could even smell her perfume, but then I paused. The bed was neatly made, and no clothes lay piled haphazardly on the chair in the corner. Danuta was a notorious slob, something we'd laughed about frequently as we'd gotten to know each other's more intimate habits in Vilnius. I'd espoused the theory that she actually suffered from rare Dirt Blindness, and was simply incapable of seeing the detritus she left. Yet here... there was no mess. There were not even clothes in the wardrobe.

Puzzled, yet not concerned, I turned back to the main living area and saw that a layer of dust coated the kitchen table. Dishes sat, forlorn and unused, in their rack by the dry sink.

Maybe she moved back to her old flat. Maybe she changed her mind about living with Aron.

Then I took a closer look at the desk, a lovely roll-top, with numerous small drawers and shelves that gracefully embraced all that written correspondence demanded. Someone had left the roll top open, and a letter in Danuta's handwriting lay there, lightly covered in dust. I'd never seen this letter, for I knew each one of her missives by heart. Next to the letter, a practice book lay open. In it, someone had painstakingly copied each word of Danuta's letter, multiple times.

I flipped through this book, confused, for with each iteration, the handwriting looked more and more similar to the original. That's when I spotted the envelope, propped against the back of the desk.

On it, in handwriting that was unmistakably Aron's, was written: *My Dearest Samuel.*

Aron: Helwan, Egypt, October 23, 1942

Sean's urgent shout had been cut off mid-word, as the gates of hell opened. I later learned that Operation Lightfoot had begun. It was the great British push that Operation Bertram had been conceived and planned — successfully, it turned out — to conceal.

All I knew then, though, was the sound of artillery, but not the deep and distant earth-thrum I'd heard so many times, with one ear pressed to the floor of my foxhole, or in the trench in which I worked at night. This brain-jarring earthquake lasted for twenty minutes. The sand danced next to me with the concussion from what I later learned were 1000 field guns firing simultaneously. The muzzles flashed in the now-full darkness. Frame-by-frame, as if in slow motion, I watched the sand jump off the toes of my boots, as if brushed by an unseen hand. At the far end of the minefield, close enough that I could see and feel it but far enough to be harmless, a mine detonated from the shockwaves. A piece of hot shrapnel landed next to my leg, and another mine went off next to the first, possibly triggered by the shock of the proximate explosion. Then, a third exploded at the other end of the field.

I twisted my head wildly and looked around. In all directions, dark blobs took shape, shaken free of their sandy camouflage by the incessant rumbling. I watched with horror as the anti-tank mines, the triggers for which were notoriously sensitive, according to the cursory training we'd received before they turned us loose with our shovels, emerged from the sand. They revealed themselves, as all secrets must, with a cold malevolence that threatened redemption, rather than nurturing it.

CHAPTER 30
Aron: A Hollow Victory

Tel Aviv, September 30, 1942

> *My Dearest Brother,*
> *If you are reading this, then I should celebrate victory. You are alive, and you are safe in Tel Aviv. For this, I should be — indeed, I will be — jubilant, for you are my only remaining family. I love and cherish you more than I've ever been able to express, certainly more than I've ever shown — especially in the worst of my moments, which you undoubtedly recall even better than I do. For these I will apologize and, hopefully, somehow make amends.*
>
> *You reading this letter is a victory, yet the pretense under which I brought you here, and the truth which I must now reveal, must make this victory hollow. Please know that all I did, I did for love of you. Perhaps this will comfort, but I understand that it is more likely to enrage.*
>
> *You were a sharp-witted boy, and I gather you have grown into an even smarter man. Thus, I will now simply rip the bandage off the wound to reveal the festering truth that you probably already know: Danuta is dead. The bulk of the letters you carry with you were written by me.*
>
> *I am sincerely sorry for this loss, Samuel. In my correspondence with Danuta, I was able to form the impression of her charm, her strength of character, and her devotion to you. In my selfishness, I could only wish for myself a love that could compel me to make such a journey as yours, or a lover willing to undertake such a journey as Danuta attempted. I have known loss, Samuel, but I realize that I have not known — nor will I likely ever know — loss of this depth.*
>
> *Here are the facts I know: After learning of her capture aboard the Vatan, from the father and son with whom she'd been traveling, I received a short postcard in April of 1941 from Danuta, postmarked Ravensbruck Concentration Camp in*

Germany. Thereafter, I heard nothing directly from her. All my inquiries – and please believe me that I made many, many inquires through the Red Cross, through my connections in the Zionist leadership, and through any possible avenue that presented itself – came to nothing. I even volunteered to travel to Europe as an emissary to the Zionist movements there, but was rejected owing to... certain personal reasons, by the Zionist leadership.

Finally, early this year I met a woman in Haifa who had been released from Ravensbruck the previous winter. She provided convincing evidence that she had known Danuta under her Hebrew name Lea Rachel Cohen. Danuta had revealed her true name and origins to this woman, you see, making her identity ironclad. She also confirmed Danuta's death, although she refused to elaborate on the circumstances, despite my strident requests. She had seen Danuta die with her own eyes, she claimed, and there is no reason to suspect deception.

Again, although I cringe at the hollowness of these words, I am truly sorry for your loss.

Once they captured Danuta, and being the impetus for her travels, I realized I must act. I realized that surviving the many trials you were likely to endure on your way here, Samuel, would require motivation far greater than any I, your estranged brother, could provide. I believed, and in time, I believe that you will concur, that Danuta – even in death – could provide you with the strength to overcome these trials. The fact that you are reading this vindicates my ends, if not my means.

I will not presume that you want anything further from me, Samuel. I do not know if I will return from Egypt, nor whether you will choose to maintain contact with me if I do. I doubt you'll appreciate what drove me to such lengths of duplicity, nor should you. I was your older brother, and I cruelly betrayed your trust more than once over the years. I am still your older brother, and I have again betrayed your trust, if this time for a more noble purpose.

You may have the full use of my flat until you decide what you'd like to do. Should something happen to me, I have prepared a will leaving ownership of all my property to you. In the interim, I left a sum of money with the neighbor who let you in, which should be more than sufficient to get you started if you decide to leave, or provide for your needs if you stay. And I fervently hope – please believe me – that you will choose the latter.

Samuel, please know one thing: if fate should bring us together again, and you choose to give me the chance, I will work tirelessly to repair these bridges that I've destroyed. I will see you for what you are, not for what you symbolize. I will not ask for, nor expect, anything in return.

Please accept again my most sincere condolences and humblest apologies.

Your loving brother,
Aron

CHAPTER 31
Aron & Samuel: Love, Hate, Forgive, Repeat

Samuel: Tel Aviv, January 20, 1943
   They're fighting back.
   The rumor I heard must have licked at Tel Aviv's heart like flames, heating hope and igniting optimism. The papers carried no official word, but—had I been listening—I could have felt the street thrum with the news.
   They're not just waiting to be taken anymore, they must have been saying. *They're fighting back.*
   These rumors, of the first shots fired in the Warsaw Ghetto by Jews on Nazis, must have mixed with the news of Rommel's continued humiliations at the hands of the British, following his crushing defeat in El Alamein.
   If the German war machine could be stopped in North Africa, they probably gushed, *if Stalingrad was retaken, and if Jews — our brothers and sisters! — were actually fighting back in Poland....*
   This is what they must have been saying, but I wasn't listening— not really.
   I was on a different plane of existence, in a universe wherein the fact that Danuta was no more became the sole source of light, heat, and air. No other news interested me except this. I rediscovered it hourly, reminded of her at every turn, even though she'd never even breathed Tel Aviv air. She was here, even in this bed, whose pillow the glorious luxury of her hair had never graced. Over the course of almost two years and 5000 kilometers of misery, I had constructed her life here in minute detail. Now, my mind seemed determined to perpetuate this story—certainly easier to consider than the truth of her suffering and death on a lice-infested wooden bunk in Ravensbruck.
   It was easier to see her in Tel Aviv than to recall that her death had been at my hand. It was easier to picture her here than to consider that she would not have been on that ship, had she not been on her way to join me in Palestine. It was easier to imagine her in this kitchen than to recall that

they wouldn't have taken her to Ravensbruck had she not assumed a Jewish identity... for my sake. She may well have still been safe in Vilnius with Adrianna, she may well have survived the war, and she may well have been on her way to Tel Aviv now — *if only, if only, if only...*.

These thoughts circled endlessly in my head, hungry sharks around flailing prey, just waiting for the opportunity to tear at exposed flesh. And oh, I offered so much exposed flesh at which they could rip.

I saw her everywhere. Her shadow flitted from room to room, always just beyond my peripheral vision, as I sat at the still dusty kitchen table cluttered with dirty cups and an overflowing ashtray. Every time I touched the door handle to leave the flat, I felt the warmth where her hand had just rested. She briskly turned each corner, just ahead of me and maddeningly out of sight, every time I went to the kiosk on King George Street to get more cigarettes. I heard her breathing next to me in the depths of the night, and was puzzled anew each time I stretched out a hand to discover cold mattress instead of warm flesh.

In the months following my arrival in Tel Aviv, I preferred this universe, a place in which Danuta still lived. I ignored the outside world, with its burgeoning optimism over Germany's inevitable defeat and the meaning of this to Jewish national aspirations. Though still a devout Zionist — my conversion during my travels had been complete — I simply had no room for ideology in this parallel universe.

In this warped place, even the telegram from Aron, which had arrived two weeks ago, had barely registered.

> *Hope you are well. Release January 20. Coming home. Will you be there?*

I'd ignored the implications of this missive, but now I reached for it instinctively with my right hand —

When will I learn?

I sent yet another dirty cup to its death on the hard stone floor. Its corpse lay sadly along with its fallen compatriots.

Aron will be here in just days — perhaps today.

Would I be here? Had I ever truly been here? How was I to feel about the man who had nearly killed me as a child, saved me from certain death in the *gulag*, yet left me alone in a world without the one thing for which I had chosen life? Was I to strike him, embrace him, spit on him? What was he to me, in any case? A brother in name only, who'd not played a role in my life for two of my three decades; a brother who'd never taken me into account in any of his own life decisions, yet presumed to imprison me now in this world without

Danuta. He had betrayed me that day on the banks of the Vistula—whatever the origins of his rage—and then abandoned me in 1931. I owed him nothing, and felt for him less.

Tears rose in my eyes, and I looked up at the winter sunshine streaming through the grimy windows of my brother's flat.

Has he loved here, as I loved in Vilnius?

The January chill traveled up my legs from the cold floor as the sharks circled round and round. I took my head in both hands, and rocked back and forth like an infant in a vain attempt to make them stop.

Then, I felt her breath on the back of my neck. This time, I did not turn to catch a glimpse. Rather, I stayed still, and she leaned closer. I smelled her perfume. A lock of hair brushed my ear, and a warm, soft hand rested lightly on my shoulder. Her voice—glorious, dusky—whispered in my ear.

"Yes," I agreed out loud, startling myself with the conviction in my own voice. "Yes, of course, I remember. My darling, you're right, as usual."

Then I turned, and I could see her smug smile.

Tell me again how right I am, she seemed to say.

I was nine years old that day in 1926 when I got lost on the Kozlowski Brothers' beach, on the banks of the Vistula. Aron was 14. I learned later that this all happened only months after the bloodless coup that brought Jozef Pilsudski to power. Back then, this fact would have, of course, carried far less weight than the excitement of going to the beach with my older brother, the promise of ice cream, and the slap and curse that followed my getting lost and his being paged to retrieve me.

We left the beach through the wooden turnstile. Aron, red-faced and sweating, still grasped me tightly by the wrist. He tugged me forward with such urgency that my shoulder ached. I sobbed breathlessly yet silently, following his slap and vicious reprimand. Tears and snot mingled and ran into my mouth, making me choke.

I was not yet of an age where I could be angry with my revered older brother, despite his behavior towards me. Rather, I simply reeled from the sheer hurt I felt from his cruelty. What had I done to deserve it?

It was a short tram ride back to Praga on the number 17 line. Aron was too impatient to walk. The car was sweltering in the afternoon sun. Aron made me sit by the open window, so as to keep me from bolting.

The smell of sweat, wood polish, and cigarette smoke overpowered me, and the backs of my legs stuck to the leather seats. I tried to count the automobiles that went by — one of my favorite tram games — but in short order we debarked into the fresh air of Wybrzeze Szczecinskie Street.

I didn't notice the group of boys at first, but Aron's insistent tugging, which had abated since we'd gotten off the tram, suddenly increased.

What have I done now? Why do you hate me so much?

The raucous voices shook me from my self-pity.

"Hey, here are some Jew Swine, now! Jew Swine, come here for a minute! Come here, Jew Swine!" The biggest of the boys was Aron's age, or perhaps older. I could see the familiar yellow leaflet clutched in his hand. They'd been all over the city recently, so ubiquitous that even I had noticed. It contained a large caricature of a swine, headlined in capital letters "SWINIA KUPUJE U ZYDA" — *only pigs buy from Jews!*

"Ignore them," my father had said about the leaflets, which — I later learned — were part of an economic boycott launched by a political party. *"They are the undertow, boys, and we won't allow ourselves to get sucked down to their level, will we?"*

Now the undertow had caught up with us, even though Aron had quickened our pace so dramatically that I trotted to keep up. Despite the effort, I didn't complain. I was scared, but it was a fruitless effort.

They quickly surrounded us, eight of them, all far bigger than me, and many bigger than Aron.

"Look, it's a Jew piglet, along with his Jew Swine. Do you suck your swine's teats, little piglet?" The largest boy leaned close to me and grabbed my face.

Up close, I could see his greasy hair and the wide gap between his front teeth. His breath smelled of garlic. He forced my cheeks into a sucking expression that elicited renewed laughter from the other boys.

Encouraged, he squeezed my face tighter. "What else do you suck, Jew piglet? Huh?"

More laughter.

My cheeks began to hurt, and tears came into my eyes. I looked around wildly for Aron.

Why isn't he helping me? Does he hate me that much?

Now I started to cry for real, and pawed pointlessly at the strong hand that held my cheeks in a vice grip.

That's when the cry sounded, a wild thing that would have put Johnny Weissmuller — my idol after I saw him in *Tarzan the Ape Man* — to shame. It came from nowhere and everywhere at the same time. The boy's hand released my cheeks suddenly as a beach towel closed over his head. I fell back, and saw the wild thing, which seemed to be wearing my brother's clothes, land on the boy's back. The wild thing rode him like a rodeo steer, the ends of the towel, anchored around the boy's face, its reins.

The rest was a blur. Aron seemed to have four arms. He was thrown clear of the larger boy, who untangled himself from the towel and backed away, clearly shaken. Aron charged back into the circle of confused boys with another wild call, and they scattered. He stood in the middle of the street, elated, and called after them, "That's right, you shits. Nobody fucks with the Jew Swine's piglet! Beware the Jew Swine! Fear him!"

Then he turned to me, bent down, and wiped my tears. He took my hand gently, and we walked back in the direction from which we'd just come, away from home.

He bought me ice cream.

This is what Danuta's soft voice had reminded me. *"He bought you ice cream."*

I had recalled the terror of being lost in the crowd. I had recalled Aron's slap and cruel words. Yet I had never examined my memories further. The partial memory had suited my life's narrative well, and never warranted further digging. My brother hated me. My brother tried to kill me. My brother abandoned me. This was my life — or so I'd believed.

I wiped the tears from my eyes and lit another cigarette, the match clutched in my left hand, my stump stabilizing the matchbox. The smoke crept towards the ceiling, and I tracked its path with my eyes. Outside, the sun had faded, and the blacked-out city remained unlit. The gloom crept through the cracks between the *trisim*, permeating the flat and pressing down with all its weight.

I stood and turned on a light, which forced the darkness back and revealed... a flat in a sorry state of cleanliness. In that illumination, I suddenly understood that the essence of any sibling relationship — possibly any *human* relationship — consisted of four simple, interconnected pillars: *Love. Hate. Forgive. Repeat.*

Somewhere along the way, I had forgotten three of these four pillars. Danuta's gentle redeeming wisdom, I realized, had reached me from beyond the grave.

Shall I tell you again how right you were, my darling?

I gathered the cups from the floor, cleared the ashtray, and took the first steps towards cleaning the mess that surrounded me, and for which I was at least partly responsible.

Aron: Tel Aviv, January 20, 1943

I exited the El Alamein minefield vastly different than I entered it.

I'd run in with abandon, fleeing demons both visible and unseen. I'd cowered, helpless and trembling, as the anti-tank mines emerged from the sand, shaken free by the shock waves of the artillery barrage that signaled what would be a turning point in the war. The mines had revealed themselves, and the shock of doing so had caused some to self-destruct — nearly taking me with them. Yet after twenty minutes of hell, the barrage had ended, and the deadly mines surrounding me lay on the sand, fully exposed in the faint starlight but *utterly intact*. They'd been shaken into a parallel universe, one in which they were uncovered but still fully capable of fulfilling the task for which they'd been created.

I stared at them for what seemed like hours, my thoughts awhirl, until Sean's voice reached me.

"Do you want me to order you a picnic lunch, or are you planning on coming out of there?"

I looked around at the exposed mines one last time, then at the dark figure on the horizon, whom I knew to be Sean, and understood what I needed to do. I stood with confidence, all traces of drunkenness vanquished by terror and revelation. I walked purposefully, cautiously, yet unafraid from the minefield in which I'd been cowering for only thirty minutes but living for over thirty years, and embraced Sean in the gathering darkness, ignoring the stares of the other dark figures around us.

The oil-burning steam engine that had pulled us faithfully from El Qantara, the sleepy town by the Suez Canal where we'd switched trains, gave a final hiss and jerked to a halt in Jaffa. I had offered to cover first-class tickets, but Sean insisted we travel like regular soldiers, and bought us an uncomfortable 3rd class wooden bench on which I'd found no sleep for the duration of the nearly ten-hour trip.

He had no such problem. As we stopped, his head—which had fallen repeatedly, sweetly, onto my shoulder as he slept—jolted from the window, onto which I'd gently moved it for propriety's sake.

I was exposed, but not forgetful that I'd created the parallel universe in which I now lived.

It was late morning, and only a short bus ride from Jaffa to my flat, where I presumed Samuel awaited me. "I'm not ready," I blurted as we walked out into the hazy winter Tel Aviv sunshine. The smell of the sea, once so familiar as to be indiscernible, now seemed pungent. It smelled of life—rich, luxurious, decaying and vibrant simultaneously.

We each carried an army duffel bag slung over a shoulder, which made walking cumbersome.

Sean found a quiet corner on the platform, and dropped his bag. When I followed suit, he turned and put a hand on my shoulder. "It's not like you have a choice, my love. He's in your flat, presumably. There's also a war on, you may have noticed, so it's not like there's anywhere to run. And wasn't it your wise father who used to say, 'wherever you go, there you are'? There's no hiding from this, so let's go."

He was right, of course. I *was* here, and I suddenly grasped that I was eager not only to meet Samuel but—in a very real sense—*me*. New Aron—the alter ego I'd unconsciously invented even before I'd moved to Palestine—and Old Aron, his ostensible predecessor, had gone. They'd coalesced in the terror of the minefield and had become one Aron—an Aron who no longer needed the dichotomy of New and Old, but was rather the sum total of his experiences, good and bad. I was nearly whole for the first time in my adult life, and eager to reach the one part that I felt would complete me.

Only one question remained: did that part want *me*?

Sean bought a Palestine Post before we boarded the green Egged bus, and I perused the headlines over his shoulder. In Warsaw, prolonged bursts of gunfire from the Jewish ghetto had given rise to fears of a massacre. Chile, pragmatic and sensing the clearly changing tide of the war, had broken off diplomatic relations with the Axis powers.

Diesel fumes masked the smell of the sea as the bus jolted through the tightly packed houses of the Neve Zedek neighborhood, then emerged onto the slightly wider streets branching off Rothschild

Boulevard. Street scenes once familiar seemed foreign after my months in the desert.

Has the city changed, or have I?

"Bloody hell! They're limiting us to four eggs a month and 500 grams of coffee. Bloody barbarians!" Sean read the new food-rationing announcement and tried to lighten my mood.

I smiled wanly at his effort, and returned to my reverie.

Sean returned to his paper.

My mind raced. *He doesn't want me. He hates me. Why wouldn't he hate me? What have I ever offered him but rejection, pain born of my own self-loathing, and distance? He will see me only as the person who took Danuta. He hates me. Can I blame him?*

Sensing my turmoil, Sean placed his hand on my shoulder in reassurance, without averting his eyes from the newspaper. The quietly supportive, intimate gesture jogged my memory, and my eyes suddenly filled with tears.

What if he does *want me?*

In 1928, I was 15 years old and already so deep in the emotional pit in which I would live for the coming decades, that I had trouble seeing out. I was in Vienna, where my father had been trying to persuade me to allow the eminent Dr. Eugen Steinach to "fix me," as I understood it, by mutilating my genitals.

"I could force you. I could have you restrained," he'd finally croaked in consternation, his hoarse whisper breaking the solemn silence of the clinic's wood-paneled waiting room. His eyes showed the shock of sudden paternal impotence. He'd just realized that he could no longer control me, and would be unable to rectify what he saw as a glaring yet wholly rectifiable injustice.

"You could, Father. I suppose you have the power, legally." My voice remained preternaturally calm, despite the burning knot in my gut. I could feel the muscles in my jaw, taut and straining with the effort of keeping my voice low. "You could, but you won't. You won't, because you'd never be able to face yourself if you did. And you certainly couldn't face Mother."

His face was ashen. "But this is your *life* we're discussing, Aron. Your entire life. Surely you can understand that. Don't you *want* to change?"

My efforts at propriety lapsed, and my voice broke. Heads in the waiting room turned as I blurted, "Do you think I *like* being different? Do you think it's easy thinking... what I think? Do you think it's easy feeling... what I feel? Of course, I *want* to change, but even if I could, it wouldn't be like this. Not with some monster cutting me!"

During the long train ride back to Warsaw, I was too numb to think. It was only when I walked into the flat, and saw that smirking face, that I found myself wholly focused on a convenient object of wrath. Samuel had known of Father's plans, I was sure. He didn't deny it, seeming instead to revel in my misery. He had betrayed me. *He* was at fault. More importantly, as always, he was proximate. When I confronted him, he at first cowered, as I expected him to do. Then he rebelled, which surprised me, but I could no longer take comfort in blaming Samuel for my own shortcomings.

I sat in my room that entire next day, alternating between rage and anguish that I was woefully ill-equipped to understand. Samuel was at school, Father at work, and Mother flitted in and out of my room like a moth seeking exit but inexorably drawn back to a candle flame. She left food, but removed it when I didn't eat. She embraced me, but quickly withdrew when I stiffened at her touch.

The shadows grew long in the afternoon, and still I stared out my window over the Vistula. Clouds had gathered, and rain seemed imminent. I didn't hear the door to my room, and started when the small warm hand rested on my shoulder. It remained far longer than necessary, hesitantly seeking to comfort. I turned red-rimmed eyes to find my brother looking sheepish. He thrust a folded paper into my hand.

"I brought this for you," he said. "Antoni Wawrzaszek asked me to give it to you. And I stopped at Mr. Brzezicki's store on the way home, and bought some of those chocolates that you like. There was a tram accident right in front of his store, and you wouldn't believe how many people stopped to look... and it was... it was... you know...." His voice trailed off as he recalled that the context of our current dialog remained far removed from the mundane. He turned to leave, and I let him go without a word.

I let him go without a word.

How could I have forgotten this? I pressed my cheek to Sean's hand surreptitiously before he removed it from my shoulder.

The bus grounded to a halt at the corner of Allenby and King George. We shouldered our duffels, and shuffled down the narrow steps into the street.

I let him go without a word.

Moments carry staggeringly disproportionate power. A single fleeting moment in battle, or in parliamentary debate, can change the course of nations. A moment of distraction by a pilot or a surgeon can irrevocably impact—or even end—lives. A glance, a word, a gesture—in just seconds, these can alter the trust built brick by brick over decades.

In that moment, fifteen years previously, Samuel had reached out to me, and I had turned away. His ten-year-old psyche had realized its mistake, and he'd clumsily tried to make amends. The note from Antoni had been a brief, carefully worded missive of encouragement. I read it, then discarded and forgot it. In the fog of my angst, I never wondered how Antoni—the sole person I knew then who could have possibly hoped to understand—had even known of the events in Vienna. Clearly, I realized now, Samuel had told him—not from spite, but rather from love and concern.

And I turned him away.

We trudged down the hill towards Bugrashov Street. On the corner of Ben Tzion Boulevard, they'd already erected a small monument to the 130 victims of the Italian bombing I'd witnessed less than three years earlier. It served as a testament to another single moment of devastating gravity, the destructive ripples of which spread far, far beyond its own temporality.

Suddenly, they were everywhere—reminders of moments that I'd let slip by unexploited, unfulfilled. The post box on the corner of my street, into which I had not placed so many of the letters I'd written in my own name to Samuel. The neighbor's door, which I'd never knocked on. The countless conversations I'd not had with the people closest to me, who would have been happy at my approach.

We turned onto Buki Ben Yagli Street, and I reached down to squeeze Sean's hand, my gesture hidden from prying eyes by our bulky duffels. I'd captured this moment, I realized. I looked into his eyes, and mouthed "I love you," then watched as his puzzled expression morphed into muted pleasure. Another moment claimed. And I silently vowed that it would not be the last.

Even though there will always be moments that escape our grasp, it is in our sole power to minimize their number. Regrets for moments past serve only our own vanity. It is emotionally simpler to bemoan their loss *ex post facto* than to snare them before they pass. For in the ultimate equation, which carry more weight: moments lost, or moments gained?

The answer was clear, and as I crossed the threshold of my building for the first time in months, I shed two decades of regrets over moments lost. The load on my back lightened despite the duffel, and my step quickened towards the door to my flat, wherein a whole world of moments worthy of capture waited.

EPILOGUE
Samuel

Tel Aviv, May 13, 1943

"I have a story to write. Would you like to comment, in an unofficial capacity? Yes, that's right, anonymously.... Sorry, it's not *my* fault that you're so low-level that your name is primarily familiar to the janitorial staff.... Uh, yes, it *is*. But you do work in *Kofer HaYishuv*, which technically makes you a source, even if you're a dick. So listen, here's what I'm leading with: 'Tide Turns in North Africa: Allies Triumph in Tunis, 150,000 Axis POWs, Von Arnim Surrenders'. I'd like an insider quote from within the *Yishuv* leadership, so what have you got for me? Wait... did you just fart? I could hear that, you know. Jesus, the acoustics in your office must be miraculous. You could stage a fucking symphony in there. God, what a pig."

Five minutes later and I have my quote, and hang up with my brother. I turn my attention back to the Polish language typewriter on my desk. I've become reasonably adept at one-handed pecking, but am still trying to convince Henryk — Henryk Rosmarin, former Polish Consul General to Palestine and now my employer — to hire a typist. He claims that *Nowiny Dnia* — Daily News, Palestine's first Polish-language newspaper — has a limited circulation, comes out only three times a week, and primarily regurgitates translated news from the wires. Thus, by his logic, there's no need for staff beyond myself. It's hard to argue with this logic, but I persist.

I persist because, despite being in Tel Aviv for just six months, and only actually living a life of any consequence for three of them, I've figured out how things work here. I have the right combination of balls, brains, and shitty typing skills that one needs to make a real splash in our budding journalistic community. To be honest, the prosthetic hand doesn't hurt. It gives me a certain wartime panache — eliciting a winning mix of admiration and pity that I'm not ashamed to exploit to the maximum.

The Polish newspaper job, which I owe to my brother's connections in the burgeoning Polish immigrant community, is a good foot in the door. Still, I have my eyes on the Hebrew-language press, where the real future is. I'm taking Hebrew lessons three times a week with the indominable Hava, whose strictness is mitigated only by her fantastic cup size. I insist on speaking, reading, and writing Hebrew at every possible opportunity. The key to learning a new language, I quickly realized, is not to be ashamed of looking like a complete ass. Yes, I call window boxes tomatoes, and loudly. Yes, I did publicly ask for a vagina of water from a waitress. Nonetheless, these instances are diminishing—notably the vagina incident, which really only *could* happen once.

I wasn't angry with Aron. More accurately, I *was* angry, but my anger dissipated so quickly that it may as well never have existed. Our meeting in January, when he came into his spotless flat looking ready to hug me sloppily and cry, was anticlimactic. We'd both arrived at the conclusion that, yes, the other *had been* an asshole for twenty years, but that our own personal asshole-ness had been of equal measure. The asshole coefficient of the universe having thus balanced out, we were rapidly able to move on with the occasionally messy yet largely fun business of being adult brothers.

Let me correct myself: I *am* angry. I'm angry that, despite over a thousand years of rich Jewish history in Poland, the Poles turned on us so viciously and wholeheartedly—making it impossible for Jews to live in Poland as full human beings. I'm angry at how people who were once our neighbors played such a prominent role in helping the Nazis hunt us down—even as they themselves suffered at Nazi hands. I'm angry that the society in which we were raised made it triply difficult for my brother to find his way. Being a Jew in Poland was daunting, being a homosexual Jew was impossible, and being a homosexual Jew living in a home where the futile hope of ever fitting in— 'integrationism,' in my father's lexicon—was a supreme value, was simply inhuman.

Would I have fared better as an adolescent, under such strains? I fear not, and by a long shot. So, I'm angry, but not at Aron, and I'm committed to doing my small part to ensure that this new society which we are building on the shores of the Mediterranean treats its Jews, its homosexuals, and, indeed, its one-handed widower journalists, far better.

Aron and Sean are still thankfully, discretely, together—thankfully, owing to the fact that I like Sean, but mostly to the fact that Aron would be insufferable without Sean's mitigating, calming presence; discretely, since theirs is still not an enviable arrangement. Sean is still a British soldier, and although his previous demotion and punitive transfer quashed the promise of a sterling military career, and he is essentially a mid-level bureaucratic functionary, his 'unnatural' liaison with a Zionist is still illicit and officially forbidden. As is Aron's relationship with a representative of His Majesty's Government in Palestine, despite his low-level status in the Zionist hierarchy. They're cautious, however, and Aron's neighbors are considerate and understanding. They manage to spend nearly every night together.

Much has changed for me. One thing has not: along the moon path I travel, I am still accompanied by four ghosts.

Jacek visits me weekly in dreams that begin with him still in his ammunition crate. "Hey *malpeczko*," he calls. "You gonna let me out of here, or do I have to get my three-year-old niece to beat you up?" These dreams end less humorously, usually with his hands on my throat, much as my own hands — yes, they *were* mine — once encircled the throat of an anonymous prisoner on the Pechora River.

Igor and Viktor visit, too. They float in partially inflated life preservers, sink beneath the surface of black water, and constantly re-emerge to call each other "butt face" and "shit-breath" before sinking again. I watch them appear and disappear, until one or the other finally tells me to stop wallowing and get on with it.

Danuta, of course... not a day passes that I don't hear her wise voice at least once. Not a night falls that she is not with me. I no longer suffer phantom pain from my missing right hand, yet I constantly feel her hand caressing my invisible appendage. The silent hall of the small flat I rent on Bugrashov Street knows the rustle of her silk nightgown well. She is both here and not here, and I am alternatingly confused, devastated, and charmed by her presence and absence.

Even in my devastation, however, I persist.

I persist and I write. By day, I write in *Nowiny Dnia*. By night, I painstakingly reconstruct the play I started so long ago in Warsaw. I do this because I *am* my words. I am Samuel Katz, and I was not born of great words. I was not born of a writer whose words illuminated thousands of nescient eyes. I was born of a man who had thoughts of inherent value and the eloquence to express them, *yet chose to remain unheard*. It is this, I believe, that drives me to be heard in his stead. If I don't express my truth, one thing is certain: no one will hear it. For me, there is nothing worse than not being heard, For if no one hears me, if no one follows me along this illusive moon path that I so relentlessly pursue, who am I?

Acknowledgements

Every novel comes from a personal place, yet *Moon Path* is perhaps an exception in sheer depth, if not in essence. During the entire course of the book's writing, my family and I devoted ourselves to helping a very special woman in her daily battle with Metastic Melanoma, which had spread over the years from a small mole on her thigh to her brain. Despite this, shortly before I finished *Moon Path*, Michal Ben-Ari Greenberg — my wife of 20 years, mother of my children, my best friend, and the most strong-willed soul I've ever known — lost her struggle. I was with her at the end. She was as valiant, stoic, and beautiful in death as she was in life.

I owe heartfelt thanks to many people who helped me bring *Moon Path* into the world. First and foremost is Michal, who's patient transcription of semi-legible handwritten testimonies retrieved from the murky depths of the *Hagana* archives in Tel Aviv gave me a firsthand feel for the real people who played a role in the Northern Plan. Second is my amazing and indefatigable son, Segev, who's depth of insight far exceeds his 17 years. At every juncture of *Moon Path*, even in the darkest hours of Michal's illness, he was there to offer ideas, patient encouragement, and sometimes just a sympathetic ear. I could not have done it — the book or the caregiving — without him.

I'd also like to thank my surrogate alpha-readers, who stepped in to take Michal's place after her death: Jeremy and Belinda Gerber, Jon Kohn, my mother Ronnie Greenberg, and my unstoppable mother-in-law Einat Benari. And of course, my solid core of beta-readers deserves my recognition and eternal gratitude: Robin and Jay Epstein, Amy Ariel, Daniel and Nomi Sherman, and all the rest. Finally, I owe sincere thanks to my editor, Dave Lane (aka Lane Diamond), whose relentless and patient persecution of my grammatical and editorial transgressions — in this and my previous two books — would do justice to any Inquisitorial court.

I was entranced by the idea of The Northern Plan (or "Haifa-Tobruk," or "Masada on the Carmel" — choose your moniker) from the moment I heard about it some decades ago. I vowed to use the plan as a backdrop for a novel one day. Once I started researching in-depth, however, I quickly learned that it was a plan never truly put into action, nor even wholly fleshed out. Despite this, as a Zionist, I see the Northern Plan as a psychological turning point in the creation of the Jewish national home. In the shadow of the unfolding horror that was the Holocaust, the Jews of Palestine came to the visceral realization that there was — quite literally — nowhere left to run. This ethos — perhaps conceived previously but certainly gestated during this short yet intensive period Haviv Canaan called "The Two Hundred Days of Dread" — continues, I believe, to shape Israel to this day.

I was surprised to find how little written material was available (in Hebrew or English) about Tel Aviv's closeted homosexual community in Mandatory Palestine. Despite some outstanding insights drawn from journal sources and indirect references, I was forced to take broad literary license (Michal would have said "make it up") regarding the lifestyles and attitudes of these pioneers of what has become a diverse and vibrant community, and a true source of national pride. LGBT historians, take note: there is work to be done!

Finally, being rather pedantic (Michal would have called it "anal retentive") about even the most minute historical detail, I relied heavily on written sources in the creation of *Moon Path*, most of them in Hebrew. Along with an incredibly long list of articles and online sources, the following books were invaluable during the writing of *Moon Path*.

1. Begin, Menahem. *White Nights: The Story of a Prisoner in Russia*. New York: Harper & Row, 1979.

2. Canaan, Haviv. *Two Hundred Days of Dread*. Tel Aviv, Israel: Mol-Art Press, 1974.

3. Wasserstein, Bernard. *On the Eve: The Jews of Europe Before the Second World War*. London: Profile Books, 2012.

4. Dagan, Shaul. *The Northern Plan*. Tel Aviv, Israel: Ministry of Defense, 1994.

5. Ratner, Yochanan. *My Life and Me*. Tel Aviv, Israel: Schoken Publishing, 1978.

6. Elam, Yigal. *Hagana: The Zionist Way to Power*. Tel Aviv, Israel: Zmora, Bitan, Modan – Publishers, 1979.

7. Solzhenitsyn, Aleksandr. *The Gulag Archipelago*. New York: Harper & Row, 1985.

8. Sumakai Fink, Amir and Press, Jacob. *Independence Park, The Lives of Gay Men in Israel*. Stanford, California: Stanford University Press, 1999.

Steven Greenberg
Kadima, Israel
May 2019

About the Author

Briefly....

I am a professional writer, as well as a full-time cook, cleaner, chauffeur, and work-at-home single Dad for three amazing teenagers. Born in Texas and raised in Fort Wayne, Indiana, I emigrated to Israel only months before the first Gulf War, following graduation from Indiana University in 1990. In 1996, I was drafted into the Israel Defense Forces, where I served for 12 years as a Reserves Combat Medic. Since 2002, I've worked as an independent marketing writer, copywriter and consultant.

More than You Asked for....

I am a writer by nature. It's always been how I express myself best. I've been writing stories, letters, journals, songs, and poems since I could pick up a pencil, but it took me 20-odd years to figure out that I could get paid for it. Call me slow.

After completing my BA at Indiana University – during the course of which I also studied at The Hebrew University of Jerusalem and Haifa University – I emigrated to Israel only months before the first Gulf War, in August 1990. In 1998, I was married to the wonderful woman who changed my life for the better in so many ways, and in 2001, only a month after the 9/11 attacks, my son was born, followed by my twin daughters in 2004. In late 2017, two weeks before my 50th birthday, my wife passed away after giving cancer one hell of a fight.

Since 2002, I've run SDG Communications, a successful marketing consultancy serving clients in Israel and abroad.

Website: www.StevenGreenberg.info
Goodreads: Steven Greenberg
Facebook: StevenGreenbergAuthor
Twitter: @GreenbergSteven
LinkedIn: SDGCom (Steven Greenberg)

What's Next?

Steven Greenberg always has at least one book in the works. Although we don't yet know the specifics, we know one thing: like all his other books, his next one will be a compelling literary and/or historical fiction piece sure to keep you turning the pages. Please stay tuned to developments and plans by subscribing to our newsletter at the link below:

www.EvolvedPub.com/Newsletter

More from Steven Greenberg

*One woman's quest for truth reveals a dark
family secret long buried in Prague's Nazi past.*

GALERIE
Amazon #1 Bestseller in 4 Countries!
WINNER: Pinnacle Book Achievement Award, Fall 2015 – Best Fiction
FINALIST: Readers' Favorite Book Award 2016 – Historical Fiction

Every family holds to secrets, but some are far darker, reach deeper, and touch a rawer nerve than others.

Vanesa Neuman is the daughter of Holocaust survivors, and her childhood in the cramped intimacy of south Tel Aviv is shadowed by her parents' unspoken wartime experiences. The past for her was a closed book... until her father passes away and that book falls literally open. Vanesa must now unravel the mystery of the diary she has received — and the strange symbol within — at all costs.

Set against the backdrop of the Nazi occupation and the Jewish Museum of Prague — Adolf Eichmann's "Museum of an Extinct Race" — Galerie is fast-paced historical fiction in the tradition of Tatiana De Rosnay's Sarah's Key. From Jerusalem's Yad V'Shem Holocaust research center, to the backstreets of Prague, and into the former "paradise ghetto" of Theresienstadt, Vanesa's journey of understanding will reveal a darker family past than she ever imagined — a secret kept alive for over half a century.

More from Evolved Publishing

We offer great books across multiple genres, featuring high-quality editing (which we believe is second-to-none) and fantastic covers.

As a hybrid small press, your support as loyal readers is so important to us, and we have strived, with tireless dedication and sheer determination, to deliver on the promise of our motto:
QUALITY IS PRIORITY #1!

Please check out all of our great books,
which you can find at this link:

www.EvolvedPub.com/Catalog/

Thank you!

CPSIA information can be obtained
at www.ICGtesting.com
Printed in the USA
BVHW032020230719
554211BV00002B/60/P